"... a glorious page-turner. Damning sε
the Florida Panhandle, and desperate cha
A keen observer of the human spirit, Haskew's world of grief and redemption is a
gut-punch. Like the deftly drawn landscape—live oaks smothered in Spanish moss,
dusty limestone roads, and bottomless sinkholes of cold, translucent water—this
book is pure poetry, each line an absolute masterpiece. I guarantee that Winston
and all his souls will wander with you long after you finish this beautiful book."
   —Kim Bradley, author of *Spillway*, 2022 Florida Book Award Silver Medal

"An intriguing combination of Southern suspense, police procedural, social
history/social critique, and spiritual odyssey, *Winston's Book of Souls* is full of twists
and surprises all the way through, beginning with an insurance salesman's
discovery of a dead body in the North Florida Panhandle of the early 1960s. The
sense of immersion in history is intense, the setting is rendered with exquisite
precision and accuracy, and the characters are compelling yet believable in their
very ordinariness as they struggle to work through local dilemmas even as larger
events make themselves felt in this time of national and global changes. I couldn't
put it down."
   —Claire Bateman, author of *Wonders of the Invisible World*

"Haskew's debut novel offers a rich exploration of time and place, of the power of
human connection, and of the lasting impact of secrets. In its opening pages,
Winston's Book of Souls pulls you into a journey through 1960s Florida with its lush
landscape, treacherous sinkholes, violent storms, and racial divides. In this setting,
you'll find yourself compelled to keep turning the pages to uncover the truth behind
a mysterious murder, whether secrets will out in the end, and if one man's faith in
another is strong enough to change longstanding bigotry."
   —Heather Marshall, author of *When the Ocean Flies*

"*Winston's Book of Souls* takes readers on a page-turning, twist-filled journey
through 1960's Florida in the compelling company of two immensely relatable souls
struggling to find their moral center during a time of national racial divide. Set in
the lush landscape of the Florida Panhandle, this novel brims with mystery,
intrigue, and drama, driven by long-guarded secrets that refuse to stay asleep."
   —Jo Watson Hackl, author of *Smack Dab in the Middle of Maybe*

"What is at stake when one dead man's life insurance policy is bogus, an off-the-
books money maker for a desperate agent in need of quick cash and hope for a
better life? . . . Haskew's Southern-suspense voice is pitch perfect in this, her debut
novel, where what must be made whole is more than one man's stuttering career.
Justice, family, and freedom hang in the balance at every turn."
   —Arthur McMaster, author of *In the Orchards of Our Mothers*

"Once you meet the folks in Pineville, you will recognize some of them, and others
will make such an impression that you will want them as your neighbors. The story
takes place in the 1960s, in the rural south, with the overlay of racial tension. Yet
the main character, Winston, an insurance salesman, is a beacon of hope for easing
this tension while also dealing with his own moral dilemmas that play out over the
novel. The twists and turns keep the reader guessing as more interesting characters
are introduced, with relatable interactions, events, and daily dramas, both large
and small. When the story ends, the reader will hope that a sequel is in the works
because these characters and their small-town life and death events will stay with
you for a long time."
   **—Shirley Ann Smith, Ph.D., author of *Navigating the Labyrinth: Teacher
Empowerment Through Instructional Leadership***

WINSTON'S
BOOK
OF
SOULS

a novel

TERRESA COOPER HASKEW

WINSTON'S BOOK OF SOULS
Terresa Cooper Haskew

Published by TouchPoint Press
www.touchpointpress.com

Softcover ISBN: 978-1-956851-78-6

Permissions and review inquiries: media@touchpointpress.com.
Rights: info@touchpointpress.com

Editor: Liam Lassiter
Cover Design: Sheri Williams
Cover images: Shutterstock
Author photo: Chantilly Lace LLC

References to Dale Carnegie's *How to Win Friends and Influence People* and Dale Carnegie quotes used with permissions from Dale Carnegie & Associates, Inc.

Connect with Terresa Cooper Haskew online:
terresacooperhaskew.com

First Edition

Library of Congress Control Number: 2024932450

Printed in the United States of America.

In honor and memory of my father, W. W. Cooper, whose storytelling and long career in the insurance industry inspired these fictional events and gave life to my protagonist, Winston Taylor.

For my mother, Margaret Ann Cooper, who has always supported my writing and urged me to never give up on this novel.

Were it not eternally dark we would see him, ninety feet down in crystalline seventy-two-degree water where his body abides within a disintegrating shroud, confined inside a silt-covered car. Here he waits, kept company by the remains of mastodons and their ancient human hunters, layered beneath the limestone and strewn through the maze of tunnels, caves, and springs known as the Florida aquifer.

1961

Chapter 1

The woods were quiet, save for rising wind through planted pines—millions of fringed limbs whispering the same ancient language. His father had taught him windy days were good to catch a buck in the brush. The old man had been right.

Winston headed for the power line clearing. Florida Panhandle sand sifted into his polished wingtips. The Winchester slapped against his back.

At the spot where the deer had stood, rich red blood spatter and bits of hair confirmed his hit. He examined the tracks and touched the telltale crack in the right hoofprint—the signature of the big daddy he'd been trailing for weeks.

Blood droplets led him into a shady copse of pines, the ground spongy with hoof-churned straw. Early autumn's air smelled of pine sap, tinged with the musk of an animal on its last run for life. Another three hundred paces and still no deer. He hoped to be gone with his kill by dark.

In the distance, through the green and brown palette of planted timber and thickening scrub, something big and blue caught his eye. He stopped, watching and listening for movement. Nothing. Five quiet steps. Five more. He had no desire to be mistaken for game. "Hey!" he shouted. His voice echoed. Mockingbirds twittered the only reply.

The blue shape materialized as a faded Ford station wagon with rusting bottom panels. The vehicle sat at the edge of an unpaved road, twin to the spot where he'd left his own car, now nearly two miles away. Similar logging roads bisected these thousands of acres of timberland owned by Buckhead Paper Company.

Winston inched closer to the blue wagon and called out again. A buzzard flapped up from a sycamore, its own stalking interrupted. Someone else must be hunting here, may have already discovered his deer—a damn claim jumper. Though he'd only intended a quick stop after work to scout for tracks, the ten-pointer had suddenly appeared. He'd looked the deer in the eye. It had called to him. The whitetail was his, fair and square.

He approached the vehicle from the passenger side and peered across the empty front seat, where the driver's door hung open, framing a pair of legs sprawled in the sand. "Hey, now," he said and hurried around to the figure on the ground. "Hey, buddy. You ok?"

A Negro man lay face up and motionless under the waning October sun. His eyes were partly open, as though squinting into that crystal ball of light. A glistening hole gaped in the torso. A shotgun lay nearby.

Winston's heart was like the runaway deer. He whirled around, rifle in hand, half expecting to see someone pointing a gun at him. He looked down the dirt road in both directions and as far into the trees as he could see. For a long time, he stood completely still, listening to the tangle of forest. He and the dead man were apparently alone.

The shooting appeared accidental. Had the fellow pulled the gun barrel-first from the car? Maybe he'd dropped it when he stepped out. Winston moved around the scene, noting shuffled footprints and blood spray on the sand. A thin line of interested ants.

He crouched to study the face. Maybe mid-twenties. Medium complexion. Not bad looking, even in death. Many Negroes peopled Winston's life insurance sales, but this fellow did not look familiar.

Though the dead man wore a camouflage shirt, his pants were paint-stained khaki, shoes shabby lace-ups spotted with color. Winston glanced down at his own fancy footwear, his own nice work trousers. His white dress shirt was protected by the camouflage jacket he kept handy in his car. Maybe this guy had also succumbed last-minute to an instinctive call to hunt. Dove season was open after all—the shotgun was a weapon for shooting birds.

Whatever the circumstances, Winston knew his involvement in a mysterious death could put him at risk. He'd worked hard for respect, at work, and in the community. His reputation was impeccable. Pretty much. Well . . . as far as anyone knew.

Turning away, he was struck by the thought that he was standing on the edge of a deep chasm of choice, where one misstep could land him in a dark and terrible place. Still, something within compelled him to stay.

Winston rested his rifle on the car's blue hood and lit a cigarette. His hands trembled. He thought of Ruthie when he smelled the Zippo's fumes, the lighter her anniversary gift to him. The regular inhale and exhale of the smoke soothed his alarm over what lay at his feet—a man dead as a runover dog.

This was a real dilemma. This man was someone's son. Maybe someone's father. Lives were about to change forever with the news of this terrible accident. Winston paced, trying to decide what to do—the deer nearly forgotten.

Circling past the Ford's side mirror, Winston caught a glimpse of his own anxious face: smooth, broad forehead now furrowed like an old man's, olive skin paling under stress. He grimaced at his reflection, thin lips exposing a sharp bottom incisor that pushed forward from the rest of his otherwise orderly teeth. Ruthie labeled him good-looking and tough, but where was her handsome, fearless man now? Right here, someplace he shouldn't be, sweating and thirsty—a fool in the woods.

The dead man had been much more prepared for his outing. The Ford's front floorboard held a full jug of water, top sealed with a paper twist. Inspecting the mouth of the clear glass container, Winston chose to believe the rim was clean, untouched by the dead man's lips. He drank deeply, then rested the bottle against his chest. His eyes roved over the station wagon's interior—keys dangled from the ignition; the back held all the tools of a painter's trade, evidence of a hard-working man.

He couldn't just leave the body there for the buzzards—an ugly pair on the ground, not twenty yards out, already waiting for a flock of reinforcements. Winston waved his arms at them, shouting "Hi-yah! Hi-yah!" One flew high into a pine. The other watched him without fear.

"You nasty bastard."

He lifted his rifle and shot the black scavenger. The bird flapped around in the dirt, then was still. Winston realized if he left to get help, one wild thing or another would make mincemeat of the corpse. Unforgivable in his book.

Though not a tall man, Winston was lean and strong, with the carriage of a military drill sergeant. But moving a dead body proved harder than he'd imagined. He dragged the hunter to the tailgate, shoved paint cans aside to make room, then rolled the ruined body onto a paint-spattered drop cloth. He wrapped the rough fabric around the uncooperative corpse and heaved the bundle into the wagon. The dead man's protest registered as a wet, sticky noise. Winston braced himself against the back bumper, drew in a few deep breaths, then sent his lunch tumbling into the sand.

When he wiped his lips on the hem of his hunting jacket, he discovered the camo was streaked with blood. A brownish drip colored the leg of his good pants. He peeled off the jacket and threw it into the cargo hold with his new-found friend and the man's shotgun, then slammed the tailgate shut.

Chapter 2

As he cranked the Ford, Winston wondered about the man's identity. The glove box contents had offered no clues. Maybe his home was just down the main road. Maybe they were going to drive right past it on the way to Pineville. He steered the wagon down the sandy logging road, toward the location of his own car. The sky's previous blue was now a faded gray.

Take it easy, buddy, he thought, reassuring the dead man behind him. *I'll get you to town. Get you cleaned up over at Fern's—they'll put you in a suit. You'll be looking good for your family.*

Keeping his composure was somehow easier by imagining the passenger behind him was upright and breathing. That the man knew Winston was trying to help. The reality of driving down a darkening road in the middle of nowhere, with a bloody corpse at one's back, would be hard for anyone to handle.

Winston pictured the young man's mother wailing at the coffin: "Lord Jesus, no! He ain't nothin' but a boy." Could see her caressing the cold face, maybe draping herself over the corpse. Death was hard to bear for those left behind . . . and who *were* those people who would mourn? Could they afford a funeral? Did they have life insurance? The need to know was a small fire inside him.

Winston's black Studebaker waited in the distance like an old friend. He pulled up behind the sedan and put his rifle inside, back in its case. But when he opened the Ford's tailgate to retrieve his bloody hunting jacket, the shrouded corpse nearly rolled out into the dirt. Partially open eyes peeked over the paint-crusted canvas, keeping watch. Who *was* this fellow?

He pulled back part of the tarp, tilted the body, and with great foreboding, wiggled free a limp leather wallet. Inside, a State of Florida Driver's License: Jackson Smith. Twenty years old.

Tallahassee address, fifty or so miles from Pineville—not even in Winston's insurance sales scope. But his name . . . his name rang a bell. Smith was common. But Jackson . . .

Winston headed back to his own car, to the front seat, to his Bayside Life Insurance debit book. The black leather book, easily eight inches thick, contained the inventory of all his policyholders. Ruthie called it Winston's Book of Souls.

"Honey, the people listed here aren't dead," he had often argued.

"I know that," she'd pout, but she firmly believed that the people he insured had entrusted him with their very souls. "They're paying for your protection. You're like their guardian. They feel safer when you insure their lives."

Her words echoed as he grabbed the book by its rolled leather handles, laid it on his car's hood, and opened the thick covers. Little leather alphabet tabs separated the sections. He flipped to the S's and ran his dirty finger over page after page of the green-lined paper. Quite a few Smiths populated the pages: Grayson, Mollie, Ethel, Deacon, Roger, Barry. Jackson . . . JACKSON SMITH. Right there, in his own handwriting: Jackson Smith, with a cross-reference to the policyholder, Mabel Griffin.

Winston's pulse quickened. Mabel was Jackson's grandmother. She owned a policy on her grandson, who lived out of town. A student, wasn't he? He thumbed through the wallet again and found a FAMU student ID. Black dread rustled within him. Jackson was a Bayside Life Insurance customer all right—he was one of Winston's "special policies." Holy shit. He clapped the debit book shut and threw it into his sedan.

Back at the Ford's tailgate, he stared awhile at the now-named remains. Then he tucked the wallet within a fold of the shroud and closed the hatch. He tossed his stained camo jacket into his own car and slid back into the idling station wagon. Winston Taylor and Jackson Smith gunned it down the unpaved road, the vehicle fishtailing in the deep sand.

Winston's whole body trembled. Here he was, hauling ass to town to do a good deed for a man whose very identity could ruin him and his whole Taylor household. What the hell was he to do? He slowed the car to a crawl.

∽

Blue Sink.

The name floated into his head the way answers appeared in the window of Mary Carolyn's Magic 8-Ball. Blue Sink. An ancient erosion of limestone bedrock, filled with water, created a deep sinkhole. Such holes were common in this part of Florida, but Blue Sink was larger than many. The natural pool was a summer hangout for high schoolers. A place to get drunk and skinny dip. The sinkhole's banks were so steep that swimmers hauled themselves straight up and out by clutching tree roots. The supposedly bottomless hole was also an illegal dump site for broken appliances and furniture, or anything one needed to disappear. Blue Sink. *Signs point to yes.*

$\backsim$

Winston realized he'd long since passed the fork to Blue Sink. He slowed down to reverse direction, executing a three-point turn on the sandy road, trying to stay off the softer shoulder. The wheels began to spin. He gassed it, whining tires throwing a rooster tail of sand behind him, digging deeper and deeper into the dirt. He threw the car in reverse, laid on the accelerator, then snatched the shifter into drive, trying to rock the car out of the ruts. Next thing he knew, the station wagon was almost bottomed out.

Winston shoved the driver door open and hopped out into the deep sand. "Goddamnit!" He kicked the back bumper, which was nearly touching the ground. His toes shrieked inside his previously shiny shoes.

On his knees, he began digging out the tires with bare, cupped hands. Then dirt flew when he used a metal paint tray as a shovel. He gunned the engine, trying again to rock the old car out of the ruts, but the wagon buried its own

10

undercarriage in the soft sand like a baby refusing to budge from the womb.

Winston wrapped his arms around the wheel and rested his head. Despite the chilly evening air, he was sweating from his efforts, and the smell of Argo starch drifted up from his damp shirt. Ruthie had ironed it just this morning before she and Mary Carolyn left for the asthma specialist in Gainesville. To the best of her knowledge, Bayside Life was paying her husband enough to afford their daughter's fancy doctor. No more best guesses out of old Dr. Wiles, Pineville's favored family physician. Wiles was good for chicken pox and measles, but worthless when Mary Carolyn's little lungs struggled all night in the steamed-up bathroom. Too many times Winston had held her small body near the scalding shower spray, looked into her wide panicked eyes, and promised she'd be okay.

"But I can't bweeve, Daddy."

They *needed* that specialist. But Winston's earnings were not enough. No siree. On one of those particularly awful nights, Winston had conceived of a plan to help cover his daughter's medical care. Ruthie knew nothing of his arrangements, and nobody had been hurt in the bargain.

"The bargain you made with who?" Dead Man Jackson asked from the back of the wagon.

Winston sat up straight.

"God don't usually bargain," the voice mused.

Winston looked over his shoulder, relieved to find an empty back seat. Was he losing his mind? Had he bargained with the devil? Cut a deal for Mary Carolyn's relief? He didn't recall any specific arrangement like that. But he knew he couldn't let *this* deal, this plan, fall apart now. Not here in these lonesome piney woods. No way. He had to get to Blue Sink.

In evening's growing gloom, he picked up armloads of fallen branches and pine boughs. He dug the wheels out again, front and back, and wedged wood beneath the tires, creating a sturdy base for traction. Then, in case it might help, he prayed for God's will to be done and refrained from asking that it fall in his favor. When the Ford's engine rumbled to life, he remembered to pray for Jackson's soul, too, the one that should have been safe in that holy Book of Souls. He had failed them all.

Though some of the branches flew from beneath the spinning wheels, enough held their place that the car was soon rolling on top of the road. Winston floored it. A half mile later, the Ford began to vibrate.

Thump, thump, thump. The wheel shook in his hands, steering nearly impossible. A flat tire? A fucking flat? Did his prayers just fall on deaf ears? The back passenger-side tire was now running on the rim. One of the broken limbs he'd used for traction must have jabbed into the spinning rubber. The tire wouldn't make it to Blue Sink.

Chapter 3

The spare was in the back with Jackson. Weak yellow dome lighting offered little illumination for retrieving the tire and jack and wasn't helping Jackson's complexion either. Winston leaned in over the ripening corpse and located the wing nut securing the extra tire. His position allowed little leverage, and the nut refused to budge. He needed more room.

"Everybody out!" he ordered. His head spun like he'd just downed a six-pack of Busch in one sitting. "Time for a pit stop!"

His mouth curled up at the corners as he snugged the body in the paint tarp and dragged it out of the wagon. *Wouldn't it be some shit if somebody happened to drive down this road right now? Just happened to drive by and see me and a dead man. The two of us just sitting here, communing in the moonlight.* Winston's teeth gleamed. If somebody just happened by on their way to the store for a gallon of milk, say, or a loaf of bread, they'd see them both clear as day. He laughed a little at his ridiculous thoughts. The joyful noise of his own voice was startling.

Like somebody would just roll up and offer help. He snickered.

"Excuse me, sir, I see you have a flat and a dead man on your hands," Winston said aloud in a deep, snooty voice. "May I offer you some assistance?"

Fucking hilarious.

Winston's shoulders shook with laughter. He laughed until tears ran down his face, howled until no sound came from his mouth. He slid down into the sand, slapping his own thigh. He looked over at the half-wrapped mummy. Could this shit get any worse?

The distant rumbling of a truck wiped the silliness right off his face.

Winston listened so hard his ears rang. Unsure if the truck was coming closer or moving away, he dragged Jackson around to the far side of the car, out of sight. He located a pair of pliers in a beat-up box of tools and climbed into the cargo area to wrestle out the spare. The tire changing set him back no more than twenty minutes, helped along by the tiny flame of the Zippo. Its limited light revealed what darkness had tried to cover. He kissed the lighter before dropping it back into his pocket.

With Jackson back in his bunk, Winston made a wide-open run for Blue Sink. The Ford rattled and clanged, shaking with the challenge. His headlights bounced across the rutted way, and he watched carefully for the sinkhole turnoff.

∽

Winston stopped the car near Blue Sink's edge. He cut the engine and lights. On the last leg of this trip, he'd rolled up his window against the chill. But ol' Jackson had begun giving off an odor in the closed car, so he'd put the glass back down. Now he sat at the wheel, shivering with cold and fear.

He'd come to dump the body, to prevent his own ultimate ruin. But was this the right thing? He still had time to change his mind, to turn around and take Jackson home. He turned everything over again and again in his head.

The sound of crickets flooded in, and he could hear tiny rustlings everywhere on the forest floor—a million little creatures on their nightly missions, doing whatever it is they are called upon to do for survival. And Winston was just one of the many, just one little speck in the universe, holding onto his world by his fingernails. Surely God's eye was closed for the night by now. Or maybe He'd not be able to spot this one little transgression in the multitude of so many that must be happening at this very same moment.

He had thought through his decision, and he was good with it: he'd make Jackson Smith disappear. Jackson Smith had left his family to go hunting. As far as anyone would ever know, something happened along the way to the woods that made Jackson just keep on going, just keep on truckin' and never look back. No death. No funeral.

Winston started the engine and turned on the headlights. He got out and measured with careful steps the distance from the car to the sinkhole's edge. Five feet and the Ford would roll over the rim. He kicked through fallen leaves to find a long, sturdy limb. Back at the wheel, he waited, giving Jackson one last moment to protest. But the dead man had already accepted his fate. Winston shifted the car into drive, jumped out, and poked the gas pedal with the stick. The engine revved like an airplane and the 1952 Country Squire Wagon lurched over the lip of the deep, dark hole.

The splash was louder than expected. Winston shuffled to the sinkhole's edge and trembled as he watched the headlights splay on the sink's steep walls, until the car disappeared into lightless depths.

Winston's feet throbbed in his wingtips, and he rubbed his arms for warmth while he walked. His car was miles away. Maybe he'd get lucky with a passing logger out late in the woods. Maybe someone would happen along to hear his woeful tale, how he'd been out scouting for deer. How he'd become engrossed in the trail, and ultimately lost. Hey, maybe the Good Samaritan who stopped for him could use a little help in return: a good deal on a life insurance policy with Bayside Life. It could happen.

Chapter 4

After Jackson Smith's *burial*–a term that helped Winston live with what he'd done–he'd fallen ill, shaking all over. He'd thrown up several times like his body was trying to purge something foreign he'd swallowed. Ruthie exerted her wifely authority and sent him to bed. She tried aspirin and ginger ale. She watched him carefully for signs of measles–adults weren't immune–but no red spots appeared on his skin.

A week later, Dr. Wiles made an evening house call.

"What's the matter with you, boy?" he asked, his wrinkled face sagging with fatigue. He opened his black bag, pulled out his stethoscope, and listened intently to the language of Winston's heart and lungs. Then the old doctor perched on the bed's edge and patted his patient's arm.

"Listen, Winston. I know you're worried about yourself, but I don't think there's a damned thing wrong with you, physically."

Winston raised up on his elbows. "Doc! I've been puking my guts out. I wake up in the night, shivering like an Eskimo with no clothes. This's gone on too long. You know I hardly ever get sick." He flopped back against the pillows. "My chest feels weird, like my heart could just stop. And I have spells of not getting enough air. Scares the shit out of me."

Wiles sighed, then looked directly into Winston's eyes: "You're not dying, Winston. You're a strong and healthy thirty-five-year-old man."

Winston shook his head in disagreement.

Dr. Wiles raised his hand and continued: "I don't doubt what you're experiencing. These feelings . . . you're worrying over something. Or maybe you've been touched by a conflict of the spirit. It can happen."

"I'm not following you."

"Have you been overly upset lately? Maybe a problem at work, or an argument with somebody? The death of someone close to you could bring it on."

Winston shrugged.

"Sometimes people experience something extraordinary that doesn't sit well with who they are or what they believe, and the event rocks them to the core. The body might react with symptoms much like yours, especially palpitations and shortness of breath. Spirituality comes from the Latin word meaning 'breath.' You see what I mean?"

"What kind of witch doctor bullshit is that?" scowled Winston.

The doctor raised his eyebrows, then frowned. "That's not a medical opinion, my friend. I heard it in church, and I only share it with my favorite patients and fellow worshippers. Which reminds me, I haven't seen you at First Baptist lately. You might need to pray about whatever's bothering you." He tucked his stethoscope back into his bag.

"Oh! And speaking of favorite patients, Mary Carolyn is responding well to her respiratory treatments in Gainesville. Those are some damn fine doctors over there, and I'm glad y'all pursued that course of treatment. She's gonna outgrow the worst of that asthma."

Winston offered an uncomfortable smile. "She *is* doing much better. Appreciate you sending us to those guys."

It all sounded so easy. But nobody had a clue what it was costing to keep his daughter with a specialist, or the things he had done to make that happen in the first place.

"But what about my situation, Doc? Don't you think I need to see a specialist or something? I can't lay around here forever. I've got a job and a family to feed."

"Despite what you're telling me, everything sounds good. If the feelings with your breathing and heartbeat continue, let me know." The doctor headed for the door.

"What am I supposed to do in the meantime?"

Wiles turned. He studied his shoes for a moment, then raised his head. "You remember that Bible story about Jesus healing the paralytic at Bethesda? Tells the paralyzed guy to pick up his bed and walk, and miraculously, he can walk." Wiles pointed his finger at Winston. "My best advice for you is to shake this off and get up off your ass. Take a shower and shave that raggedy beard. Go sell some life insurance to people who just might need it."

By Friday Winston thought he'd survive. He cleaned himself up and headed to the office. He knew his boss, Roger Johns, would be more than happy to have him back.

"Well goddamn, Winston, I thought you'd died or something," Roger said. He leaned back in his chair, looked Winston up and down, and grinned. "Glad you pulled yourself out of that swamp fever, or whatever was wrong. I've had a helluva time keeping up with your accounts and taking care of this place by myself." He slid a red pencil behind his ear. "And to top it off, the home office has been chewing on my ass."

"I hear you. A rough couple of weeks for me, too." Winston took off his narrow-brimmed fedora. "I'm better. I gotta get my head back in the game. See what's going on with my territory." He wriggled out of his jacket. "I hate that you had to take care of my work. Ruthie said you called several times."

"I tell you what, pal, your being out sick really drove home what a big damn territory we've got. *You've* got, mostly. Widespread, I mean." Roger got up and sharpened his pencil. "Maybe I need to push the home office again for another agent. Give you more time to work on new business." He knew Winston's talent was in his talk—the man could sell anything.

After a long but pleasant catch-up, Roger sent Winston out the door with a hearty slap on the shoulder. "Knock 'em dead, man," he cheered. "Make us some money!"

∽

Winston started with an easy route, collecting a few premium payments from policyholders on the outskirts of Pineville in a modern development of small concrete block homes— Spring Lake Heights.

Mrs. Williams, a humpbacked widow, led him into her cramped living room which reeked of cabbage. He perched on the edge of her Afghan-draped sofa, opened the debit book onto his lap, and carefully recorded her cash payment, twice checking the amount he'd written. He hoped she didn't notice the tremble of his pencil.

The old woman prattled on about her grandchildren, the youngest just beginning to walk. Winston nodded and smiled, though inside himself he watched his own footsteps following the blood trail of the buck he'd shot. He longed to revise his path, which had taken him to the station wagon, to the dead man sprawled in the sand—one of his very own "special insureds."

Jackson Smith was special, all right. Maybe it was Winston's good luck that he'd stumbled upon that scene. Something had led him there. Maybe fate had given him a break, given him a chance to fix his royal screwup.

"Thank you, Mrs. Williams," he said, zipping her payment into his money pouch. He rose from the couch to go, and his eyes drifted over a hodgepodge of framed family photos. "Hope you get to visit those grandkids over the holidays."

～

Winston could think of nothing but what he'd done. He had the shock under control now, mostly. But his smooth solution for saving himself—cover up the "special policies"—was not enough. What else did he need in order to protect his own ass? To keep his story straight? Fear still ran through him; he could smell it in his sour sweat. Though the idea scared him, he needed to see Mabel Griffin.

Chapter 5

Hampton Springs was more than twenty miles from Pineville. Mabel lived on a remote stretch of rutted, hard-packed dirt. Small houses huddled just off the road's edge, some nothing more than abandoned wooden shacks. A few appeared shaggy with peeling, faded paint. Mabel's house, however, stood out like a posy in a bed of dead weeds. A robin's-egg blue welcomed Winston, with its yellow steps and stoop. It made sense; her grandson had been a painter.

"Insurance man," Winston called, squeaking open the screen to knock on her closed front door. He stood back, waiting, debit book in one hand, fedora in the other. In a moment, the door creaked open. Mabel pushed up her thick glasses and peered at him, her eyes oversized and wavering behind the magnification.

"Mr. Winston! Come on into the house. So cold out today."

Winston stepped into the main room, which was a small kitchen and living area. The walls were painted a glossy apple green. A soap opera played on the console television. She lowered the volume.

"Good to see you, Mrs. Griffin! How you been?"

"Oh, lordy, Mr. Winston. I got enough ailments to keep you here all day. I know you didn't come here for that," she smiled.

"I've always got time for you, ma'am." Winston sat in a cane-bottom rocker close to a small propane heater, dropped his book and hat at his feet. He rubbed his hands together to warm them and gazed at a small picture on the side table: a young colored boy, smiling shyly at the camera.

"Honey, you a good-lookin' white man. I think you get better-lookin' ever time I see you," she cackled.

"Well thank you, ma'am. But I think it's time you got some new glasses."

"These eyes be seventy-two years old come spring—Jesus let me live that long. I don't think they's enough glasses in this world gonna improve what I sees. But I knows a handsome man when I sees one."

A red flame crept up Winston's neck and into his face. This was their typical banter—Mabel Griffin was clueless about what had happened. Hopefully, she would never know that he was a participant in her coming grief.

Mabel disappeared into her bedroom and returned with a large red pocketbook. She dropped it onto the metal kitchen table and rummaged through the bag's contents, removing a round tin of Copenhagen snuff and a yellowed handkerchief. Her hand surfaced again with a thin, scarred wallet. She called Winston to join her.

Winston sat down at the table, opened the big debit book and pulled the stub of a pencil from behind his ear. He located Mabel's account page; her life insurance coverage was in the amount of $500. She'd been his customer since the day he joined Bayside Life. "How much?" she asked, though they'd done this countless times.

Winston told her: same as always. She looked at him, her mouth open, waiting. "It's $1.76 on your policy, Mrs. Griffin. And . . ." Winston flipped to Jackson Smith's page. "And it's another $1.25 on your grandson." Jackson's "special policy" was for $1,000, double his grandmother's coverage. Based on mortality tables, his premium was a bit lower due to his youth and good health.

She nodded like she remembered, counted out ten ones, and handed them over.

Realizing her confusion, Winston took the cash, pulled off three bills, and handed back seven. "Need a penny?" he asked. She dug around in the red bag again and produced the copper coin, smiling like a child finding an Easter egg. He took a deep breath.

"How's your grandson doing? He still in school?"

"Oh, yes," she said, taking a seat. She nudged the can of Copenhagen back and forth along the edge of the table while she talked. "Been going to college. I can't call the name of it. Forgetting too many things these days."

Winston's face flushed hot again.

"A good boy, my Jack. He been painting houses to help feed hisself. Shamed to say Suki, my girl, never was much of a mama. But the boy come see me a few times since he been grown. Brung me a little money once. Worried 'bout his old granny. I'm all that boy's got left for family."

Winston reminded himself he was not responsible for her grandson's death—he'd only cleaned up the mess. That thought made him feel a little better. But the small payment that now lay in his hand, money Mabel had saved for Jackson's insurance, brought him great shame. The amount looked insignificant in today's light. He knew it had not been paltry, though, when added up for more than a year. And thrown in with a number of his other "special policy" premiums. Still, his gut tightened.

Winston recorded both payments in the debit book. The notation was the first legitimate entry for Jackson Smith's special policy account, though Mabel had no way of knowing that. He'd sold the policy to Mabel Griffin, betting her grandson—a young, healthy male who rarely made an appearance at his grandmother's door—would never be an issue, expecting the guy to live a long life. Winston was so confident in the longevity of all his special insureds, in fact, that the insurance coverage didn't even exist. But the premiums did. And where did all those "special" premium payments go?

He closed the book and tucked the pencil back behind his ear, then asked: "You seen Jackson lately?"

Mabel shook her head. "Not in a couple months. But he'll be back soon. He always comes back."

Winston sat in his car, rubbing his forehead. How could he possibly just move on like nothing had ever happened? Ruthie always said things looked better in the light of day. He thought he'd find out for himself.

Chapter 6

Winston parked his car near the edge of the Buckhead logging road where two weeks earlier he'd come to scout for deer tracks. That day had been warm and bright. Today the sky was a low ceiling of gray clouds. A cold front was moving through, kicking up a stiff, biting wind. Turkey oaks clustered at the edge of the planted pine forest, littering the ground with rusty leaves. He stepped out into the chill, grabbed his jacket off the back seat, and clamped his felt hat onto his head.

He walked, watching for any trace of the buck he'd shot that day, and wondering why he'd even pulled the trigger. He rarely hunted out of season. But remembering was like trying to repeat a dream. The animal's eye looming through the scope was what stuck with him.

Finally, a brown bloodstain was visible in a cluster of low palmettos. Another further along. He detected a faint odor of something dead. Maybe his deer, fallen somewhere in a thicket. Buzzard bait. But Winston was not there for the deer.

His feet continued on the remembered path, coppered with fallen straw, all the way through that tract of tall trees. All the way to the second logging road where he'd discovered the body of Jackson Smith. The walk was longer than he recollected.

Winston moved out of the stand of pines and into the dirt road. All was quiet except for the whistling wind. He stood very still in the place where the body had lain. He could almost see it.

Again, he considered the idea that Jackson Smith had not been alone when he died. That someone had been hidden, watching him deal with the dead man. But there was just no sign of that. No evidence, really, that anything malicious had occurred here. What he had not erased himself, wind and animals had. He cupped his Zippo's flame and lit a Camel, the tobacco a comfort.

One more stop to make.

Trees hemming the narrow entrance to Blue Sink whipped in the weather. A frantic limb screeched against the passenger door. Winston winced at the likely scratch. At a safe distance from the sinkhole, he turned off the engine and fired up a smoke. He rolled the window down and sat, watching the birds and hurried squirrels as he considered his situation.

Why in hell had he ever thought that hiding the body in Blue Sink was the best solution? Only crazy people did shit like that. Was he crazy? No. Confused and disoriented, maybe. Desperate. But he knew that if he didn't get mentally on top of this, crazy might come knocking. He shouldered the car door open and stepped out.

Years had passed since he'd seen the sinkhole in full light. Here, a mixed cluster of live oaks, buckeyes, and bigleaf magnolias reigned over pines, holding court near the mouth of the sink. Spanish moss draped crooked hardwood limbs like ruffled gray shawls lifting and twisting in the air. Wind bent the limber pines at dangerous angles. A small dust devil took shape, lofting sand and debris, then spun itself out. Winston stamped out the cigarette butt and moved toward the water.

He surveyed the area where he'd started Jackson Smith's station wagon rolling into the sinkhole. No gouges or scrapes were noticeable on the earth's surface. Any tire marks were covered by leaves and straw. Winston baby-stepped toward the sinkhole rim, afraid he'd see a car roof bobbing at the surface. Or worse, Jackson's bloated body floating like a marshmallow in a drink from hell.

The terrain was extremely uneven. He grabbed onto a bush and bent to peer down into the deep sink. His head dizzied. He stepped to steady himself and the soft soil collapsed from beneath his leather-soled shoe.

A cry flew from his mouth as he fell, sliding sideways down the steep embankment. The ground was alternately rock and sand, and he scrabbled at the earth to stop himself. A rotting stump, jutting from a shallow ledge, caught him at the waist, knocking the wind out of him. His eyes bulged. He croaked for air. *What the fuck!* His fingers gripped a sapling that sprang from the sinkhole wall, and he lay like a fish out of water, gills opening and closing on nothing.

When his diaphragm recovered and he was able to breathe, he raised his head and looked down into the sinkhole—a liquid dark blue. In his dazed state, the hole appeared as an unblinking eye, a god gazing placidly back at him. The water's surface, protected from the wind, was smooth and free of debris. He lay still against the cold ground. The wind was gentler here, and he could hear groundwater trickling into the sinkhole. If someone had to die, this was not such a bad resting place. Surely better than molding over in a damp, underground vault.

Winton's abraded palms stung. Several fingernails were laced with blood. His ribs throbbed against the stub of the tree that had saved him. Hitting the water wouldn't have killed him, but wet clothes in icy air might. And how would he have explained the sopping clothes to Ruthie?

He lay a moment longer, considering the safest way out. The ledge offered a bit of wiggle room. He held onto the stump and the sapling and rose to his knees. Protruding roots and limestone cavities offered handholds. He climbed carefully back to the rim, finally standing on solid ground. His legs trembled.

At his feet, in a smooth patch of sand, lay a buckeye—a shiny brown nut-like seed pod. He picked it up, turned it over, and his thumb found a home in its slight hollow. A perfect fit. The nut was inedible, poisonous even, but his daddy always said buckeyes brought good luck. He pocketed the find, a reminder that a self-correction was in order, that he needed to step carefully from here on out. He would not fall again, today *or* tomorrow. As long as he kept the secret of what happened here at Blue Sink, all would be well.

1963

Chapter 7

Winston woke with a gasp, a man breaching the surface, lungs hungry. His chest heaved. The water had been cold and dark except for the headlights of the submerged car. He trembled violently; his undershirt was soaked.

The window air conditioner blew icicles over him. Ruthie lay like a corpse on the far side of the bed, the chenille spread tugged up to her chin. She was oblivious to the sinkhole dreams he'd been surviving for the past two years. The station wagon filling, sinking—his night vision keen as a sniper's, peering into the car's flooded cargo area, seeing the tarp-wrapped body bumping against the headliner.

In this night terror, Jackson Smith fought the wrapping of cloth. Struggled for air, his mouth open against the back glass of the wagon. Winston had jumped in, thinking to save the man he'd thought was dead, the man he'd consigned to rest forever in a natural sinkhole in the middle of a forest. A decent burial, or so it seemed at the time.

Winston watched the dark outline of his sleeping wife. Ruthie was happy in this life they'd built together. He'd be damned if he'd allow that two-year-old corpse to come undone . . . or cause his own undoing.

The Bayside Life office sat still and silent this early Friday morning. Winston stood just inside the glass door, letting his eyes adjust to the dimness. The smell of pencil shavings and stale cigarette smoke filled the room. He breathed deeply, then flipped on the lights. He knew he was lucky to be here.

Roger Johns had hired him seven years back and taught him everything he knew about life insurance. But Winston was born with the gift of gab, and the sometimes not-so-delicate art of persuasion. After Roger's promotion to district manager and move to the home office in Jacksonville, Winston had taken charge of the Pineville office, with a significant and much needed pay raise.

Winston started the coffee brewing, sat down, and yawned. He looked around the crowded workspace. Three heavy oak desks and rolling chairs took up most of the space. A large green and white Bayside Life logo decorated the back wall. Policy documents and correspondence almost buried the wire filing basket on his desk. His one employee's workspace fared no better.

Angus F. Larkins, A. F. to his friends (if he had any), was a bespectacled, overweight man with slicked-back gray hair, reminding Winston of a well-preened owl. *Who-Who?* Before he'd moved to the home office, Roger had hired A. F. to support Winston in Pineville. Winston had wanted to do his own hiring but was reluctant to challenge his boss's decision. Now Winston wished he had.

A. F. was a whiner and a shirker, a distasteful character. The old man whistled when he breathed and spoke with a husky, whiskey voice. His inappropriate jokes and hoarse laughter were irksome. And he never smelled *clean.* A. F. wouldn't survive much longer at Bayside Life if Winston had any say-so.

The third desk, once Roger's, was vacant except for boxes of the company's customer trinkets: pencils, rulers, packs of sewing needles, and brochures. Winston had been told that low sales in this poor region of the state didn't justify adding another agent. He disagreed but had yet to figure out a way to change this.

While the percolator gurgled through the last of its cycle, hissing out the satisfying aroma of Folgers, brewed dark as river water, Winston doodled on a lined yellow pad, recalling last night's dream of dread. He sketched a mummy with eyes and drew a water line above the body. The secret that must always remain under wraps. Then, with a cup of black coffee and a lit Camel, Senior Agent and General Manager Winston Taylor flipped his desk calendar to Friday; another fine October day of hustling customers.

⌒

"Sorry, boss," A. F. rumbled, arriving almost forty-five minutes late. "Car trouble this morning. Gotta work on that carburetor again tonight."

Winston tossed a ball of paper into the wastebasket. "That story's getting really old, A. F. I'm about fed up with your crap." He'd lost count of the old man's tardies. "Your excuses need as much work as your sales pitch." A. F. was like an anchor, dragging their office down to drown for lack of new business.

A. F. Larkins enjoyed Bayside Life's employee benefits: a decent salary, gas and clothing allowances, and a nice commission on new business sales. Trouble was the company received a minimal return on investment—the agent had sold only a handful of significant life insurance policies during his tenure, and rarely met the monthly goal for small burial contracts. He was, however, diligent about collecting existing customer premium payments. Yeah, Winston kept a close eye on the man's debit book, monitoring the regular balancing of his accounts. You can't outfox a fox.

"Our sales are way down again this month," Winston said. "Roger's under a lot of pressure to fix it; he's putting the heat on me. So, I'm asking YOU. . ." Winston glared, pointing at Larkins. "What are you gonna do to help the situation?"

A. F. rearranged the top of his desk, refusing to engage. The wall clock ticked.

Winston was suddenly up and rushing at A. F. He grabbed the back of the man's chair and sent him rolling away from his desk. A. F.'s gray face went white.

"I'm talking to you, and you by god better listen!" Winston growled. He walked away, then back. He took a deep breath, then let it out in a whoosh. "You're digging your own grave here, man. You gotta do something to help save yourself."

A. F. fished for something inside his ear. Winston waited. Their eyes finally met.

"What you *need* to do, first, is get your ass to work on time. Then you *need* to focus on selling our existing customers some additional coverage."

A. F. mumbled agreement.

"Talk to 'em about their relatives. Help these people see what a fix they'd be in if a family member fell over dead. Lemme give you a good example." Winston was cranking up his sales engine. "Say you're going to see Gladys Latham—she's one of your good customers. She and her no-count husband are insured, but what about those kids?"

"I already asked her about the kids. She ain't interested."

Winston's grim smile was punctuated by his rogue bottom incisor. "That's what they all say. So next time you go see her, you come down with a case of amnesia. You start tap dancing on her something like this: 'Mrs. Latham, you ought to think about buying a little policy on your son. Otis is getting older. Won't be long before he'll be out running with his buddies. He'll be borrowing his daddy's car, driving fast and crazy, getting himself into situations where you can't protect him.' See, that's shit mamas don't wanna think about. You'll get her attention like that." Winston was on stage now, pacing in front of A. F. who was nodding along.

"Then she's gonna push back a little, look at you like you're crazy, and tell you there ain't no way they can afford more insurance. It's all they can do to pay for what they got on her and her old man. If he was to get sick and die, or get killed driving home drunk some Friday night, they'd just have to have something to keep a roof over their heads, food on the table. Like that.

"But you can't let that stop you. They've damn sure got money to buy that liquor on Fridays. So, you push it again: 'Well, Mrs. Latham, I hear what you're saying. But I'm telling you, if something bad, *heaven forbid*, were to happen to your boy, you couldn't afford NOT to have life insurance on him.' Trust me, she's gonna be glued to you."

35

A. F. bobbed his head, but his eyes wandered to his wristwatch.

"So, then you ask her: 'How'd you begin to pay for a funeral? Or even buy him a coffin? Think about it, Mrs. Latham. I'm just suggesting a small policy, enough to cover a burial if it was ever needed. The weekly premium won't cost you much more than one of those pints Mr. Latham carries around with him on Friday nights.' You might give her a little wink here like you're kidding, but you ain't."

⌐⌐

Once A. F. was out the door, his breath chuffing like a train, Winston walked around the room, listening to the silence, eyes returning again to that empty desk collecting clutter. He needed an extra agent. Or at least a different agent. Somebody who could actually reach the low-income households, whites and coloreds alike. A. F. Larkins just did not have the touch. Many white customers found him distasteful. A couple of colored insureds voiced unease. Winston didn't have time to manage all the accounts and collect all the premiums, though many policyholders only wanted him—Winston Taylor—knocking on their doors. A. F. was a problem.

Over the past two years, Winston had worked hard to prove his worth and keep his reputation clean, if not spotless. He'd finally settled up all those "special policies" he'd collected on in '61. A loan from banker David Morgan had helped him pay back the premiums and activate all those bogus policies he'd "sold."

When he'd asked David for the loan, he'd cited gambling debt, which really wasn't much of a lie. While the reason he needed the cash was embarrassing and hard to say, Winston knew he'd not be harshly criticized for it—he and David occasionally played poker together at the Starlight Motel. And surely the banker had been impressed that Winston had acted responsibly by covering the debt and making regular payments on the loan.

Making amends for what he'd done to Mabel Griffin might never be reconciled. While he could have turned her business over to A. F.—out of sight, out of mind—he held her accounts close, and kept collecting the premiums. Mabel's memory was rapidly decaying, but she still justified Jackson's absence with college and his painting business, never doubting that her grandson would be back.

Winston often thought about the law coming for him. That somehow, they'd find out about his disposal of Jackson Smith's body, his covering up the death. He'd lose his job. His family. His future. But as Dale Carnegie said, "Today is the tomorrow you worried about yesterday." Ninety-nine percent of the things we worry about never happen. Thus, Winston kept the secret, and so far, nobody was the wiser.

Chapter 8

Louis Fisher whistled down the dirt lane to Fina Creek, a small finger of the Foley River. The path was less than a mile from the boarding house where he'd grubbed garden worms that now knotted themselves together inside a covered paper cup. He carried his cane pole horizontally at his side, preventing the tip from snagging on overhanging live oak limbs and swags of moss. The beaten trail rose slightly nearing the creek bank, then sloped again to the water's edge.

Louis slung his baited line into the tea-colored creek and lowered himself onto a rotted log. He watched the orange bobber drift, quivering in the slow current. It's like his life, he thought—lead weight holding him down, in danger any minute of being jerked under. He rolled his head around and loosened his shoulders. Relaxed his mouth. *You one lucky boy to even be here today,* he told himself. A free bird. Your black ass could've been behind bars. One misstep and still could be.

The sounds of nature calmed him, the singing of birds he could not name, the abrasive cussing of crows. A breeze stirred pine needles and rustled small leaves on the overhanging oak. Unlike the upstart pines, some of the trees in this hammock had weathered storms much worse than his own.

A broad maple canopy across the creek was just beginning to tease with tinges of red. November was near, but North Florida still steamed in warm humidity. Louis wasn't complaining. If he were still holed up in the Georgia hills, he'd be wearing a jacket by now. The climate of Pineville required less layering. Somehow, he needed to get back to the core of who he was, to shed the invisible weight of secrets.

He studied his hands, their smooth tops, long slender fingers—a businessman's hands. But the flip side told the truth—a laborer's callused palms. Etta said he was "aristocratic," with the good looks of famous Sam Cooke. If he could only sing like the guy, he smiled to himself.

A turtle floated just below the creek's surface, head poking up like a snake, then vanished. Out near the middle, a fish rolled the water. Louis lifted his pole, bringing up the line; the worm still showed signs of life. With a practiced flick of his wrist, he swung the line further out and let the lead sinker carry it down into the depths, the bobber stopping the bait from reaching the bottom. A peace crept into him; his eyes grew heavy. He thanked the Lord for this Friday, his forty hours at the papermill finished.

A quick rustle of leaves. Over his shoulder, a young woman approached, slender in a gathered gold skirt and a sleeveless white blouse. Her creamy brown arms swung easy at her sides. "Hey, Louis," she said in a low voice. "Catchin' anything?"

Louis grinned. "Looks like I mighta caught me a pretty girl," he said, laying down his pole and standing up. She walked into his arms and he ran his hands over her back and down the mound of her rump. His wide mouth covered hers as he lifted the side of her skirt, his fingers seeking the elastic of cotton panties beneath. Then she pulled back, laughing.

"Damn, girl. Don't be playin' with me, now." He pressed his forehead down against hers. "You know I got this here long pole and I do know how to use it."

Etta rolled her eyes at his exaggerated speech, her teeth dazzling against dark red lipstick. "I ain't playing with you, Louis. I'd do it with you right now on the bank of this creek. I ain't proud."

"Bubba'll whip my ass if he catches me messing with his little sister. Or worse, he won't give me a ride to work. Buckhead's a mighty long walk. You good, baby, but I gotta eat."

Etta broke a thin stem from a wild azalea growing on the bank. One by one she pulled off the leaves, watching Louis thread a slick worm onto the hook's barb. He threw the line back out.

"Why you always so worried about somebody knowing your business? Bubba ain't got no say-so over me. Gramma Ruby, now, she's a different story." She tickled him with the tip of the switch and he swatted it away.

"Keep my business to myself. I got big plans, girl. Nothing gonna mess 'em up. I've saved me almost enough for a down payment on a car. Got that money in the Citizen's Bank downtown. Nobody can touch it." Louis lifted the pole and slung the line sideways to plop the bait just beneath an overhanging oak limb.

"Well, this is big news," she said, one eyebrow raised. "How come you always acting all poor-like?"

"Cause I am. Been broke mostly my whole life. Only way out's to work and save. And I'm gonna get me a better job. Buckhead's steady money, but I ain't staying in that stinking mill for long." He wiped the worm juice on the leg of his pants. "You watch. I took some business classes a while back. I know more'n you think I do. I ain't gonna be just another colored boy in a mill."

The pole dipped in his hands, bobber gone beneath the dark water. He snatched it, setting the barb. The limber cane bent like a shepherd's hook; he fought the swift tugging. A yellow-breasted sunfish, bigger than his hand, glistened up to the surface. The fish wriggled in the air, then resigned itself as Louis slid his palm over the slick scales, fingers smoothing down fins, extracting the barb from the fish's lip. He ran the stringer's metal tip into the gaping mouth and out through the gill, then released the fish into the water. He tied the stringer to a protruding tree root.

"Just like that, Etta. I'm gonna catch me a business job. Just like that, baby," he said, taking her hand and leading her along the bank into the nearby thick cover of tangled shrubs.

Chapter 9

"Winston! You need to get ready," Ruthie yelled from her dressing table. "The parade starts at ten. We've gotta be on the float at least a half hour early."

At the kitchen table, Winston heard her calling. He slumped over his coffee, seeing his whole Saturday disappear before the day even started. He'd rather be hunting, or just wandering in the quiet of the woods. He set his cup in the sink and trudged to the bedroom.

Ruthie turned from her mirror. "Don't look so excited," she said. "You should be proud. The Bayside Life sign looks good. A little small, but people will still know you supported the school."

Ruthie was Morris Elementary's part-time secretary, and chairman of the school's involvement in the county Pine Tree Festival parade. She'd made him call Roger and beg for a sponsorship. Equally awful, she'd coerced him into riding on the float with her and Mary Carolyn along with possibly twenty-five rowdy, costumed kids.

In exchange for the Bayside Life contribution, Winston had promised he'd staff a company table, handing out pamphlets and trinkets. He knew full well nobody would buy an insurance policy at the festival, but the company's presence might open the door for future new business. Ruthie was happy. Roger Johns was happy—he'd laughed his ass off. Two birds with one stone.

Winston reluctantly put on his raggedy costume, a cross between a hobo and a scarecrow. He had drawn the line at face paint. He watched Ruthie tease her dark hair until it stood out all over her head. She blackened a tooth with costume wax and drew a large mole on her chin. An elastic band would hopefully hold a tall witch hat in place. Mary Carolyn, a miniature Dorothy from *The Wizard of Oz*, tapped around the house in her homemade ruby slippers. Just shy of nine thirty, they all piled into the Comet.

"Step on it," Ruthie said.

The Foley County High School band led the parade down Main Street. Their brass and bass booming echoed off the town's weathered brick buildings. The sheriff's impressive, mounted posse left a heavy odor of dung behind clopping hooves; clowns picked up the piles. Spectators filled the sidewalks, clapping and waving at the scores of floats rolling past. Shriners wearing tall red fez caps zig-zagged through the streets in loud, smoking go-carts, revving engines and honking horns. Miss Pineville in her sparkling gown and sash rode atop the back seat of a convertible, waving a white-gloved hand.

Morris Elementary's float was a raised flatbed trailer decorated like a pine forest. Students were safely belted to the sturdy would-be trunks. Witch Ruthie sat at the float's front, stirring an empty black cast-iron cauldron with a canoe paddle. Winston and Mary Carolyn hugged the last tree at the back, right in front of a large sign labeled "See How We Grow."

Winston marveled at his birds-eye view of downtown.

Most every Main Street business was open, welcoming parade-goers, hoping to catch their attention before they dispersed to the festival grounds. The parade passed O'Keefe's corner drug store, where Mary Carolyn's asthma medicine was dispensed. Then there was the Poll Parrot shoe store, next to Diana's Dress Shop—Ruthie's favorite destination. Henry's Ham House—Winston's main daytime eatery—didn't need a sign; the sweet smell of smoking pork was unmistakable. He grinned and waved at Henry, who stood in his apron at the restaurant's front window.

"Hey, Winston!" rose up frequently from the streets. "Win-STON!"

He enjoyed the recognition. Many people knew him. Trusted him. He was an active Chamber of Commerce member. The product he sold and managed was important to people's lives. There stood his Bayside Life office to prove it, next to Bell's Jewelry, where he was secretly making payments on a gold bangle bracelet for Ruthie's big Christmas gift.

Winston had elevated his life for sure but understood that many more rungs awaited on the proverbial ladder. When the time was right, an exciting opportunity would be within his grasp. In the meantime, he'd do anything to protect what he'd already achieved and let nothing stop his continued ascent. The Sheriff's Department, across and down the street, was a constant reminder of what his life *could* be.

〜

A colorful trail of tents sheltering game and food booths dotted the Pine Tree Festival grounds. The air was thick with scents of cotton candy and sizzling fish. Squealing, costumed kids ran amok. From his company's banner-draped table, Winston people-watched while he devoured a plate of fried shrimp with hushpuppies and slaw and washed it down with a river of sweet tea.

The Bayside Life post, positioned across from the food service area, provided a front seat view of Miz Ruby's always-popular seafood stand. The shrimp and oysters, freshly caught off the nearby Gulf coast, were lightly breaded and fried to perfection. Her cooking was legendary.

Ruby Wright, an enterprising businesswoman and pillar of the colored community, owned and operated Miz Ruby's Rooms, Pineville's only boarding house for Negroes. She also owned a small motor court with a café—Miz Ruby's Roadhouse—for the same clientele. Her facilities were listed in the Negro travelers' *Green Book*, which ensured year-round occupancy. Ruby was an ageless widow, her tiny build belying her power. Winston observed her and a couple of her aproned helpers furiously plating orders.

One clean-cut young fellow, someone Winston hadn't noticed at the time he'd bought his own lunch, was schmoozing the customers, chatting easily and switching idioms as needed to upsell Ruby's offerings.

45

"How 'bout *two* dozen of them oysters? They little and real salty this year," the server said to an older colored lady, his face lit by a wide smile. Then, looking up at the next in line, a tall white man whose belly hung over his belt: "You, sir, surely need more food than your tiny little wife there. May I recommend the Captain's Platter, with a dime off the dessert?" He made the key lime pie sound so good that Winston headed for a slice.

"I been watching you," Winston deadpanned.

The young man, in the process of dumping a fry basket of golden hushpuppies onto a tray, startled.

"Who, me?"

"You're quite a salesman," Winston grinned.

Visibly relieved, the guy grinned, and he hurriedly wiped his hands on his apron. "Thank you. What can I get for you, sir?"

Winston bought two slices of pie—one for Ruthie if she ever caught up with him.

"'preciate your business," the young man said, making change. "Hope you'll spread the word. This seafood was just caught; it doesn't get any fresher. And Miz Ruby uses part of the proceeds to help feed the needy."

Winston nodded. "I'm sitting right over there, at the Bayside Life Insurance table. Come see me if you get a break. Let me show you what *I'm* selling."

Miz Ruby, elbow-close, said, "Don't you be messin' with my hired help, now. This boy's as good as it gets." She winked at Winston.

People swarmed the festival grounds like ants, and the food lines lengthened. Winston stretched his legs on a loop through the area, madness everywhere. Parade float winners were announced from the stage with the microphone squealing intermittently. After a port-a-john visit, Winston made his way back to his table.

A number of people stopped by to talk, including Sheriff Jacob Ramsey—a nice connection, though not necessarily a friend. The sheriff rested his hand on his holstered gun while he chatted about the turnout and the good-natured crowd. The conversation was light, but Ramsey always made him a bit nervous. And Winston had been trying for a year to sell the sheriff on a burial policy. No luck.

Deputy Dan Nettles, likewise working the festival, was a different story. Dan lived a block down from the Taylors, also on High Street. The two occasionally hunted and fished together or barbequed on summer weekends. They often ate breakfast together at Henry's Ham House, which was situated within walking distance of both their downtown offices. Dan had no time to entertain Winston today. He passed with only a wave, headed with purpose into the hodgepodge of people.

Most who dropped by to visit with Winston were friends or customers. A few were strangers. He pushed Bayside Life giveaways onto everyone: rulers, pencils, thimbles, or packs of sewing needles. He did get a few referrals he'd follow up on in the next week. Ruthie sat with him briefly, taking a break from the kiddie games. Mary Carolyn looked delirious; she gave him a sticky blue cotton candy kiss.

Ruby's seafood salesman approached, minus his stained apron. "Hey, Mr. Taylor, I'm Louis Fisher." His handshake was firm. "Hope you enjoyed your lunch."

Winston chatted him up, learning Louis was raised in North Georgia by his father's sister who had just passed away. He never mentioned what happened to his parents, and Winston didn't ask. Louis said he'd migrated further south, looking for a change of scene and warmer weather. He'd found work at the Buckhead mill but considered the job temporary until he could get better established. Meanwhile, Miz Ruby had been mothering him at the boarding house.

The boy was self-confident and obviously intelligent. Winston admired that. Louis talked with his hands, bringing the conversation to life. As Winston watched those dancing hands, the light in Louis's eyes, the image of another young colored man floated up, one he'd found lifeless on a sandy road. Might he have been filled with this same potential? Winston blinked hard to refocus.

No use trying to sell Louis on insurance. The guy was single and apparently disconnected from family. He handed Louis a handful of business cards and a wooden ruler stamped *Measure Up to Your Future . . . BAYSIDE LIFE INSURANCE COMPANY*. Winston asked him to spread the word.

"You know something funny, Mr. Taylor. I've got an old green canvas bag, a zip-up pouch, from Bayside Life. Kind of a coincidence, meeting you here today."

"Where'd you get it?"

"I don't really remember. Mighta belonged to my granddaddy before he passed. I've had the bag for years. Used to keep my little cars in it when I was a kid. Then it was my money sack. Still is."

"Yeah, we sometimes deliver new policies in those. I use one to hold cash from my weekly collections." Winston crossed his arms. "So, someone in your family did business with Bayside at some point in time. Huh . . . I'm thinking we've only been selling in Georgia for the past couple of years." He cocked his head at Louis and asked, "Did your family ever live in Florida?"

"No telling," Louis said.

Chapter 10

"You knew damn well we wouldn't write any new business at that festival," Winston laughed into the receiver. "You sure made me look good with Ruthie, though. You know what I mean?" He wiggled his eyebrows for effect, even though Roger was 150 miles away.

"My confidence in your ability to sell yourself just went out the window," Roger said dryly.

"Ow! You know I could sell ice to an Eskimo," Winston laughed again. "But seriously, Ruthie was thrilled with the Bayside contribution. If Ruthie's happy, I'm happy."

"Yeah, yeah. We all know you're the best. But what have you done for *me* lately?" Roger asked. "We gotta jack up our sales numbers. The Mid-Florida region is mowing us down. They got all those well-preserved blue hairs. Easy as nettin' goldfish from a tank in the five and dime."

Winston tapped a pencil against the top of his debit book. "I know, boss. New business is pretty flat. Something's gotta change." He swiveled around in his chair, wrapping the phone's black coiled cord around him. "I been thinking hard on this, and I think we can't keep Larkins much longer. I've pushed him and pushed him. The harder I push, the tighter he pulls his head into his shell. He does fine with collections, and I sweep behind his accounts. He's not cheatin' us. But the man has no balls. He just cannot hold sway to make a sale."

"I hear you . . . but he was the best candidate at the time," Roger said. "I know you didn't have any real say-so when we hired him. In hindsight, that was a bad decision on my part. But he was the only one with any real sales experience. It was slim pickings."

"He mighta had the sales experience, but he didn't necessarily have the skill. You're right; you had to move fast. And it's not like you had a lot of options."

"What we *did* do right was put you in charge there. New business has been a problem in Pineville for a long time. You've made a difference, Winston. I'm not unhappy with your work. You've moved the needle."

Winston felt the pat on his back and smiled to himself. "Appreciate that. Like I said, I've been turning this over in my mind for a while. A. F.'s carrying quite a book of old business. If we let him go today, I'd be screwed. We'd be screwed. We need a reasonable exit plan for him."

Winston opened the door to the idea of filling the office's vacant third chair. Roger's hackles went up immediately. No way to get approval. No way to justify. But Winston persisted.

"Just think about it, Roger. Looking for a third agent makes sense. We're not under any pressure to hire because A. F.'s not going anywhere on his own. He'll sit here till his wife cashes in on his life insurance. Let's find some young guy, full of piss and vinegar—you know, spunk! Charming and enthusiastic. I can teach him how to sell. He can shadow me awhile. You could come over and work with him, too. Once he's up and running, we could let the old guy loose. You wouldn't be carrying three of us for very long."

"Where do you propose to get somebody like that? Most of those young'uns are hightailing it out of there to Tallahassee, or Gainesville. Parts unknown."

"I *know* I could find somebody better than who we've got."

Winston hung up the phone, filled with hope.

⌒

A. F. Larkins pulled into the parking lot of McCrory's and sat with the heater running. This year's November weather was brutal from the beginning. He couldn't get warm; his feet were two blocks of ice. Five minutes, he promised himself. The heater would do the trick. He looked at his watch. 11:25 a.m.

He squinted at the storefront, trying to read the sale signs pasted in the windows. A young woman approached the entrance, holding the hand of a little girl who skipped along beside her. The child was dressed warmly: tights beneath her plaid dress and a red, hooded carcoat.

A. F. adjusted the heater vents, glanced at the glove box, then his Timex. 11:27 now. He watched the woman help the girl up onto a black mechanical horse that stood near the store's entrance. Saw the mother search her handbag, and obviously drop a coin into the slot. The horse galloped. The child raked the red hood back and off her head. The woman pushed open the heavy door and disappeared inside. The little red jockey rocked back and forth.

It would be easy for someone to pluck that kid off the horse and run. He imagined how it could happen; pictured himself on a tropical beach somewhere, sun toasting his pasty skin. Sipping a rum-laden cocktail while he counted the ransom. But A. F. was only daydreaming. Writing scenes in a story called "Ways to Have an Easier Life." Anything would be better than beating the bushes in this godforsaken place. Bunch of poor people, stupid people. He had to figure it out soon; he sensed the end of his road wasn't too many miles away.

At the half-hour, though still cold inside, the feeling was returning to his feet. He knew if he pulled off his socks, he'd find his toes the same blackish-purple—poor circulation and other health issues he refused to think about. His doctor had warned that if he kept on this same path, he could lose both feet. A slow decline. A hell of a life. He tried not to dwell on it and kept his feet covered from his wife's prying eyes.

A. F. popped open the glove box and removed the flask. The pistol he kept there slipped to the front of the compartment—his protection. Sometimes he thought of interesting ways to use it. Liquor trickled between his lips, then down his throat. Heat seeped into his core. The woman came out of the store to fetch the kid and A. F. nodded approvingly. The world was looking up.

Chapter 11

Ruthie was pregnant. After years of hoping for a second child, the Taylors were surprised and thrilled. Mary Carolyn, now seven, was his angel baby, but Winston was hoping for a boy.

Though barely showing, Ruthie was already planning the nursery. She and Priscilla Nettles, Deputy Dan's wife, pored over magazines for decorating ideas. Mary Carolyn's dolls were "expecting" too. Winston stayed out of the way.

Over morning coffee, Ruthie seized Winston's arm and blurted: "We're going to need a bigger car, Winston. I want a station wagon."

His eyes widened. No way his family was riding around in a station wagon. He didn't think he'd ever forget that blue Country Squire . . ..

"We can trade in my Comet. Surely it has some value, but what do I know about cars?" Ruthie shrugged. "With a wagon, we'd have more room to spread out. Space for a playpen and a stroller. Suitcases for family vacations. Priscilla says she just loves hers."

Winston took a slow sip of coffee, set his cup down, and looked at her. Ruthie's skin seemed to glow. A thick, dark ponytail spilled over her shoulder, and lay against breasts that already swelled beneath her flannel robe. How could he explain that he never wanted to drive another station wagon? Ever? That they looked like coffins on wheels? That the very finding of a certain old blue station wagon might somehow bring the downfall of them all?

He stood and pulled her up from her chair. Kissed her face, her neck. He held her tight against his chest for a moment too long. She leaned back, frowning up at him.

"What?" she asked. "What's wrong?"

"Nothing," he said, searching her eyes for any hint that he'd unknowingly let his secret slip. "I'll think about it," he said and then quickly left for work.

Deputy Dan Nettles pushed through Winston's office door: "Working hard, or hardly working?"

Winston's right hand was a blur over the black Underwood adding machine. Quick staccato clicking, followed by the downstroke of a wooden-handled crank produced a satisfying crunch. He glanced up from his desk, raised a finger, peered at a green page of the open debit book, and rolled out another series of rapid-fire calculations. Narrow white paper spooled out of the machine, coiled, and spilled over the edge of the desk.

"Your timing's perfect." Winston pushed back from his workspace and rubbed his temples. "I could use a break."

"Where's your hired help? You ought to have him running that machine. How come you ain't out beating the bushes?"

"How come you ain't out chasing criminals? Probably a robbery going on right now somewhere in the county."

"Shit. I come here to hold *you* up. Or hold you hostage."

"Whaddaya mean?"

"Priscilla sent me. She and Ruthie have been arranging the rest of your natural life ever since that rabbit died."

"If anybody asked me, I'd say Ruthie needs to quit mashing the gas. This is all too fast. The two of them are either huddled over fabric scraps or pictures of cribs. Or talking baby talk on the phone. I got hit up this morning for a bigger car."

"Funny you should mention it . . . I'm supposed to lean on you a little, talk you into the wagon. I thought you might wanna hop in the patrol car with me—let's at least run over to the Ford place, see what they got."

"Aw, man, I wish I could."

"Don't make me have to handcuff you."

⌒

They cruised through Emerson Ford, ogled a '63 ½ Ford Falcon Sprint—a 260 four-speed—then stopped at a new white Galaxy station wagon with chrome trim. A bit shorter than a hearse. Winston read the sticker and said "no thank you" to the $2,500 new car smell.

Billy Emerson himself appeared on the lot when he spotted the patrol car.

"What's wrong with that pearly white one?" Emerson laughed, and spit tobacco into the gravel. "I think it's real clean looking. And stays a whole lot cooler in the summer than a dark color."

Deputy Nettles spoke up: "I'm trying to get him interested in a wagon. They're gettin' another kid come spring. He won't know what hit him. He better do this while he can think straight." Dan elbowed Winston, who just shook his head.

"I can't stomach that price, Billy. You gotta do a whole lot better than that," Winston said.

Emerson looked at the sticker. "I could maybe do twenty-two. Can't go no lower. Besides, you don't sound like a real buyer."

"You got any used ones?" Winston asked, looking around.

Billy looked over at the deputy. Hesitated, then: "Truth be told, what we got used ain't worth nothing. I probably can't give 'em away." He looked at the deputy again and back at Winston. "I tell you though, rumor has it that ol' Abe across town just got a nice one on trade-in."

Deputy Dan looked at him incredulously. "You gonna give away business to a Negro?"

"Look, I know you guys. I ain't got what you need and Abe might. I ain't doing it for him. I'm doing it for you."

Amazing how the presence of a uniformed man with a gun makes people want to do the right thing, Winston thought.

Dan and Winston rolled into Abe's Used Autos and parked the patrol car at the small glass-front office. Old Abe made his way slowly toward them, his once-tall frame hunched over a walking cane. He welcomed the two men, then waved to another person still inside the office. A young man came out and stood beside Abe.

"I got a young'un here I'm trying out part-time. Louis Fisher. Teaching him the ropes. Hope you don't mind if he shows you around. I got to where I can hardly get from one side of this place to the other."

Winston and Louis, who recognized each other, shook hands. Winston explained to the others how he'd met Louis at the tree festival. Louis shook the deputy's hand, too, but kept his eyes on Winston's face.

"What you doing working over here for Abe? I thought you were out at Buckhead?"

"Yessir, I am. Just took me a day off over there to help out here. Mr. Abe's teaching me how to sell cars. This is just a side job, but I'm learning a lot."

"The boy done sold hisself a car last week," Abe grinned. "He don't take no for an answer."

"Yessir. But I'm still trying to get the hang of it."

Abe cackled and shuffled back into the office.

Winston pushed his hat brim up and leaned back against the patrol car. He confessed to being a reluctant customer—his wife was interested in a station wagon, but he didn't care much for them.

Dan laughed at that. "I thought you'd learned by now who's in charge of this new baby show."

Louis's eyes darted to the deputy's face, then back to Winston. "Well congratulations, sir. A new baby! Can't blame you for holding back on such a big vehicle, but Mrs. Taylor might be right to consider a bigger ride."

Dan's eyebrow went up, and he smirked at Winston.

"Family's everything. You don't want 'em all squished up in the back of a sedan on a long trip to grandma's house. They'll need room to spread out. Space to haul all the paraphernalia," Louis said, opening his arms wide as the word. "I'll be honest. We ain't got much here to meet your needs. Got a used '55 Ford wagon, beat to hell. An important man like you shouldn't be seen in such. But we do have one you might like."

Important man. Winston couldn't help but smile at the comment. The fledgling salesman was already on his way to slick. Dan slid back into the patrol car to check in with the dispatcher while Louis led Winston to the front of the lot.

"This the one I'm talking about. A '59 Chevy Parkwood. Owned by an elderly white lady over in Mayo who just passed away. God rest her soul. Her son traded it in on something smaller. The guy was nuts in my opinion," Louis said, then quickly looked at his feet. "Sorry. No disrespect, sir. But Mr. Abe made out great on the deal."

The station wagon shimmered in rich bronze paint with a white top, white fins, and teardrop taillights. The tires were white walls with decent tread. Winston walked around the long body, finding no dents or scrapes. His throat felt dry.

"The lady didn't drive it much. Twenty thousand miles— like new for a four-year-old car, especially with her living out in the country. Six cylinders, three speed." Louis's voice softened to add, "Too bad she didn't get to enjoy the car a little longer."

Winston looked at him but didn't respond.

"This is what Chevy calls the 'middle member' of their wagon lineup, moderately priced. Made for the average

American family. You know, Mr. Taylor, besides your growing needs, this might be a real good time to think about buying."

"Why's that?" Winston asked.

"Well, I heard President Kennedy talking lately about how many Americans are on the path to prosperity. Gotta feeling you one of 'em." Louis bowed his head again and said, "No offense, sir. Maybe you already there."

Winston shrugged. "None taken."

Winston watched Louis's face, studying the way the man talked. He realized he was much more interested in the salesman than the car. The guy was good.

"Six-passenger, and the cargo area's gonna hold aplenty. I knew a guy who used to drive one. He near lived out of that car." They walked to the rear. "Let me show you," he said, unlatching and letting down the tailgate.

Time stopped. Jackson Smith's dead eyes peered over a painter's cloth, staring straight into Winston. He shut his eyes, swaying under the memory of the body he'd once dragged out of the back. He braced himself now against the Chevy, hoping Louis didn't notice.

"Don't mean to pressure you, Mr. Taylor, but whatcha think?"

Winston bit his bottom lip. He lifted the tailgate and slammed it shut.

"I gotta get back to the office, Louis. Nice car. Like I said, I'm just looking. Thanks for your help."

Winston headed back to the patrol car, fumbling in his pocket for the buckeye, and slid into the passenger seat. He rubbed his thumb over the smooth nut until his pulse slowed.

～

Louis Fisher's own hands were shaking by the time Winston and the deputy left. Cops made him nervous. Once upon a time, he'd lived unafraid. But things had happened . . . The move to Pineville had been a big step toward creating a new and fearless life. That life, however, was still under construction.

A longing . . . no . . . a grief welled within Louis. He had lost so much. He walked through the sales lot pretending to inspect some of the cars, then returned to Abe's office with that perfected Louis smile back on his face.

Chapter 12

While Winston's Book of Souls housed critical information on all his insureds, he also relied on Pineville's community grapevine, which covered their small town like kudzu. When little Lucinda Morgan was critically injured, Winston heard about it within hours. He headed straight to the hospital.

David and Melissa Morgan huddled in a corner of the surgical waiting room, holding hands and leaning into each other. Melissa's face was a swollen red mess, and she buried her nose in a wad of soggy tissues.

Winston was allergic to illness, injury, or any form of human misery. He rarely got sick himself and expected people to carry on regardless. Despite his aversion to the anguish of others, Winston was very good with customer care. He straightened himself and approached the Morgan family.

David Morgan saw him coming and stood up.

Winston grasped Morgan's hand. "David, I am so sorry to hear about Luci. How is she?"

David's eyes watered. He motioned Winston away from the seating area. "We don't know yet. They're working on her now. A head wound. Some internal injuries."

Winston swallowed hard. "What in the world happened?"

"Her horse. I never should've let her have it. But she'd begged us for years," he said, his voice cracking.

"She fall off?"

"No. They were in the stall together. We never worried . . . Luci was always cautious. But the horse apparently spooked . . . ." The father bent his head and sobbed.

Winston put his arm around David's shoulders and offered him his own clean white handkerchief.

"I'm gonna shoot that fuckin' horse," Morgan rasped into the thin cloth.

Melissa Morgan looked up into Winston's face as he spoke to her, but he knew she wouldn't remember anything he said. Nothing could change what had happened; his own experience was proof. He squeezed her hand.

"Please, just pray," she said.

Back at the office, Winston gazed out the front window, thinking about David Morgan and religion.

Two years ago, David had responded quickly to Winston's request for a loan—the banker thought the money was for gambling debts. What he didn't know was that the loan was really needed to activate the "special policies" Winston had sold, those bogus insurance policies that if discovered could have brought Winston's whole world crashing down, ruining his family and career. The banker had been professional yet sympathetic, and Winston thought of him as a savior.

Now David was facing his own awful situation, and Winston had no way to help. If something terrible happened to Winston's only child, he'd lose his mind. Mary Carolyn meant more to him than anything on earth, except for Ruthie.

Winston opened his debit book. He fingered the "M" tab and flipped to David Morgan's account page. Morgan was paying on a $10,000 life insurance policy for himself with wife Melissa as beneficiary. Melissa's page showed her coverage at $5,000. Winston put his pencil point on eleven-year-old Lucinda Lynn Morgan's policy value: $1,000. A thousand dollars was nothing in exchange for her life. For her little soul. Yeah, the cash would cover the cost of a funeral if she didn't make it. But the prominent Pineville banker David Morgan didn't need that money to bury his only child. He had plenty. Surely a compassionate God wouldn't let her die. *What a damn shame for them all.* Winston felt like ripping out the page.

Melissa had asked him to pray, but Winston was not a prayerful person. He bucked the rules and rote of organized religion. Sure, he knew "The Lord's Prayer," but so did most everyone else in the world. How could God begin to figure out who was talking? Every human saying the same thing. Winston attended church at Easter and Christmas, and on the Sundays Ruthie guilted him into it. He worshiped in the wild, he liked to say. Out in God's country—in the woods or on the water. Ruthie let him get away with it.

He did think about God a lot. Had conversations with the Man in his own way. Since the burial of Jackson Smith, he had become much more aware of God's far-seeing, far-reaching power. He knew he was being watched, too, but sometimes wondered by whom. Or what. No matter who was judging, the verdict wasn't in yet. So today, he prayed for Luci Morgan, and for her family. For whatever his prayers were worth.

Chapter 13

Winston had won. The Bayside Life home office approved the hiring of a third salesman for the Pineville office. Winston would cull applicants and interview the cream of the crop. Roger Johns would oversee the process.

Advertisements were out in the *Pineville Times* and *Capital Democrat.* So far, no "crop" of candidates had materialized, much less cream. A few resumes and calls trickled in. One from a woman. A lone female knocking on doors in the middle of nowhere? Probably not a good idea.

Winston met with a middle-aged man who clumped into the office with a serious limp, despite the six-inch rise of one black shoe sole. The candidate sounded bright enough, but spit flew from his mouth when he talked. Winston nixed him—they already had a cripple in A. F. Larkins.

Determined to find someone sharp, Winston kept crossing off applicants. Part of the problem was Pineville. Buckhead Paper Company easily drew people for the mill jobs and for logging, but who wanted to move to Pineville for an insurance sales position? Nicer opportunities existed in nearby Tallahassee and Gainesville. If potential candidates were *from* Pineville and the surrounding area, they were likely already dug into a job. If not, they probably couldn't stay employed. So much for his big speech to Roger that he could find someone better than A. F.

～

On a chilly November Wednesday, one Ricky Swain answered the ad. Winston brought him in immediately. Swain was a door-to-door Wide World Encyclopedia representative.

The candidate's handshake was firm, eye contact direct. Average build. He had a nice smile, though his lips were chapped and cracked—a lip-licker. Pale, thinning hair disappeared into a colorless complexion. Anemic-looking. The cuff-linked white dress shirt was crisp, striped tie impressive. Cordovan shoes could use a polish. Winston was instantly at odds, both attracted and repelled by the most promising candidate thus far.

Swain sat at the empty desk, quietly filling out the company application. Winston glanced at him several times, taking stock. Guessed his age at late thirties, considering the hair's slight silvering in overhead lights, the forehead furrows of concentration; close to Winston's own age. Swain handed over the completed form and Winston parked him with a cup of coffee and a brochure on Bayside Life.

Back at his own desk, Winston reviewed the application. Ricky Swain was actually 42 years old. High school education. Almost two years at the book company, covering three states—was Swain the man who'd sold Ruthie their own Wide World book set? Swain had noted previous employment with Fulton Brush Company. A *brush* company? Not married. Probably couldn't keep a wife if he lived out of a suitcase. Winston studied Ricky's face for a moment. Swain sensed the stare, looked up from the brochure, his face reddening under the scrutiny. Winston waved him over to his guest chair.

"Your application looks pretty good. Let's talk about you."

Ricky cleared his throat. "Well, first let me thank you again for this chance to come in. I haven't finished reading your booklet here, but it looks good. Bayside Life has an excellent reputation, too. I believe you all could benefit from my—"

"Excuse me," Winston interrupted, cutting through the bullshit. "From the way you talk, I can tell you're not from around here. Where'd you grow up?"

"Ohio. Moved around as a kid. Cambridge. Akron. But Dayton's where I call home."

Winston thumped the application. "I see you're currently living in St. Pete. Nice city. Successful guy like you, why move to this part of Florida? You've lived in much more interesting places." He leaned toward Ricky. "I'm not gonna lie to you. Living in this small town, in this poor part of the state, can be rough. Unless you're a family man. Or a hunter, or fisherman. I don't see you as an outdoorsman, though."

Ricky's smile was weak. "Well, I'm just not happy right now with all the traveling. I've decided it would be nice to settle down somewhere. I'm a salesman. You're looking for a salesman." He licked his mouth, dried it with the back of his hand, then sealed his cracked red lips with two passes of a Chapstick tube.

"When I call Wide World, what do you think they'll say about you?"

"You're going to call them?"

"Well, yeah. Is there a problem?" Winston asked.

Ricky coughed. Took a drink of coffee. "I'd rather they not know I'm looking for a move."

"Why not?"

"Well, if you call them and then don't hire me, I'm screwed. They'll be suspicious I'm going to leave. They like me now, but I could fall out of favor."

"Okay. But that's the only way I'll be able to verify what you tell me about your sales record. So, let's talk about that now. Lay it out for me."

Ricky painted a picture of himself as one of his company's best. Nice commissions with a decent salary. Bonuses every year. Winston was definitely interested. But something didn't feel quite right. It's hard to shit a bullshitter.

"How come you're not married?"

The silence was a beat too long.

"Why does that matter?"

"I'm allowed to ask," Winston said. "You're nice-looking enough. Likely a decent guy." Winston's eyebrows were up with the hanging question.

"Well, I . . . I'm just gone so much that I can't find a woman who'll tolerate it. It's not because I don't like women. I like them a lot. And I don't have any problem with them inviting me into their houses. Even those home alone all day while the husband's working and kids are at school." He swallowed hard.

"Fair enough," Winston said, grinning. "I'm just trying to get to know you. Your sales experience looks good; you're seasoned. Professional. But it takes a certain kind of person to drag a debit book around all day, calling on both the well-to-do and the dirt-poor—whites and coloreds alike. To make real connections with people."

Winston opened the black cover of his debit book, fanned the pages, hearing a dry whisper of voices—Mabel Griffin, Jackson Smith, Luci Morgan—those souls he knew were his responsibility. "This ain't one and done, Ricky. We don't sell and move on." He paused, looked back at his book, then into Ricky's face. "Speaking of colored folks. What's your sales experience with them?"

"They buy my books, too, whenever I venture into their neighborhoods."

"Let me tell you, Bayside Life doesn't redline; we sell insurance everywhere, to anybody who'll buy. Color doesn't matter. What are your sales percentages from coloreds? Your best guess."

Ricky answered quickly: "Oh, probably about five percent."

Winston's eyebrows went up. "Because they typically don't buy encyclopedias, or because you don't try to sell them?"

Swain's pale face was now a glistening pink. "I've tried, but not many can afford our books." He clutched the coffee mug with both hands.

"Here in our sales region, colored insureds are forty-five to fifty percent of our business. Their income levels generally run lower than average, but they're still critical to our team's success. Unlike peddling encyclopedias or boar-bristle hairbrushes—this bears repeating, Ricky—we can't walk away once we sell a policy. The sale is just the beginning of the customer relationship." Winston stood up. "And there's much more business we could have with the Negroes, with the right person to reach them. That's what I'm looking for."

Winston asked Swain where he could find him, in case he wanted a second interview, or more.

"I've got a room over at the Starlight Motel. I'll be working here maybe two more days, then I'm moving up into Georgia. But I'd sure love a chance to work with you."

"Today's Wednesday, so if I haven't contacted you before you leave town, give me a call on Monday."

After lunch, Winston sat at his desk, mully-grubbing over the lackluster response to his job advertisements. Thinking about Ricky Swain, his best candidate, at least on paper. But something felt wrong. *Something.* His eyes landed on Swain's empty cup resting on the desk corner, and he pictured the man's cracked red lips, the pink tongue darting out quick as a snake. Unattractive but not unusual. So what was the problem? When he touched the mug's handle, the answer came: Ricky Swain had a cruel mouth.

He pulled his debit book close and thumbed through a few customer accounts. He whirred the pages, then let the cover drop. Winston's livelihood . . . his life . . . was inside this book. Ricky Swain was probably a very good salesman, but would he be a good shepherd of Bayside Life's people?

Winston admitted to himself that he had not always taken such good care of his customers. But he'd righted his wrongs after that head-on collision with a dead man—Jackson Smith. Knowing his own faults, Winston was often suspicious of others. His signals about Swain were more than that, though.

Winston had a strong need to get to the bottom of everything, to have a deep understanding of people around him. He loved digging for information, for knowledge, panning for gold until he came up with a fat nugget. Surely this was an innate gift, one he might use someday for a calling higher than sales. He knew he was an outstanding salesman and could always support his family with that talent. But he didn't think he'd ever rid himself of the fear of being caught for skimming. No matter what he'd done to correct his mistakes. A job change might be in order, though the thought of leaving Bayside Life felt like a foolish move.

Winston tapped a Camel out of the pack, then stopped himself. He opened his desk drawer, found a toothpick coated with rubber eraser dust, blew it off, and ground the wood between his molars. He followed the news enough to know studies were beginning to show smoking would eventually kill you, or make you wish you were dead. Ruthie was after his ass to quit, and Winston had no intention of dying anytime soon. He ran his hands down his middle, feeling for any loose flesh or fat. Seemed his morning sit-ups were keeping him pretty trim. He reckoned ditching the cigs would be good for him. But quitting wasn't likely.

✍

Mid-afternoon, something big and dark rolled up the street and pulled into a parking space in front of the insurance office: Miz Ruby and her fancy black Cadillac Eldorado. Winston grinned. That lady tickled the shit out of him. Ruby was one more successful businesswoman, and a do-gooder with a benefactor's colorblind eye. The Caddy was her symbol of triumph. Winston thought she deserved it.

He watched her get out of the car, expecting her to head to the jeweler next door. She surprised him by making a beeline for his office. He opened the heavy glass door.

"Miz Ruby, you sure are lookin' good today! To what do I owe the honor of your company?" Winston helped her remove her wool coat.

"You are quite the charmer, Winston." Lines crinkled around her eyes and mouth when she smiled. Otherwise, her skin was a flawless creamy brown beneath a halo of white hair. She sat down in front of his desk.

"Can I offer you some coffee? I was thinking about making some to wake me up from my big ol' meat-and-three over at the Ham House."

"No thank you. I just ate, too. Nothing quite that heavy."

Winston opened his debit book and flipped pages, looking for her accounts. Ruby Wright was one of his biggest customers, paying on policies for herself and a number of family members.

"I didn't come here to talk about my insurance, Winston."

He stopped turning pages and shut the book—hooked.

"I've come to you about the job opening you're advertising." Her tone was professional.

Winston's eyebrows went up. "Really! Is there a problem?"

"No problem. This is somewhat delicate, though. I have someone I wish you'd consider for the job." She raised a hand to the string of pearls around her neck, fingering each like rosary beads.

"Who would that be, ma'am?"

"Do you recall meeting the young man who helped out at my festival seafood booth? You talked to him. His name's Louis Fisher."

A Negro?

"I remember him well, Miz Ruby. A fine-looking guy. A smooth talker." Winston leaned back and crossed his arms. "I know he works for Buckhead, but I saw him the other day selling cars over at Abe's Auto. He definitely put the whammy on me. Tried really hard to sell me a nice station wagon for Ruthie. But I'm not quite ready to trade, and I can't stand those damn station wagons." They shared a laugh before he asked, "What's your interest in Louis?"

Ruby cleared her throat. "It has come to my attention that Louis and my granddaughter, Etta, are very fond of one another. They don't know I'm aware of this *relationship* between them. Do you understand?"

Winston nodded, and she went on to tell him that though Louis had an elusive past, he was obviously very smart, and industrious. Ruby wanted to help him for that alone, but also because if the relationship with her granddaughter flourished, she wanted a good, steady job in their future. Etta was bright, too, but her eyes were not on education and employment.

Rarely at a loss for words, Winston took a moment to process what she'd said. Ruby was asking him for a business favor. But the magnitude of the request was significant.

"Wow," Winston finally said. He dug a Camel from its pack and lit it. He took a long drag, then ground it out in the half-full ashtray on his desk.

"Miz Ruby, I truly don't know how to respond to this. So many thoughts are running through my head about how this could be a good thing. But it might also come back to bite me."

Ruby said she understood. Her only request was that Winston *consider* Louis for the job, adding, "I see something good in this young fellow. The paper mill is what keeps our town alive, but this boy needs to be using his brains, his charisma."

"Well surely Buckhead will realize that, over time. They have office jobs there, too."

"You know that's not going to happen. Buckhead's hiring philosophy is that Negro employees are beneficial as long as they're kept out in the mill. Management is not enlightened enough to hire a colored man for an office position. And if they did, he'd never be allowed to rise up in the ranks."

Winston pushed the cigarette pack around on his desk, thinking. Then he handed Ruby one of his business cards, said "Tell Louis to call me by tomorrow morning. I'll talk to him." He helped Ruby into her coat and walked her to the door.

"Thank you, Winston," she said. "I won't forget this."

A quick update call to Roger Johns sparked excitement over the encyclopedia guy. Thumbs down on the female, and the fellow with the big shoe. Roger sounded pleased, until Winston dropped the caveat that Ricky Swain put out a strange vibe.

"What do you mean, a *vibe*? What the hell, Winston. Can't you just take things as they are? Why've you always gotta be looking for something sinister, some hidden meaning?"

"I know, I know. But I'm telling you, something was hinky with him. I believed his sales story. This was just something subtle. I'm gonna call Wide World, just to make sure he wasn't trying to pull the wool over my eyes."

Roger reluctantly agreed to calling the encyclopedia people, saying he hoped Winston's suspicions were wrong. He thought Swain sounded solid and a good, quick fit, somebody who wouldn't need sales training, only an orientation of the life insurance business. He said he was ready to fill the position and move on.

Winston did not mention Louis Fisher. That was a whole 'nother thing.

Chapter 14

"Wide World Encyclopedia. Happy Thursday!" said a perky voice. Winston gripped the receiver, scanning the application for the name of Swain's supervisor.

"Good morning. Daniel Davidson, please." He fitted a toothpick between his teeth while he waited.

Davidson came on the line, and Winston explained the reason for his call. He asked about Ricky Swain's sales performance. After a long pause, the supervisor put Winston on hold.

Davidson returned with: "I'm sorry, but I can't help you. I've been advised to forward any questions about Mr. Swain to our Human Resources department."

"I'm not really interested in the HR basics," Winston pushed back. "I was hoping you might share something real, like his track record. He sounds knowledgeable enough." He sucked on the toothpick. "I'm also wondering about commission structure, whether we can realistically compete for him. I'm talking to you, manager to manager."

"I understand. But I can't comment. Let me transfer you to HR. Best I can do."

Winston heard a clicking and waited. Finally, an authoritative voice—Vincent somebody, an HR director—spoke into his ear and said the Legal Department was now in charge of the Swain file. Vincent could only confirm Swain's employment. The start date matched what the candidate had written on his Bayside Life application. But according to company records, Ricky Swain's employment had ended a month ago.

"He's not employed with you anymore?" Winston frowned into the phone.

"No sir. His end date was—"

"I heard you. His application says he's still employed. He told me so himself this morning."

"I'm sorry, Mr. Taylor. He is not."

"Something's wrong with this picture," Winston said, biting hard on the toothpick. "What happened?"

"I just can't divulge any of that. But let me ask *you* something. What type of insurance position are you trying to fill?"

"Sales. A debit route covering several North Florida counties. Cold-calling and collections."

"The employee would be entering the homes of your customers then . . . likely in rural areas?"

"Yeess . . ." Winston's brow puckered into several hoed rows.

"Where the customers might be women, home alone?"

"Highly likely."

"Well, you never heard me say this, but if I were you, I'd be looking at my other candidates. That's truly all I can tell you." The line went dead.

"Be damned," Winston said to the empty room. He replaced his toothpick with a Camel. Smoke formed a thick haze around him as he turned what he'd heard from Wide World over and over in his head. He lit another cigarette from the stub in his mouth.

The "something" about Ricky Swain began to take shape. He dialed the Sheriff's Office and left a message for Deputy Dan.

Late morning, Dan and Winston met for pie and coffee at the Ham House. Pecan for both; coffees black.

"Not sure what's on your mind, but I'm happy to listen if you're paying for this," Dan said after a big swallow of pie. He washed it down with coffee. "Almost as good as my mama's."

Winston nodded, shoveling in another bite. He wiped his mouth. "Just wanted your take on something that happened. I interviewed a guy for my vacancy. Most qualified person so far. But he lied on his application."

"Then don't hire him," said Dan. "What's the big deal? People lie all the time when they're trying to find a job."

"Nuh-uh. It's not that. My gut's talking to me."

"So, you're a detective now."

"No, you are. Well, next best thing." Winston laid out what had happened. How he'd followed up on the guy's application. How everything he'd heard led him to think something sinister was going on.

"Like what?"

"My antennae's standing straight up." Winston leaned toward Dan and dropped his voice. "Like maybe the guy's casing homes he calls on, then breaks in later. Or maybe he's assaulting women after he's scoped out their houses."

"Damn. That's exciting. But pretty far-fetched, don't you think?"

"You wouldn't think so if you'd heard the higher-ups at Wide World . . . and the one who implied the guy shouldn't be entering homes where women were alone. He didn't *say* that. But I'm telling you, Swain is suspicious."

Dan corralled the last pie crumbs with his fork and licked them off the tines. He took a clean napkin from the dispenser and wrote down Swain's name. "I'm gonna do you a favor. Get someone to run a check on this guy, see if any BOLO's have been issued. Look at unsolved crime bulletins for B&E, peeping. Maybe assault. If you're right, could be the company's protecting its reputation, keeping anything like that under wraps."

"Exactly. They wouldn't want that stigma tied to their door-to-door sales force."

"No shit, Sherlock. I'm no psychiatrist, but I'm diagnosing you with a chronic paranoia disorder." He grinned and rolled his eyes. "Lighten up, man! Sometimes I wonder why Ruthie even keeps you."

∽

When the sun's late afternoon rays pierced Bayside's glass front, a spit-shined Louis Fisher sat across from Winston. Not exactly nervous, Winston thought. Excited.

"You sell that black wagon yet?"

"No sir but won't be long. A young couple keep visiting, even drove it once. I think they're trying to get up the cash."

"You'll get it sold. You're persuasive." Winston skimmed over Louis's application again.

"I see you took some college courses at Florida A&M. Business stuff." Winston leaned back, laced his fingers together. "Why didn't you stay? Smart guy like you, you could've earned a degree."

"Foolish, I know. I got bored with school and sick of not having any money. I guess I lost my stride. When I quit FAMU, I went back to my aunt's house in Georgia—she pretty much raised me. I did some odd jobs there awhile. Then I decided to head back to Florida. Find a better path for myself."

"Hell of a place you picked. Pineville."

Louis shrugged. "I heard about Buckhead looking for workers. The pay's pretty good. One of my goals is to grow my savings. That's why I ended up at the boarding house— I'm putting as much money as I can in the bank."

"Rooming at Ruby's was a wise move, then," said Winston. "In a lot of ways."

Louis leaned forward, held Winston's eyes. "Mr. Taylor, what I really want is to work my way out of manual labor. Get into something more respectable. I ain't afraid of hard work. No, sir. But I wanna better myself. I think sales is a good place to start." A pulse beat at the side of the young man's temple; his fingers gripped the edge of the desk.

Winston nodded. "It's worked for me. And there's room to grow at Bayside Life." He sighed. "Louis, I like you. There's something about you I can't quite put my finger on, but I still like you. So, I'm gonna be brutally honest."

Louis nodded, his expression stoic.

"The home office may not approve the hiring of a Negro man to work in this neck of the woods, in this capacity. You know what I mean."

Louis exhaled, bowed his head for a moment. "Mr. Taylor, I appreciate this conversation we're having here. I'm lucky to be sitting across from you right now. What you're saying ain't nothing new for me. It's not." Louis's smile was genuine. "I got some thoughts I'd like to share, though."

"Do tell."

"One reason I've stayed in Pineville, besides the paper mill job, is the community of good people. There's harmony here, despite the civil rights turmoil. I'm not saying it's not a good fight. Maybe you feel different. But here in Pineville, people resolve their differences. Color is not necessarily the deciding factor in success or failure. Look at Miz Ruby! And there's Mr. Abe for example. Pineville feels like a safe and healthy place. I'd like to stay here awhile."

Winston let him continue.

"You need a third agent. I know I'm the one could make the most difference here." Louis tapped his own chest as he talked. "I'm the one who could touch the coloreds. So many people here you probly aren't reaching 'cause you're a white man. I think if you give me a chance, Bayside Life sales'll go through the roof." The young man's face glistened.

Enthusiasm. That's what they needed. Winston soon closed the interview, making no promises.

∽

The hunt for a new agent was time consuming. Winston was tired. He hadn't made a single policy sale in over a week. His collections were falling behind, but he didn't want A. F. touching his best customers. He'd kept the man out in the field during the interview process. Told him to report back Friday. Tomorrow.

Winston reached to turn off the lights, but the phone rang. *Fuck.* It was Roger Johns.

"Curiosity was gettin' the best of me. What's happenin' in our prestigious Pineville operation?"

Winston managed a chuckle. "I was hoping to dodge you another day." He filled Roger in on the morning call to Wide World Encyclopedia.

"No shit! I gotta hand it to you, your instinct was dead on. Something strange about this. So, I guess we just walk away from Swain."

"Well . . . I'm thinking about that. I'm leaning toward stalling him a little. I can't really say why." No need to tell Roger he had Deputy Dan checking out Swain. That would send Roger into a tailspin. "Maybe they're dealing with an employee lawsuit or something. Who knows what's happening? But I think the guy is a strong candidate. I'd like to keep him dangling while I wait for a few more applicants to surface. I could get him to come back for a second interview, maybe in a week or so. Let him defend himself."

"I guess I'll leave that decision up to you. You're on the front lines. And you seem to be a seer of some sort," Roger laughed. "You had any more responses to the ad?"

"Yeah . . ." Winston hesitated. "I've had one other guy in here. Louis Fisher. Young guy. Got some business classes under his belt. He's working two jobs now. Out at Buckhead and a part-time gig selling cars."

"Well, damn. What's the hem-hawing about? He got a lead shoe and one eye?"

Winston was not ready to mention that Louis was colored. "Kind of complicated, boss. He might not be suited for a job like this. He's extremely ambitious. Just not sure if we got him that we could keep him."

"Jesus, Winston. Just fuckin' find somebody."

Chapter 15

After breakfast, Ruthie left for Gainesville—Mary Carolyn's asthma checkup. Their daughter's breathing issues were few and far between. Winston headed to the office, happy for Friday.

A. F. Larkins showed up at his desk a little after eight, his punctuality a small miracle. He was surely hearing the proverbial footsteps, and if he wasn't, what a fool. Winston hoped he'd brought in a sack full of cash and a new policy application or two.

The two worked together, calling accounts—a reckoning of the money they'd collected all week. Later, Winston would deposit the cash and checks into a Bayside Life account at the Citizens Bank of Pineville, where the funds would then be transferred to Jacksonville. No mathematician, A. F. almost always needed more than one run-through to reconcile. They finally balanced cash against the debit book ledgers, and A. F. asked about the status of the interviews. Winston's answer was vague. A. F. had no need to know.

Just before noon, the men split up. A. F. knocked off for the afternoon, said he needed to drive his wife to a doctor's appointment. Winston locked the office door, dropped the collections at the bank's drive-up window, then headed home.

⌇

Solitude. With Ruthie and their lively little girl in residence, the Taylor house was rarely quiet. Winston turned on the television to catch the Saturday weather forecast; temps in the thirties expected by four in the morning. The baloney and mayonnaise white-bread sandwich he put together was a treat.

Winston pulled his hunting clothes from a camo duffel bag and shook out the wrinkles. He spread them across the living room couch, ready to go. The jacket was newer than the rest of the clothes, deeper greens against his favorite faded pants. He'd burned the jacket he'd worn the day Jackson Smith died.

Shotgun shells rolled inside the box Winston retrieved from the hall closet's top shelf. He assessed the contents: 175-grain soft points. Plenty for tomorrow. Half an ear picked up something on TV about the President being in Dallas. Who cared? He had little interest in government or national politics.

Early tomorrow morning he'd be hunting deer on Clark Bishop's land. Clark was one of his well-to-do insureds—a Pineville gas station and fuel oil company owner. Mary Carolyn attended school with the Bishop kids, played with

Angela, Bishop's youngest daughter. This was Winston's kind of politics—work and family.

He examined his rifle, wiped off fingerprints with a flannel rag, then slid the Winchester into its case. Passing through the kitchen, he noticed lunch crumbs on the counter. He hesitated, then swept them up with his hands, dumped them into the white enamel sink, and headed back to work.

∽

Winston settled at his desk, and Dan Nettles called: Ricky Swain might indeed fit the description of a person of interest in a couple of out-of-town B&E's and a sexual assault, but nothing in Foley County. Detectives were interested in finding out more about Swain—wanted to see Winston at the station. They agreed on three o'clock.

My oh my, Winston smiled, reveling in being right. Something *was* weird with Ricky Swain. But he, Winston, needed to quit trying to be a detective, no matter how much he enjoyed it. Quit running like a hound after a fox every time his intuition whispered. Lately his office days unfolded like episodes of *As the World Turns*. Exciting, but he wasn't making any money for himself or the company. And Thanksgiving was next week, another interruption of momentum.

He also needed to wrap up this interview crap. In his mind, Ricky Swain was already out of the picture. No new resumes had trickled in. For now, his best option was Louis Fisher, but a Negro was a long shot—Roger would probably have a stroke if Winston even brought up hiring a colored man. Tomorrow, in the deer stand, in the peace of the woods, he'd think hard about this. Listen for answers. Or warnings in the wind.

An insured's family member called to report her mother's death. She needed the payout for the funeral. Winston fell into his funereal mode—quiet and consoling. He explained the process to the beneficiary, then notified the death benefits group in Jacksonville. *Too bad,* he thought. *But we all gotta go sometime. One less premium payment coming in, too.* He had to get back on the street.

Two-fifteen. Winston lit a cigarette, gazed out the window. The usual foot traffic on both sides of Main looked somehow different. He watched a couple of people walk hurriedly to cars. Several gathered on the sidewalk, animated. Two women appeared to be crying, hands covering mouths. A car stopped in the road, the driver shouting at the gathered pedestrians. What was going on? He stubbed out the smoke and gathered a notepad and pencil, and Ricky Swain's application.

The phone rang again, shrill and unnerving. His body tingled. He snatched up the receiver. "Bayside Life Insurance. Winston Taylor."

Ruthie was on the line. Crying. Ruthie almost never cried. Winston's heart hammered.

"What Ruthie, what?" His voice rose with her sobbing. "What the hell! Is something wrong with Mary Carolyn?" Winston was almost shouting. "Is the baby okay?"

"It's awful, Winston."

He steadied himself against the desk.

"Somebody shot the President. Somebody shot President Kennedy."

Winston's ears rang. The President? Relief washed over him. This had nothing to do with his family, with his life. He slumped into his chair.

"What the hell, Ruthie? How do you know? Where are you?"

He clenched the receiver, listening to his overwrought wife, still at the doctor's office in Gainesville. She'd seen it there on TV: coverage of the presidential motorcade. Three shots at Kennedy—hurt bad. She'd called as soon as she could; the line for the pay phone was long.

They talked for a moment, her voice thick and wet. He soothed her a little, then told her to dry up the crying, to get out of there. She pushed back—she'd stay a little longer, watching for an update. They'd be on the road soon. Winston hung up, light-headed with relief: his girls were okay.

Even though the attack on Kennedy was not his to carry or solve, disquiet grew within him—the President should be above injury or death. Winston knew qualified people would get to the bottom of what had happened this day in America. Surely Dallas doctors would save their leader. But the uneasiness in his belly twisted like a snake.

Winston headed straight for the Sheriff's office. So many people on the streets—some wandering like the lost, some hurrying as though seeking safety. Someone repeatedly honked a car horn. The Presbyterian church, normally locked tight on Fridays, stood with doors flung open like arms. Winston sprinted on to the station. The duty officer, expecting him, unlocked the door to the administrative area and waved him in. Uniformed deputies and officers in street clothes filled a large meeting space, all eyes on a portable television elevated at the front of the room.

Walter Cronkite's distinctive, commanding voice now graveled heavy and hopeless. President John F. Kennedy had died at two o'clock, eastern standard time. The always-professional news anchor pulled off his black-rimmed glasses, looked up twice, perhaps at a clock. He took a second to control his emotions, swallowing hard. He cleared his throat, said Vice President Johnson would soon take the Oath of Office, becoming the 36th President of the United States.

The President was dead. John F. Kennedy. Assassinated.

The whole room was silent, all mesmerized by what played before them in grainy shades of gray. Winston looked around for Dan. Across the room, the officer lifted his hand in silent recognition. All the men stood at attention, hats in hands, a few with tear-streaked faces. One or two with a smirk. In a corner, two secretaries held hands and cried.

Sheriff Ramsey turned off the television. He cleared his throat, then directed every non-law enforcement person to leave the room. Dan caught up with Winston at the doorway and whispered that the whole department was now in crisis mode, preparing for fallout from the President's death—potential rioting, shootings, or who knew what. He said detectives were still interested in Swain, but it would have to wait. Was there any way to keep him hooked regarding the job, hopefully holding him in Pineville or nearby for a couple of days? Winston would try.

Chapter 16

The phone was ringing when Winston unlocked his office door: Roger Johns, wanting to commiserate on the death of Kennedy. Were the Russians responsible? Should the country be preparing for battle? They danced around those ideas, then Winston reeled the conversation back to Bayside Life business. He shut his eyes and explained that he'd mentioned Ricky Swain to Dan Nettles at the Sheriff's Department. Now Swain might be a suspect in several cases, and Winston found himself involved. He gave Roger the details.

The line went quiet for a moment, then: "Unbelievable," Roger said. "What a shit show." Winston braced himself and waited.

"Goddammit, Winston! Why did you let yourself get tangled up with the cops? I give you a golden opportunity to hire another agent, and you turn it into an investigative tangent, trying to sniff out a crook. Meanwhile your collections are behind and sales are tanking and this is BULLSHIT."

Rubbing at the tension gripping his neck, Winston said: "I don't blame you for being pissed, Roger. But think about it. Swain is the best applicant we've had come through the door. I *knew* something felt off when I met him, but I still thought he might be a good possibility for us. Maybe the only candidate worth hiring. We can't risk taking someone on without calling past employers. It turns out it's not such a bad thing that my instincts were right, and that I thought it important to call that encyclopedia company and verify that Swain was on the up and up. I think my actions to protect Bayside Life and our customers shouldn't be considered a negative. I'm not sorry I checked with local law enforcement either."

"Do I need to drive over there?" Roger finally asked. "Talk to the Sheriff?"

"Nothing to do now, Roger. It's the weekend. Nothing's gonna happen here with the cops, probably not for a couple days. The Kennedy situation trumps all."

"I betcha the guy'll be gone by tomorrow, latest."

Winston took a deep breath. "I'm thinking I could try to reach Swain now, over at the Starlight Motel. Hopefully, he's still in town. Jack him up for a second interview on Monday. Maybe you could be here for that."

"You mean a real interview?"

Winston rolled his eyes. "No, just to hold him here. But we could do a mock interview. He's got no idea the cops are interested in him."

Roger made thinking noises, then said "I'm saying yes to a Monday meeting. Let me know if he agrees. Try for mid-day or after. But I'll talk to Brian Benson about it. Get back with you tonight or tomorrow on whether I'm coming. Brian may want to come, too. This could be very dicey. We need to keep Bayside Life in the best possible light. Always."

⌒

Winston phoned the Starlight Motel. Myrna, the day manager, confirmed Swain was still registered and transferred the call to the room. Swain answered after several rings.

"Glad you're still in town, Ricky! This is Winston Taylor." Winston pictured the man's lips cracking into a smug smile.

"Mr. Taylor! Good to hear from you. Just got back to my room from making the rounds. Made a fast pass through a subdivision called Pembroke Pines. Then Spring Lake Heights. Big development. Never saw a lake, though," Swain laughed.

What kind of *rounds*? Winston felt a chill seeping through the phone line. Bayside Life had customers in both of those neighborhoods—Winston conjured up their faces. He imagined Ricky Swain casing their homes.

"Thought I'd try to catch you before you left town. I remembered you said your next stop would be somewhere in Georgia."

"Yeah, thought I'd leave in the morning. I'm tapped out here for now. I did sell three sets of books, though. At houses I sure didn't expect I would."

Three sets of books, my ass, Winston thought. The guy was a psychopath.

"Let's get right to it. I've interviewed a number of applicants, and you're one of the most qualified," Winston lied. "I'd like to meet with you again, talk more specifics. You still interested?"

"Of course! I appreciate that. I must've gotten a good reference from Wide World," probed Swain.

"I didn't call 'em. I got a really good feel for you in the interview. My gut tells me you wouldn't be working for a company like Wide World Encyclopedia if you weren't a strong salesman." Winston laid it on thick. "And I didn't want to alert your people unless we made you an offer. Our home office may still want to verify your employment history before we can actually hire you, if we reach that stage. Just a formality. Other than that, there's really nothing Wide World can tell me that I haven't figured out about you by myself."

"Thank you for that, Mr. Taylor. I think I could learn some things from you. I bet you're a manager who challenges his employees daily."

Winston laughed. "You have no idea," he said.

"I wouldn't mind being put to the test."

They agreed to meet at the office on Monday at one o'clock, then Winston immediately updated Roger, who said he'd be there mid-morning Monday. No word yet on whether Brian would come along. They'd send A. F. out again for the whole day. Winston would run down Deputy Dan by tonight. Let him know Swain was a sitting duck.

What a crazy-ass week.

⌇

Tommy something, the kid working pumps this afternoon at the neighborhood Sinclair, was no more than thirteen or fourteen. Joe Jenkins, the filling station owner, loved to give the local boys opportunities to earn money. Tommy gassed up the Studebaker while Winston went inside for a bag of pork skins and a Coke. He called out a reminder for the boy to check the tires.

Joe worked in the service bay, head and hands disappeared into the undercarriage of a Ford truck jacked high on the lift. Winston watched, stuffed the crackling snack into his mouth, then chugged from the icy Coke. The bay smelled of oil, gasoline, and spray lubricants. A nice smell. Something good about people who worked with their hands. He licked crumbs from his fingers, noted his only callous— on his pencil finger.

Joe wanted to yammer about the death of the President, about who was responsible. Maybe Castro, a delayed payback for Bay of Pigs. Khrushchev? Was he killed because he supported the coloreds? Who knew? Surely the FBI and the CIA would get to the bottom of it. Winston changed the subject—*Fix or Repair Daily* on Fords? Not true, Joe said.

Dan Nettles wheeled his personal car in next to the second pump. He drove a black VW bug, its engine singing like Ruthie's sewing machine. The deputy unfolded himself from the front seat, adjusted his holster and met Winston on the pavement, out of earshot of Tommy. Dan was on his way home for a quick dinner but would return to the station for an extended shift. He said they were scheduling extra patrols throughout the county on this historical night, particularly in the colored neighborhoods.

"Some of the Negroes are taking the assassination real hard. A couple of their pastors are meeting with the Sheriff right now. I heard they were coming to alert Ramsey of possible trouble."

"I can imagine there'd be some anxiety among those folks. But we're all stunned," Winston said, already tired of assassination talk. He tossed his snack bag into the trash drum, set the bottle in a nearby wooden crate of empties.

Winston filled Dan in on what he'd done about Ricky Swain, the plans for a Monday interview.

"I had an idea," Winston said. "Whaddaya think about one of your detectives, or even you, sitting in on the interview? Under cover-like. See Swain without scaring him off. Knowing he ain't even working for the book company anymore, you won't believe how that bastard can lie!" Winston crossed his arms. "It's crazy!"

"I don't know about that, now," Dan said. "I'd have to talk to the guys in charge. I think they want to hear from you first, then decide about bringing Swain in. We don't know for sure if he's a real suspect. He lied to you, but maybe he's an innocent guy desperate for the job."

Winston screwed up his face. "Shit, Dan. Of course, he's trying to get the job! He's hoping to disappear from his past, blend into little ol' Pineville. Start up with our women. Break into our houses. Wake up, man!"

Dan rolled his eyes. "I said Swain *might* be someone of interest. You've already found him guilty and we haven't even interviewed or investigated him. Calm down, buddy."

Winston stuffed his hands into his pockets, scuffed the bottom of one shoe on the oil-stained concrete. He agreed he could be jumping the gun, burying the guy alive in supposition. "Sorry—tough week. But just think about what I said, Dan. Talk to your guys if you can. Y'all need to take a close look at Ricky Swain, or outright bring him in for questioning. Because after the interview Monday, when I don't hire him, he's gonna evaporate."

∽

Winston entered his quiet, dim house. He found Ruthie lying on the bed, dark creeping in between the Venetian blinds. He pulled off his shoes, crawled up behind her, and rubbed her back.

"Where's Mary Carolyn?"

"I took her next door to the Frazer's. They'll let her play with their girls, stay the night."

"Mmm," he said, thinking of what they could do with the alone time, and it wasn't even full dark. "You feeling okay?"

"No."

"The baby?"

She rolled over to face him. "I can't stop thinking about Kennedy. Jackie seeing him shot to death. His blood on her."

"Yeah. I was over at the Sheriff's Department and saw some of the TV coverage—Cronkite was on. Hard to believe Kennedy's dead. What's even harder to believe is that somebody shot him in broad daylight with millions of eyes watching. And you know cops were everywhere in Dallas, keeping watch . . . Shit, our whole Sheriff's Department's on red alert in case anybody in Foley County gets crazy in the aftershock. You know, riots or whatever."

"Good god, Winston," Ruthie said as she sat up on the bed, "we shouldn't be talking about Foley County. Who cares about li'l ol' Foley County . . . this is way bigger than us!"

Winston sat up, too, and caught her hands which fluttered like two trapped birds. "Ruthie. Honey. You're lettin' yourself get too worked up. Calm down."

She pulled her hands free of his but lowered her voice. "We ought to be talking about what's gonna happen next in our country, in the world. They're holding that guy, Oswald, for the shooting. But what if they find out the Russians hired him? Or Castro was responsible? People are saying this could be another world war. That craziness last year with Khrushchev aiming a nuclear missile at Florida . . . our neighbors building bomb shelters in their back yards . . . that was more like a school bully shootin' spitballs compared to this!" Her last word ended with a hiss.

Winston drew her against him. "Stop it. There's not a damn thing any of us can do except carry on with our lives. Leave the Kennedy crisis to the people smart enough to figure it out. That's not me, and that's not you." He kissed her neck, unbuttoned her blouse. "This, now," he said, "this is what I call carrying on with our lives."

Chapter 17

Clark Bishop owned land north of Pineville between Shady Grove and Madison. Some of it was pastureland where he raised Brahman cattle with the help of an onsite foreman. This morning, though, Clark's Ford pickup with Winston in the passenger seat rolled through the dark woods Clark kept strictly for hunting. The truck's low beams lit up scrub, ancient oaks, and an abundance of slash pine.

"Cold as a witch's tit," Winston said, stepping out of the cab's warmth.

"Hey, puss, we didn't come for the weather," Clark laughed. He opened his door to spit tobacco into the dirt. "I'll pick you and your deer up around ten. This same spot. If you ain't here, I'll honk the horn and wait."

Winston assessed the elevated, enclosed tree stand with a bright-beam head lamp, then hauled himself up the homemade ladder. A ragged scrap of carpeting helped muffle floor noise. By the smell of it, mildew multiplied within the rug's fibers. He set the headlamp on the floor and made himself at home in the tight quarters of the rough wooden hut: retrieved a canteen of water and a snack from his pack, rummaged for the binoculars. If he were hunting anywhere else, with anyone but Clark, he'd be hunkered down in a makeshift ground blind. Most hunters thought it dangerous to even think of climbing a tree to spot a deer. But Clark Bishop was innovative, always looking for a better way. Winston sat like a king on his throne.

Wind whispered around the blind. He sipped the water, emptied half a sleeve of Lance peanuts into his mouth, then washed them down with a big swallow. The rifle slipped easily from its padded case with the faint scent of 3-In-One oil drifting up. Winston checked the safety and loaded the 30.06 with the 175's. He folded back the interior shutters covering three window openings and settled into the skewed swivel chair. At first light, he'd have quite a view. His Timex ticked a chilly 5:23 a.m. Shivering, he tugged the brim of his lined cap down to just above eye level. He switched off the headlamp and got still, waiting for the sky to lighten.

Staring at the black slates of open windows, he let his mind wander to his current conundrums, turning them over and over for inspection . . . Ricky Swain. A criminal? Or just desperate for a job, as Dan had suggested. Might make a good insurance agent but be damned if it'd be with Bayside Life. "Fuck him," Winston whispered. He wanted to nail Swain. He didn't need any hard evidence to know the guy was guilty of something. *Should've been a detective*, he smiled to himself; he loved a good mystery. The hunt was what always got his juices flowing, he admitted it.

Dark was losing its depth. He scanned the improving view. Nothing. The short stack of candidate applications fluttered through his head. Not much to work with. The crippled guy: a no. The woman—completely off the table. But Louis Fisher . . . Louis . . ..

Winston jerked, catching himself from dozing off. He stared hard beyond the windows. Still no visibility.

Miz Ruby—sharp; intelligent. Part of what made Pineville tick, though very few gave her that much credit. She wouldn't have come to him with a half-assed idea. Her feelings about Louis might be as keen as his own.

The few times Winston had come in contact with Louis Fisher, he'd been impressed. Personality. Physical appearance—medium build, fit, clean-cut—sure to draw the girls. Charming and well-spoken. Persuasive. No wonder Ruby's granddaughter was falling hard. But the chance of Bayside Life hiring a Negro in North Florida during these troubling times was slim to none. Maybe a stupid mistake, though. Louis had made a good point about why he was right for Bayside, and being colored might work in the company's favor. In Winston's own favor. Yeah, that's what really mattered. He yawned, rolled his head around on his shoulders.

The drawback: not all customers who needed tending would welcome a colored man into their home. Bayside might lose a few. He and Roger would have to come up with a good strategy. Maybe they'd start with Louis shadowing A. F. Larkins. Winston blanched at that thought. Maybe he'd shepherd Louis himself, build customer confidence in the duo. Then draw up a route for Louis based on customer reaction.

Shit. All this thinking was wearing him out. Winston swigged from the canteen. He needed to stop chasing his own tail. No way he'd convince Roger, much less the company's top dogs, to hire Louis.

⌢

Good, soft light now. Wisps of ground fog. Birds chirped; squirrels chased in an unseen tree. Increasing wind gusts swayed the hunting blind. Despite wool socks and liners, his feet inside leather boots endured a tingling numbness. Chapped hands stung—no patience for gloved shooting. He wanted to feel the kill. He pulled a toothpick from his chest pocket, clamped down, and ground the pick to nothing but fibers.

He stood up and stretched in place, and the ceiling quickly closed in. Back in the seat, he wiggled his frozen toes and lifted the binoculars up from around his neck, checking the view through all three windows. A distant clear-cut was visible from one of the openings—an excellent field of fire. The area appeared close enough to touch, the gaps between trees empty as far as he could see. Beyond another window, dried yellow corn littered the ground—clearly a bait station. He couldn't expect to shoot a buck at the bait, though; the big boys frequently held back at least a hundred yards, watching the does and offspring feed. Ten yards off from the corn, an antler rub on a sturdy sapling caught his eye. Some big daddy had marked his territory. Winston smiled. Good ol' Clark had set him up for success. He leaned back to wait.

Something vaporous drifted in the shadows of Winston's thoughts. What was it? Something he'd missed about Ricky Swain? Or was it Louis Fisher? He wished he had a blanket. He closed his lids, trying to coax the elusive notion to the forefront. Then it materialized, floating toward him, bloated and wet: Jackson Smith. The dead man who never seemed to die.

Winston's eyes flew open. He blinked rapidly. A distinctive flush of quail. Movement. A reflexive response: gun up at his shoulder, a right swivel, eye at scope, safety off. Three deer on the feed: magnification stroking a doe with two yearlings. A longer look now, out beyond the bait, scanning the grove of trees. Swing to the clear-cut. Lens over logs and deadfall. Crosshairs floating over brown. Sand-colored antlers. *BANG!*

Winston's ears rang. Smoke cleared. The buck had dropped where he'd stood.

The field-dressed carcass now lay at the foot of the hunting blind, innards left behind for a buzzard supper. Clark Bishop's truck rumbled up the makeshift road, and together they loaded the deer into the truck bed. On the way back to town, Winston laid out his plan; Clark agreed. They delivered the deer to Miz Ruby's Rooms—Winston's secret penance for consigning the body of a young man to a deep, watery grave.

Chapter 18

On Monday, at 4:45 a.m., Winston sat at the kitchen table sipping his second cup of scalding coffee. He'd turned on the oven and left its door cracked to warm the room; the hallway floor furnace couldn't keep up.

Sleep had eluded him nearly all night, uncertainty circling like vultures inside his head. He had little interest in the wheels of government, but the Kennedy assassination rattled him. The president would be buried today with half the world watching. That fat bastard, Jack Ruby, had killed Lee Harvey Oswald. Stepped up and shot him in front of a crowd of cops, reporters inside the Dallas police headquarters, and on live television. Winston had watched several replays; his apprehension grew with each viewing. How did Ruby have the balls to shoot the man who most likely killed Kennedy . . . and why? Sure as shit, the President's assassination was orchestrated by the Russians. Had to be. Khrushchev was probably laughing his Commie ass off. Now LBJ's running the country? All the race riots going on? America was on its way to hell.

Winston stirred his coffee with a tarnished silver spoon, watching the black ripples inside the cup. His restless night wasn't just anxiety over the state of the nation. Ruthie had never even heard him say the name Ricky Swain, but she'd probably kill him if she knew what was about to happen.

Just after lunch, he and Roger Johns would "interview" Swain. Brian Benson, Roger's boss, would be there, too. They'd worked out a half-assed plan yesterday on the phone. Dan Nettles was also involved.

Over the weekend, the Sheriff's Department had talked to several law enforcement agencies in Florida and in nearby states, all of them on the lookout for a man resembling Ricky Swain. Victims reported vague descriptions of the perpetrator—none had gotten a clear look. Commonalities, however, included unusually pale hair and skin. Various crimes were involved: B&E, peeping, and sexual assault. Law enforcement found no probable suspects in any of the cases.

Foley County cops had no real reason to haul Ricky Swain in for questioning; they had no open cases involving anyone like Swain. They had had no fingerprints from Swain to compare to those discovered at distant crime scenes. Until yesterday, when Winston remembered he had never washed the coffee mug Ricky Swain drank from during his interview. The cup was now a piece of potential evidence, with prints lifted and ready for comparison by other agencies.

Winston couldn't prove that Swain was guilty of anything, but the veiled message from the fellow at Wide World Encyclopedia, coupled with Winston's own strong instincts, said Swain had done something bad. And his friend, Deputy Dan, had faith in him. At the end of the day, Winston would either be a hero or a fool.

Fool. "Fools rush in . . ." Something about that old saying. The knee-jerk decision to dump that station wagon into the water. Winston bolted for the kitchen sink, his coffee now a bitter, rising gorge.

He wiped his mouth on the dish towel, sank into the ladder-back chair. Winston knew the ground was still shaky over the sinkhole secret. As unstable as the day he'd lost his footing and nearly tumbled into Blue Sink. Why had nobody reported Jackson Smith missing? Two years now. Old Mabel Griffin's mind had gone downhill. These days she probably wouldn't even recognize her grandson if he walked into her house, which he never would.

Something ticked like a bomb inside Winston. Putting himself "out there," calling attention to himself, was dangerous. The collective head of the Sheriff's Department had swiveled his way. He couldn't afford that kind of attention. Just as he was suspicious of Ricky Swain, was doing all he could to nail the man, he recognized that someone could do the same thing to him. He almost wished he'd never called Wide World Encyclopedia. But maybe helping catch a hardcore criminal was another chance to redeem himself for his own past mistakes.

⌁

Dan Nettles was waiting for Winston outside the still-sleeping Bayside Life office.

"You look rough, buddy," Dan said. "This is your big day, but you done gone and forgot your makeup." His belly shook.

"Can't go there with you this morning, man," Winston said, unlocking the office door. "Hardly slept worrying about this shit."

"Well, I got some news you gonna like to hear. Your man, Swain, mighta got a little careless."

"Whaddaya mean?"

"I mean somebody broke into a house over at Spring Lake Heights last night."

Winston's eyes widened. "Whose house?"

"Jason Joseph's. You know, one of the owners of that new boat showroom out on 361, like you're going to Dekle Beach."

"Yeah, I know who you're talking about," Winston said. "You think Swain was the burglar?"

"Not sure yet . . . Anyway, word spread like a neighborhood wildfire, and one old woman said she saw a strange man walking through several yards on Friday. There's an alley runs behind that place on one side of the subdivision. Backs up to a cow pasture. Less conspicuous access."

Winston nodded. He knew it well.

"The woman who saw the guy in broad daylight said he was medium build with thinning blond hair. Spooky-white complexion. She got a pretty good fix on him through her bedroom window."

That fucker, Winston thought. "What'd he get?"

"Couple guns. Old gold watch. Pearl necklace."

"So, the description fits Swain—or a look-alike. But that doesn't really help us here, does it?"

Dan rocked back and forth on his soles. "Oh, yeah. The guys who worked the break-in got some decent prints, and they think they're a match to what came off your coffee cup, though those were a little smudged. Just waiting on the fingerprint expert to get in and confirm."

Winston's mouth hung open, and he shook his head at Dan's words.

"Believe it, my friend. We're tweaking your interview plan for today. We want to get a better set of prints, just so there's no room for mistakes. Detective Brody and I think we can make this real easy. Gimme a cup of that coffee, Lucy, and I'll 'splain it to you."

At a quarter till one, Brian Benson, Roger Johns, and Winston waited in the office for Swain. The Bayside Life team was ready with a stronger plan than what they'd previously devised. Dan Nettles stood by, out of sight at Bell's Jewelry in case of trouble. Ten minutes later, Ricky Swain pushed through the front door.

Winston met him with a strong handshake and a big dose of enthusiasm. Ricky was well-dressed, professional. His cracked red lips could not stop smiling, eyes darting back and forth between the two Bayside Life execs. Puzzled. Winston introduced Roger and Brian. They both offered business cards, evidence of their status with Bayside Life. Ricky declined the offer of coffee.

Roger took the lead: "Ricky, Winston's told us all about you and your current position at Wide World Encyclopedia. That's a great company, by the way. Sounds like you've been doing good work for them."

Ricky licked his lips. "Yessir! I've enjoyed working with them. But I'm tired of being on the road all the time. It'd be nice to settle down, sleep in the same bed every night. Pineville might be a good move for me."

"You're probably wondering why Brian and I are here for this interview."

"Well, yessir, I was only expecting to meet with Mr. Taylor, so I'm a little surprised."

"Here's what might really surprise you: We've had a number of strong candidates for this position. Mr. Taylor has done all the initial interviews, but we're now down to those we feel are our best choices. I'm happy to say that you're on the top of the heap. Mr. Benson and I wanted to meet you personally so that we could make the best possible decision."

Ricky nodded, his face glowing.

"Bayside is working hard to increase business in the North Florida area. You may be just the person we need," Roger said, then paused to make sure Swain was still along for the ride. "Today we're going to talk with you in more detail about the job and the opportunities. We want to ask you some specific sales questions, more in-depth than in your first interview."

Ricky's head bobbed. "I've been thinking on Mr. Taylor's comments to me last time about working on the colored community, increasing those sales. I've come up with a couple of ideas to share with you, too."

Winston eyes met Roger's: so far so good.

"Great! I like that proactive thinking. We'll be interested in hearing your thoughts," Roger said. "At the end of this interview, we'll give you some information to take home about company benefits, top sales club parameters, that sort of thing. Since we're far from the home office, and since we want to expedite the hiring for this position, we'd like to go ahead and get you to fill out a few forms and get you fingerprinted. We'll take all that back to Jacksonville with us. That gonna work?"

Brian Benson chimed in: "Yeah, our Human Resources department has to review all that applicant information before we can make a final offer."

Ricky's excitement faltered. He swallowed hard. "Fingerprinted?"

"That's our company policy. Doesn't Wide World do that for their hires?" Roger asked.

"I've never been fingerprinted in my life," Ricky said.

"Then welcome to our world," Brian laughed. "At Bayside Life, it's routine practice."

The three Bayside Life Insurance men would all later admit to a serious case of the jitters, and outright fear that Swain might be packing a gun.

Roger Johns forged on and led Swain down a fictional interview path geared to keep the man at ease and believing. While they waited for Swain to complete the several personnel forms, Roger declared he'd left the fingerprint kit in the car and went out to retrieve it. He returned empty-handed. "I swear I brought it." This would delay their ability to make a job offer, he said, especially with the Thanksgiving holiday coming. Swain watched and listened.

Winston offered that the Sheriff's Department, just down the street, wouldn't mind rolling the prints for them. Wouldn't even charge for it. He picked up the phone and called the duty officer, just like they had rehearsed. Asked if they'd be able to do it on short notice.

The four men walked to the Sheriff's Office, chatting good-naturedly about how quickly the weather had warmed, about small-town friendliness. Winston pointed out several businesses along the sidewalk, talked about the owners—all Bayside Life Insurance customers. Swain acted genuinely interested.

Detective Brody ushered them into a brightly-lit manila-colored concrete room. A large mirror was set into one wall; a Most-Wanted poster hung nearby. Fingerprint cards and an ink pad waited on the edge of a small conference table.

"Which of you guys needs printing?"

Swain raised his hand, and Brody waved him over to stand at the table, facing the mirror. Roger and Brian sat down to watch. Winston excused himself for the restroom.

Brian joked that he couldn't trust Roger Johns as far as he could throw him. "I can't believe you forgot the dang print kit, and here we drove all this way to expedite hiring. I'm gonna remember this next time your evaluation comes due." They all laughed.

"Aw, we're happy to help you out," Detective Brody said. "We actually fingerprint people fairly often. As a service to the public, I mean."

Ricky Swain was quiet, his face expressionless.

Brody asked Swain to remove his suit coat and roll up his sleeves. "This ink can be messy, don't wanna ruin your shirt."

Winston and Deputy Dan stood in the dark room on the back side of the two-way mirror, watching Brody roll Ricky's prints. The door opened and another deputy brought in Edna Williams, Winston's best Spring Lake Heights customer. Winston put his arm around her shoulder and gave her a little squeeze.

"All right, Mrs. Williams," Dan said, "I want you to look through that glass there and tell me if you recognize anyone in that room."

Edna looked puzzled. "Aren't you going to show me a lineup, like they do on TV? Where the men come in all dressed alike?" She sounded disappointed.

"No ma'am, this is called a 'show up,' and we only do it under special circumstances, like if we can't risk losing the suspect. So, go ahead and look. Take all the time you need," Dan said.

"Oh, goodness, I don't need time. That's the same man I saw, sure as I'm standing here. The one with the ink on his hands. That man was cutting through yards across from my house and I saw him stop and put his face against the front bedroom window of Earl Sawyer's . . . Earl wasn't home . . . everybody knows he's gone to Albany, chasing some widow woman." She took a deep breath. "But anyway, I got a little worried he'd come to my place. Nettie Gilmore's little sausage dog was barking to beat the band, and then I saw him—"

"That's what we needed to hear," Dan cut in. "Thank you for coming forward, Mrs. Williams. You've truly been a help. Winston, would you show her out?"

∽

Winston returned to see Swain wiping his hands on a wet towel.

"Looks like we're done here," Winston said. Roger and Brian got up from the table.

Detective Brody examined the print cards and waved them in the air to dry.

"Didn't hurt a bit, did it?" Roger joked, then patted Ricky Swain on the back. Swain was without words, trying to scrub the ink from around his nails.

Dan Nettles entered, called Detective Brody aside, whispered something. Brody nodded.

"Gentlemen," the detective said. "We're going to need this room for another purpose, so we need you to step out. All of you, except for Mr. Swain here."

Ricky froze. Looked up at the group. "What do you mean?"

"Have a seat, Ricky," Brody said. "This is your best and final interview of the day."

That evening, Roger and Brian took Winston to the Wagon Wheel to celebrate. Over drinks, they rehashed the day's events and their part in the sting which had started with the one o'clock interview. By six thirty, Swain was the newest resident in the Foley County jail, arrested for the Spring Lake Heights break-in. His prints matched perfectly those lifted from the Joseph house. All items stolen from that home were recovered—discovered in the trunk of Ricky's Ford Fairlane. The investigation was ongoing, and the three Bayside employees swore not to discuss the case with others. Detective Brody and Deputy Nettles were already working with Wide World to match Swain's past travel itineraries and sales records with dates and places where similar open cases existed.

"Winston, I've always thought you were full of crap about a of lot of things, but now I'm beginning to believe you've got some kind of sixth sense," Roger said. "Your perceptions are spot on, and you've saved Bayside Life from a huge embarrassment and potential financial liability. Your efforts in this situation will *not* be forgotten." He raised his glass. "To Winston!"

"To Winston!" Brian echoed.

They all laughed and drank to success . . . and excess.

Chapter 19

Tuesday morning, Roger and Brian sat around Winston's desk, reviewing applications. They agreed they had few worth considering. Two more resumes had arrived the day before; nothing of interest. They kept returning to the woman. Marta Pinsky, forty-four years old, with three years of sales experience at a musical instrument store in Valdosta, Georgia. Counter sales only. Still, she would have certainly learned something about closing a deal.

Lighters clicked. The three smoked and talked. They'd seen A.F. briefly before he headed out on his debit route—it was Brian's first time to meet the man. Roger said he could see A. F.'s recent decline: shuffling gait, wheezing. Nasty wet cough. No wonder his job performance was less than stellar. Roger also said he thought Winston was a bit hard on A. F. Winston just shrugged—he'd lost all respect for his employee.

Roger stubbed out his cigarette. "Hey! Where's the application on that young guy you told me about? The one working at Buckhead. He already lost interest?"

"I was saving that one for last," Winston said. "I wanted you to go over all the other applications first. See how little I've had to work with. Then take a look at this applicant, Louis Fisher. I want you to understand why I think he's worth pursuing." Winston handed over the form.

Roger and Brian skimmed over the application together. "Looks interesting, but slim on sales," Brian said.

"Yeah," Roger agreed. "I know you, Winston. What're you holding back?"

"He's colored."

The small office was suddenly too warm.

Roger looked again at the application; he'd completely missed the question about race. "Does that make him special somehow?" he asked, one eyebrow raised.

"He *is* special, somehow," Winston said, looking back and forth between his two superiors.

"We've got a colored salesman down in the South Florida region," Brian offered. "He's holdin' his own."

Roger's face went red. "North Florida isn't even remotely similar to the demographics down at the end of the state, Brian. That whole area is filled with a bunch of Yankees. Those people aren't really *in* 'the South.'" His finger punched the air: "*This* is the South. Those northerners aren't prejudiced like the people around here. We might as well be sitting in Alabama or Mississippi right now." Roger crossed his arms and glared at Winston.

Brian motioned Roger to step outside. Winston emptied ashtrays, keeping an eye on the sidewalk: Roger studied his shoes, hands stuffed into his pockets, already settling. Brian Benson was a peacemaker.

Back inside, Roger said: "Let's start over with the colored guy—Louis, isn't it?"

Winston lightened the mood by beginning with an animated account of riding down Main Street on a parade float with a bunch of squealing kids and a witch of a wife. He wove in his first encounter with Louis at the Pine Tree Festival, and Louis subsequently trying to sell him a station wagon for Ruthie. Then he sobered with his telling of Miz Ruby's appeal to give Louis a chance at the job.

Roger interrupted to share a bit of local politics with Brian, including Ruby Wright's standing in the community and her Bayside Life significant customer status. "Winston's right," he said. "Ruby's the best reference Louis Fisher could ever have."

"The guy came to me brimming with enthusiasm. He *wants* this, a chance to challenge himself, prove himself. Rise above color. He's got a hunger in his belly that shows. You can't help but like him . . . and respect him."

"What'd you tell him?" Brian asked.

"I told him the truth! What I just heard here today. That Pineville probably isn't ready. That Bayside Life probably isn't ready. But I'm telling you, *I'm* ready. I'm ready for somebody I can train up in my way of sales, my way of customer care." Winston was now the one getting hot. "I've got colored customers that count on me. That I could call if *I* needed help. I know A. F. Larkins is out there right now, ruining some of those relationships I've built."

"Winston, you know damn well there are people here who aren't about to let a colored man into their homes. We'll lose their business. Whoever we hire's gonna have to work both sides of the street." Roger ran his hands through his hair.

"I know that. But listen. The world is changing. This big push toward equality. Look at this whole mess with the loss of Kennedy and LBJ in charge. He's always been a bleeding heart, and I doubt seriously he's as dumb as the political cartoonists make him out to be. The laws are going to change in favor of more equal rights. Maybe not in our lifetime. But it's gonna happen."

Winston let what he said hang for a few beats. Then: "Bayside Life could step up to support this. In this one small way, in this one small territory. Hiring a Negro might make the company look good at the forefront of this coming change. We'd be viewed as progressive."

"Yeah, well we'd be viewed as progressive if we let the woman in, too," said Roger. "See if her spike heels could carry her through the sand."

"No. This is bigger than that, guys. Louis Fisher has the potential to raise our sales in the colored community, and I believe if I work with him on the whites, introduce him and let him shadow me long enough, he'll be accepted on his own. Then he can enter most any house in this area and do the job he's there to do." Winston's eyes never wavered from their faces. Then, lowering his voice: "The only color I see here today, gentlemen, is green—the color of money."

Brian looked at Roger. "You know more about this territory, these people, than I do. What do you want to do?"

Roger slumped in the chair. Looked at Winston. "Is there any way we can meet with this guy before we leave town?" he asked.

Winston brightened. "Just so happens, I put a bug in his ear last night. I believe I can have him here late this afternoon."

〜

After Ruthie's excellent Tuesday night Shepherd's Pie, Winston turned on the television and collapsed onto the couch to watch *I've Got a Secret*. While Mary Carolyn played in the bathtub, Ruthie joined him, and asked him to rub her back. He offered to rub the front side, too, but she punched him.

Their easy conversation centered on Thanksgiving Dinner; the Taylors were hosting. Ruthie had invited the Swearingen family, who'd just moved into the house behind them. Dan and Priscilla Nettles were also coming. Winston hoped Priscilla would lay off the wine at dinner. Drink turned her into a loudmouth. He hated drunk women.

Ruthie droned on about the menu. Winston didn't care what they ate. She'd grocery shopped over the weekend and come home with enough to feed their whole block.

"Aren't you trying to do too much?" he asked. "You gotta think about your condition. Let Princess Priscilla do something." His half-lidded eyes were on the television.

"You're right . . . I'm so tired," she said, getting to her feet. "I can't remember feeling this way the first time with Mary Carolyn." She planted her hands at the small of her back. "Oh, by the way . . . I forgot to tell you. I ran into that man who sold us the encyclopedias. The Wide World guy."

Winston shot up from his seat. "What! When?"

"Saturday. I was out shopping."

"Why didn't you tell me! Where'd you see him?" Winston's face darkened.

"Good grief!" she laughed.

"I'm serious, Ruthie. I heard some stuff about that guy. Where was he?"

"In the grocery store. I was picking out sweet potatoes, and there he was, standing right at my elbow. Startled me. I couldn't place him for a second. He must be a good salesman, though. Do you know he actually called me by name? I was amazed."

Chapter 20

Late Wednesday afternoon, a party cranked up in the back yard of Miz Ruby's Rooms. Ruby herself was in charge, celebrating Louis Fisher's new job with Bayside Life.

With the stove already working overtime for Thanksgiving dinner preparations, Ruby improvised: a large black cauldron squatted over an outdoor fire, simmering a heavenly bog of stewed chickens. Etta brought out a sack of white rice and poured the grains into the rich, steaming broth. Older boys tended the fire and stirred the kettle contents with a long-handled wooden paddle.

Word spread quickly and Ruby's friends and family gathered for the feast, though some barely knew Louis. Ruby's older brother, Jimps, pulled Louis aside.

"We all gonna have a good time here tonight. Celebrate your big job," Jimps said in his usual deliberate manner. He spat tobacco juice into the dirt. His mouth opened and closed, searching for words. "But I gotta tell you, boy, this could be a dangerous thing you doing, getting all wrapped up with them white people."

Louis smiled. "Thank you, sir. I know you lookin' out for me. But I think Mr. Taylor'll treat me right."

"You ain't lived long as me. You ain't seen what I seen. Don't be fooled."

Ruby, overhearing part of the conversation, came to the rescue.

"Jimps! Don't you go borrowin' trouble, now. Winston Taylor's a good man. This boy's gonna be just fine," she fussed. "Git on over there and git you some perlo."

Louis raised his eyebrows at Ruby. She just shook her head.

Several liquor bottles cloaked in brown paper sacks passed through the crowd. A guitar picker tuned up; someone played harmonica. An upended metal bucket served as a makeshift drum. The best kind of party began.

∽

Night fell. Voices loosened, and songs rose. Rough renditions of "Under the Boardwalk." Some Sam Cooke—"Another Saturday Night." Etta's brother, Bubba, set up his record player on the back porch, along with a stack of albums. With the volume up, the whole yard was a dance floor. Even old Ruby swiveled her hips to "The Twist," the crowd clapping and whistling, giving her center stage.

Louis and Etta slipped around the house to the front porch swing. Louis hummed his whiskey breath into Etta's ear to the tune of "You Really Got a Hold on Me." She shivered and grinned.

"I'm so happy for you, Louis. You gonna do good. I just know you will."

Louis's teeth matched the moon. He'd hardly stopped grinning since he talked to Winston Taylor earlier in the day. What an opportunity! After all he'd endured, this job was a sign that he was on the right track.

"If I hadn't met your grandma, and then you, I doubt this job woulda ever come my way. Miz Ruby stood up and spoke for me, and I ain't never gonna forget it, Etta. Y'all like family."

"You too easy to care 'bout, mister," Etta said, rubbing his close-cropped hair.

Louis kissed her hard. Looked into her face. He wove his fingers between hers and said, "Listen. You been loving on the likes of me for a while now, and I'm not sure—"

"I didn't do nothin' I didn't want to, Louis. You a fine man; I know it deep inside me."

He pulled her closer. "Etta, I can't make you any promises right now."

"I ain't asking you to."

"I know. But I gotta stand strong on my own before I can carry anybody else. You know what I mean?"

She nodded.

"I'm crazy 'bout you. But I gotta focus on my future. I gotta make this job work out for me."

Headlights washed the house as a car turned into the drive. They both shielded their eyes until the lights were shut off. In a moment, a tall, dark-skinned man materialized at the steps. Louis and Etta stood up.

"Evenin'," said the stranger, inviting himself up on the porch.

"You here for the party? Or needin' a place to stay?" Etta asked. "Maybe we got a room open."

"Sounds like you got quite a shindig going on," he replied, tipping his head toward the cacophony out back.

He looked at Louis for a moment. Parlor light shone through the window but did little to illuminate features. "I'm actually huntin' for somebody. Heard he might be stayin' with you folks."

"Who's that?" asked Louis. The hairs on his arms tingled.

"Looking for a guy goes by Louis Fisher."

Louis squeezed Etta's hand and said "Go on out back. I bet your gramma needs your help. I'll be 'round in a minute." Etta didn't move. "Go on," he repeated until she left. Then he stuck out his hand: "My name's Louis. What can I do for you?"

The man knuckled his hat up higher on his forehead. "I'm Reginald Bevis. I was asked by a family out of Quincy to find you."

"You weren't asked to find *me*. I don't know nobody in Quincy. Ain't never been there," Louis said, swallowing hard. "You got me mixed up with somebody else."

"It's possible. It's possible," Bevis chuckled. "Been known to be wrong. You are a little young for the description I got. Can you step over by the light, so's I can get a better look?"

Louis stood still. "What's this about?"

"You know a Lettie Nash?"

Louis shook his head. "Never met her."

"Well now," said Bevis, "Lettie Nash is laying up in a hospital bed over in Quincy. The girl's got some kinda sickness. She ain't gonna live much longer. She done tole her daddy you the father of her boy. He's nigh on two years old."

Louis stepped back, shaking his head. "You got the wrong person. I told you; I've never met anybody named Lettie Nash. Never been to Quincy either."

Ruby flipped on the front porch light and stepped out the door. She introduced herself and asked the man what he needed.

"Just here in Pineville on a business matter. Thinking I might could use a room for the night."

"As you can tell by the noise, we got a big event out back. We're actually full," Ruby said. "I do hate to turn anyone away, though."

"Little gal here a minute ago said there might be a room."

"As I said, we're full."

Bevis didn't budge, and Ruby snapped: "This is *my* place of business. You need to take yours elsewhere!" She moved back into the house, held the door open. "Louis, you're needed inside."

In the kitchen, Ruby made herself taller, looked up into Louis's eyes.

"Etta said that man was huntin' for you."

"Aw, no ma'am, Miz Ruby. He said he was lookin' for a Louis Fisher, but it wasn't me. He'll just have to keep on lookin'," Louis said. "I ain't got no trouble with a woman."

"Spare me your aw-shucks show, Louis. *That* talk sure doesn't sound like the Louis Fisher I know."

He ducked his head.

"Look, if something's wrong, you can tell me. You know I'll do anything I can for you."

Louis nodded. "I swear to you, Miz Ruby, the guy had me mixed up with somebody else."

125

Chapter 21

The Taylor's Thanksgiving dinner was over. The guests had left happy with full bellies and plates of leftovers. Dan had put a governor on Priscilla's holiday drinking—Winston was relieved and pleased.

Ruthie, complaining of fatigue, crawled into bed, and Winston was right behind her. In the room's semi-darkness, he rubbed her shoulders and back, and lightly soothed her belly. Winston was in love with every inch of his wife.

Ruthie turned to him, their faces close, and Winston finally told her the full story of Ricky Swain, the encyclopedia man. She listened, spellbound.

"Oh, lord," she finally said. "And I thought you just went off to work every day with that pencil behind your ear and that black book swinging by your side, juggled numbers and made small talk with a bunch of regular-old people. I never once thought about you fraternizing with the crazies. That's scary, Winston."

"If you only knew half the shit I've waded through since I've been selling insurance, you wouldn't be able to sleep at night," he said, laughing.

"Quit teasing me . . . you know I'll sit around worrying . . ."

Winston kissed her all over her face. "I'm just kidding. But the Ricky Swain thing was real."

"What do you think about him bumping into me at the store?"

"It wasn't just coincidence. I think Swain was following you, looking for a different way to connect with me. Maybe to get even with me if he thought I wasn't going to hire him. He's a con and a criminal, and a very effective salesman. I *do* think he really wanted the job," Winston said, rolling onto his back. He ran his hands over his face. "He needed a steady income and a cover, a means of hiding in plain sight. A real reason for knocking on the doors of strangers."

"Winston, why in the world did you let yourself get involved in something as insane as this?"

"I don't know," he shrugged. "It just, uh . . . *evolved.*"

"Oh, bullshit!" she laughed. "You love digging to the bottom of everything! Sticking your nose where it doesn't belong."

"You know, you're absolutely right. I've been thinking a lot lately that I might want to do something different one day, something besides sales."

Ruthie frowned. "Like what? You're so good at sales."

"Some kind of investigative work. I don't know how I'd get into it. But I know Bayside Life has an investigations department. So do other insurance companies. And there's the Florida Department of Insurance. In Tallahassee."

"Tallahassee!" She slapped his leg. "That's my guy!"

127

"Don't get too excited, Ruthie. Just daydreams for the future. But there's something else I need to tell you." Then he wheeled out the story of Louis Fisher.

"I can't believe you hired a colored man," Ruthie finally said. "And I can't believe Roger approved it!" Her tone was one of wonder.

"I know."

"This sounds made up." She sat up on the bed, looking down at him, brushing his flattop with her fingers.

"I can hardly believe it myself. That I made it work," he said. "But this felt . . . right. Like I was supposed to do it. You think I made a mistake?"

"Not a mistake. I mean, it really shouldn't matter what color he is. But it sounds like you're already expecting trouble." The room was quiet, then she continued, "What I can't get over is your attitude about this, your pushing for this guy. Your *regard* for this man." She put her hand on his forehead as though checking for a fever. "Since when did you become so enlightened?"

∽

On Friday after Thanksgiving, Louis shined his coffee-brown oxfords and dressed in a new pair of tan trousers and a cream-colored button-up shirt. He slipped into his tweed sport coat, woven overplaids of olive, burnished brown, and black on a gray background. Miz Ruby had given him a new trench coat, for which he was most grateful. He draped it over his arm when he hitched a ride with Bubba to the Citizen's Bank.

A young teller counted out the currency, bills whooshing from the top of a green stack. She controlled the cash like a card shark, counting under her breath. Though he knew the money was his, he'd never seen it all at once like that. Satisfaction filled him. The woman placed the withdrawal inside a white envelope, smiled, and passed it over the counter. Just like that. He slid the fat bundle into the pocket of his sport coat. Then he slipped into his new overcoat and walked the two plus miles to his next destination.

At Abe's Autos, Louis found his new car waiting for him, parked smack in front of the sales office. Sun glinted off the freshly-waxed 1954 Chevy Bel Air, an ivory two-door with a green hardtop. Though the vehicle was nine years old, rust spots and dings were minimal, and the engine was in great shape. Louis and Abe had cut a deal the same day Louis was offered the insurance job. He pulled $350 from the envelope and handed the bills to Mr. Abe, the man who'd helped make the purchase possible, who'd helped make the Bayside Life job possible. Working with Abe had given Louis legitimate sales experience.

Their handshake was firm, yet Louis sensed a tingle of emotion in that skin-to-skin clasp. He did not want to let go.

Today was a gift Louis had given himself. Time to embrace his new freedom in the form of the Bel Air—his own transportation. He drove with no clear destination, but more for the physical sensation of steering, his hands holding the wheel to anywhere. The joy of having cash in his pocket. Time to remember where he'd been, but only to understand how he'd reached the present. A glorious day of private celebration.

Heading north on U.S. 221, Louis tuned the A.M. radio to WAPE out of Jacksonville, *The Mighty Six Ninety, The Big Ape!* He sang along with the top tunes, beating time on the dash with "Easier Said Than Done" by the Essex, a colored group. Negro musicians were getting good airtime on The Big Ape. The Fireballs' "Sugar Shack" reminded him of Etta— their daring daytime trysts at the river and in his rented room under Miz Ruby's roof, silent as mice. Shoot, the big back seat of his new car might be their own sugar shack, for the time being anyway. A heat throbbed through him; he cracked open the car window. Cool, crisp air filled the interior. The sky was blue and bright, the day warm enough to ride without the heater. Windshield time. Louis's life scrolled across that clean curve of the glass.

He'd taken a risk, leaving red Georgia clay, moving south to sandy Pineville. Worked two jobs. Found a semblance of family in Ruby's boarding house. Now a new employment opportunity in the world of insurance, the world of business. He, one small, dark figure in that space Bayside Life had allowed him. So much to learn; so many challenges. Great strides toward his goals.

But his current achievements were diminished by the visit of Reginald Bevis. The man hunting him down like a dog not two whole days ago, accusing him of fathering a baby, running off and leaving the mother sick and dying. And Etta had heard it, and now Ruby knew. This was no way to start a shiny new life—already tarnished by the rust of the past. He'd have to think on this. Figure out what to do. But not today.

Once he reached Highway 90, Louis steered west, passing through the small towns of Monticello, Lloyd, and Chaires before entering Leon County. Then the city itself—Tallahassee—home to Florida's capital. He let loose the memories. The place was part of his past, a good part. Until it wasn't. While Pineville was where he'd chosen to dig his feet into the sand—it offered safe harbor and stability—Tallahassee had given him lift, and knowledge. A partial education. A broader view of the world.

He followed South Monroe Street, which climbed one of the city's highest hills, to reach the FAMU campus. The school's green and orange colors fluttered from frat house balconies, on flags stabbed into the ground everywhere. Green for agriculture; orange for Florida citrus. The complex was nearly abandoned; most students had gone home for Thanksgiving holidays.

Louis parked in the visitor lot and walked the grounds, just like he'd done for the first time more than four years ago. Around the dormitories, past the student services center where'd he'd often come seeking guidance and financial assistance. A student starving for more than food. He stood on the steps of the old ivy-covered brick Carnegie Library building, his favorite place on campus. The place that housed worlds he'd never known, worlds he could only dream of.

The off-campus housing area, the only place he'd been able to afford, was almost a mile away from the main buildings. He decided to leave the car and walk. He'd forgotten how beautiful the campus was. The same magnificent live oaks still towered, moss flowing like the curly tresses of a woman in every man's dream. He could have found his house with closed eyes.

Today the buildings showed some measure of renovation, painted and re-roofed. Then Louis was there, standing in the front yard of the unit he'd shared with two other more-than-poor students; a place with no insulation, and cracks in the floor. The roach motel, they'd called it. No worse than places he'd endured during childhood.

He thought about the other boys, his two roommates—friends at first, until that night at the G&W, a lean-to produce stand at the foot of a railroad overpass, not far from their rental house. What had happened there had sown a seed of fear within him that would not stop growing.

Desperate times and foolish measures. The boys were invisible and invincible back then. Experience had changed that in Louis. Part of him longed to return to the campus, to bury his head in books. To worry only about his next test. But those days were gone. The road from Tallahassee had been rough beyond measure. Louis was a man now, creating a whole new story for himself. His stride was lengthening.

The Bel Air crawled past the G&W, which was locked up tight on this day after Thanksgiving. Louis took in the wooden structure and its faded sign, and a silent black and white film played behind his eyes: three drunk, colored men, arms full of stolen food, surprised by the old white man with the shotgun. Louis offered up a moment of silence for this part of his past, hoping for the day he could throw a final clod of dirt on the first big mistake of his life. He turned the car east and headed back to Pineville.

Chapter 22

"I told you not to call me Mr. Taylor," Winston said, glancing too long at Louis, right wheels rumbling off the edge of the road. "Mr. Winston ain't gonna cut it either."

"Yessir, boss man," Louis deadpanned.

Winston laughed. "You just beat all."

Louis laughed, too. "All right. Winston." He relaxed against the Studebaker's seat. "Just sounds disrespectful. Lotta white folks ain't gonna like hearing me saying it."

Winston frowned. "Not our problem. Our problem is sales. We gotta get out of this stagnant pattern. We need a tight, tough team to make this happen."

"Not sure A. F.'s willing to make room for me on the team," Louis mumbled.

Though inclined to agree with Louis, Winston reassured him: "Oh yeah. He'll come around. He needs a little time to accept that the world ain't flat. He'll be all right."

He'd called A. F. on Thanksgiving Eve to announce Louis's hiring. The conversation hadn't gone well. A. F. had taken the employment of a colored salesman as a personal insult, insinuating he wasn't going to help train a Negro. Winston had controlled his fury, said suit yourself. He understood A. F.'s problem with the hiring of Louis. Louis was indeed a threat.

Now Louis's first week of orientation was over. He'd devoured the handbook on personal insurance terminology and Dale Carnegie's *How to Win Friends and Influence People*. Today Winston was working from his own debit book, introducing Louis first to his favorite colored insureds. Most houses they entered were decorated for Christmas and hope was in the air.

⌒

As they drove, Winston filled his new agent in on the Briney Thomas account history. The Thomas family was high on the transfer list, an easy transition to Louis, and while Winston liked those people, he needed to hand them over. They reminded him too much of the past. Their house had been his last business stop before he found the dead man, before his nightmare began. He pushed his hand into his pocket and cradled the buckeye.

They parked in the dirt yard beneath the cover of sweeping live oak trees and kicked their way through a flurried clutch of chickens. Winston kept a sharp eye on the brindled dog, which was now showing teeth. "I ain't never trusted that mutt," he said.

They stepped up onto the weathered porch decorated with deer antlers, and Winston's knock rattled the screen door. He'd hoped to catch Briney at home, but the guy's big logging truck was gone.

Mrs. Thomas, a short, round woman with a massive brown bosom, opened the door.

"Mr. Winston! I knew it was 'bout time for you to come around," she said.

Winston introduced Louis and she hugged the young man like he was her own son. She brought them into the house, which rarely happened. While Louis chatted up the customer, Winston noticed a bird cage in the corner, but no bird. He peered through the wire at a fluff of gray fur peeking from a mound of towel.

"What you got in here, Mrs. Thomas? A long-haired rat?"

"Oh, Mr. Winston," she said, shaking her head. "Briney done brought home a baby squirrel he found in a tree he took down. Mama was long gone. Lord, that littleun's got to be hand-fed ever so many hours."

She opened the cage and picked up the squirrel. Winston cupped the tiny animal in his hands, couldn't believe it sat so still.

"You wanna sell him?" Winston asked.

"What you gonna do with that thing, Winston?" Louis asked.

"My baby girl would love this. Just love it."

"Her mama ain't gonna love it, or you, once she finds out the feedin' schedule," Louis laughed.

"Be good practice for the baby," Winston grinned. "I'll pay your premium for you, Mrs. Thomas, if you give me the squirrel and the cage."

"Done!" she said, laughing. "And I'll throw in the baby doll bottle, too!"

⌒

At day's end, Winston was optimistic about the customer response to Louis. He noted a level of communication between his new agent and the colored insureds that he himself might never experience. While he had spent several years building strong relationships in the colored community, Louis would make a quick difference with the Negroes. The white reception would take time.

~

At old man Dobbins's house, A. F. sat in the car a few more minutes with the heat running. He pulled a flask from the glove compartment and took a swig. He was already sick of Winston's new *boy*. He couldn't believe Roger Johns had allowed it—a colored guy selling insurance right here in Pineville. Couldn't believe Bayside Life even knew what was happening in their own backyard. That kid grinned every time someone looked at him, white teeth blinding.

He nipped from the flask again, closed the cap, and returned it to the glove box. Paper wrapping crinkled as he opened a piece of Juicy Fruit and pleated the strip of gum into his mouth. He chewed it into a pliable ball, thinking about Louis Fisher. The mint tingled his tongue; he swallowed the sweetness. *I'm gonna eat his darky ass for lunch,* he chuckled to himself.

Gary Dobbins, a pale raisin of a man, let A. F. inside, shutting the door quickly against the cold. A space heater hummed in the stifling living room. The agent shuffled over to its glowing grate and stood close enough his pants could've caught fire. God almighty, he sure could use a nap, right there in that warm room.

The Price is Right blared on television. Bill Cullen declared some silly woman the champion. She squealed and jumped up and down in her high heels. Women were ridiculous, A. F. thought, but she *had* won a trip to the Bahamas. Maybe he ought to see about getting on the show. Practice up on prices. One big win and he'd tell everybody at Bayside Life to kiss his ass.

Dobbins removed several bills from his wallet to pay for his and his wife's insurance, then crept into the bedroom for change. A. F. could hear Rebecca Dobbins mewling from the bed. She'd been sick with something for years. He hoped she lasted a little longer; he couldn't afford to lose a single customer right now.

With payments recorded, he closed his black book and turned to go.

"Just thought you oughta know, Gary, we got us a new salesman at Bayside Life. Might need to bring him round, time to time. Getting him trained up. Teaching him some tricks." He laughed, nearly choking on the gum, then spasmed into a deep cough. His face reddened and his eyes bulged.

Dobbins watched, nodding. "Awh right."

"You wouldn't mind having somebody new coming in, now, would you?" A. F. coughed again.

"Be fine. Be fine." He moved to open the door for A. F.

"What if he was a Negro? You be fine with a colored fellow in here in your house, your poor ol' wife laying in there in her shimmy, her drawers flashing?"

Gary Dobbins stopped, confusion on his face. "A colored guy's coming? Coming inside?"

"Could be. You never know when he might be knocking."

"Not sure 'bout that now, A. F. I might need to think on that some."

"Yeah, I thought you'd want to know ahead. In case, you know, you don't want to turn over your cash money to a stranger like that. You can always call our office. Let Winston Taylor know you don't appreciate it. You got your rights, you know. It's up to you. Y'all have a good day now."

⌒

Sparky, the squirrel, was a hit. Until Ruthie tried to feed it warm milk from the doll bottle. The baby rodent sunk its needle teeth into her finger. She squealed and flung the squirrel across the couch, deemed the damned thing old enough to eat solids, or Winston could return it to its last home.

"Why can't we just get a dog like normal people," Ruthie said, rubbing ice over her injured finger. "Leave it to you to bring home a stupid squirrel!"

Early next morning, Winston was stunned to find a stiff Sparky in the bottom of the cage. Mary Carolyn would be squalling for days. Fuckin' squirrel. He buried it out behind the utility shed before the rest of the house was awake. Told the girls Sparky must have escaped the cage and followed him outside when he went for the newspaper. *Probably looking for its mother right now,* he said. Mary Carolyn teared up, and that was the end of that. But why did he still have the eerie feeling the dead squirrel was another form of punishment?

Chapter 23

The week before Christmas, Roger Johns drove over for two days of his own orientation and assessment with Louis. He spent most of a day riding along with the new agent on his debit route and was pleased with the young man's client interaction. Winston had already introduced Louis to a select few white customers, who were mostly amicable. Roger still knew some of Pineville's policyholders from his tour of duty there, and he also made some introductions.

Before returning to Jacksonville, Roger held a lunchtime staff meeting at the Pineville office, and brought in food from the Dixie Drive-In. Greasy cheeseburgers and crispy fries. He gave a friendly pep talk about opportunities and expectations, and offered details on a quick sales competition the company was offering to kick off the new year. All sales retroactive to the first of December would be counted in with January and February numbers. The top two agents in each of the five regions would get a fifteen percent bonus and win a guided deep-sea fishing trip, tentatively set for the first weekend in March.

A. F. scowled through his meal. Louis waved his hand to be heard.

Roger gave up the floor, and Louis announced: "I got an idea." He ran a finger over the large wall calendar. "Not counting weekends and Christmas, we still got a few workdays left in the year to make a difference. I know I'm the new guy, but what if y'all let me try calling on every customer I've already met. By myself. Maybe take 'em a little Christmas gift?"

"Like what?" Roger asked, always stingy with his budget.

"Simple stuff. Candy canes. A box of chocolates."

"Where you goin' with this?" asked Winston.

"I'm thinking I wanna talk to them about the joy of giving. And what finer gift could a man give his wife than a life insurance policy? See, the cost to buy one, or increase current coverage, wouldn't cost 'em but a *fraction* of what a regular present would. But the insurance would be the promise of something huge. A promise that says: I care enough to make sure you'll be okay after I'm gone." Louis paused, eyes searching the faces of the men before him. "People get all emotional-like during the holidays. Might be an easier time to get 'em to spend money, especially if they can't figure out what to get the person they love. The women might even be easier to sell." Louis's eyebrows were raised.

Roger and Winston looked at each other, then Roger broke the spell with a laugh.

"That's crazy!" Roger said. "They'll boot you out faster'n you can say *scat*."

Winston stared at Louis, considered the idea, then said, "Come on Roger, what can it hurt? Let the man try. It's at least a unique sales approach. And he's got a point. Some of these people are really strapped for cash. A little bit could buy a lot." Winston slapped Louis on the back. "I gotta say, I never thought of an insurance policy as a Christmas present!"

Late that afternoon, before Roger left for home, he and Winston had a private talk with A. F. Several customers on the agent's route had called Winston, and declared they'd cancel coverage if a colored man knocked on their doors. A. F. received a written warning. They wanted to fire him straight out, but knew they still needed another pair of hands.

⌇

On Monday, the twenty-third of December, Winston presented year-end bonus checks to both his men. Louis's check was a small token. A. F.'s bonus was more substantial, despite the recent disciplinary action. The written reprimand had only resulted in A. F.'s even surlier attitude with Louis, and a growing coldness toward Winston. Plus, the man smelled more and more like early holiday libations.

Winston's own check was in the packet mailed from Jacksonville—his biggest bonus ever. Roger had told him the previous week that the check was coming, and why. Both he and Brian Benson were impressed with the way Winston had stood up for Louis Fisher, the way he'd convinced them to hire the man. Roger and Brian believed this was an example of Winston's continued development into a strong manager. The resolution of the Ricky Swain issue was also remarkable. Winston had shown them a previously-unrealized talent—his investigative insight. The insurance industry had a strong need for investigators. Roger said the money was an investment in the future success of the Pineville office and in Winston's destiny at Bayside Life.

∽

The Starlight's restaurant hummed with lunch crowd conversation. Winston spoke to a few people while he waited for Ruthie to arrive. Clark Bishop, headed for the register, stopped at Winston's table and recounted the story of his recent wild boar kill. At least a hundred and fifty pounds of pungent musk. Said he could smell the beast long before he laid eyes on it. Clark was planning to mount the tusked skull—the head was currently soaking in a bucket of bleach water.

Winston had lost his desire to hunt for sport. These days he'd only kill what was fit to eat. And it sure wouldn't be a stinking hog.

The clock ticked to 12:20; Ruthie had said she'd meet him at noon. Winston's excitement waned. He'd planned to surprise her with his bonus and give her credit for being the woman behind his success.

Twelve-thirty. No Ruthie. Car trouble? Her Comet had some miles on it but was reliable. Maybe a flat. Winston borrowed the restaurant's phone and called his house; he let it ring a long time. He called his own office, thinking he might catch A. F. or Louis. No help. He reached into his pocket for change to cover his sweet tea; his fingers brushed the buckeye he carried there. Something inside him rustled—a large dark bird, waiting. He left a message with the waitress in case Ruthie showed up.

At a quarter till one, Winston pulled into his own driveway. The green Comet sat inside the double garage, a separate white building resembling a small barn. Breathless with apprehension, he sprang up the back steps and through the unlocked kitchen door. "Ruthie," he called. "Ruthie!" His eyes swept the empty living room, the den. He tore into their bedroom and stopped.

The bed was unmade, covers tumbled into a mound. Winston snatched the bedding back, his ears ringing with the high-pitched quiet of the house. An irregular circle of blood soaked the mattress.

"Jesus Christ," he breathed.

Bright drops led him across the wood floor to the bathroom. Blood smeared the toilet seat. The tub's edge. The sink faucets appeared rusted red.

He hurried back to the nightstand, to Ruthie's Princess phone, its white receiver sullied. Winston dialed a number he knew by memory.

"Foley County Sheriff's Department."

"Uh . . . this is, uh, Winston . . . Taylor." He stared down at the large red blotch on the white sheets, and the blood smear on the floor where he'd stepped. "Is Dan there? Dan Nettles? Tell him it's me, Winston. I've got an emergency."

Dan Nettles's voice was a lifeline: "Man, we've been trying to reach you. Ruthie's at the hospital. She's okay, but she's hemorrhaging. Priscilla took her out there. Mary Carolyn is with the Frazer family. I can come get you."

Winston paused, then: "No. I'm headed there now."

The Studebaker's tires smoked the asphalt when Winston left for the hospital. He wanted to believe Ruthie was fine, but he knew otherwise. If the baby survived, she'd be a wreck through the rest of the pregnancy. If the baby didn't make it, a piece of Ruthie would be gone for good. Hell, he wasn't so good himself right now. The weight of a target hung heavy on his back. Why?

His mind somersaulted as he drove far beyond the speed limit. Life had been good before Jackson Smith's passing. Hadn't it? He and Ruthie were happy. He'd been working hard for Roger Johns, selling the shit out of insurance, filling his debit book with dollar signs. He glanced down at the seat where the book lay closed. The Book of Souls, Ruthie always called it. With vision blurred, he slowed and pulled into the hospital parking lot. His throat constricted, and his eyes overflowed. The blinker still tinked; he flipped it off.

God don't usually bargain.

Winston gasped, remembering those words he could only have imagined coming from the mouth of a dead man on that worst day of his life. Now the message was here again, rattling between his ears. The truth was he hadn't been filling the debit book with dollars . . . he'd been filling his pockets. And though he'd paid the money back, tried to make amends, he was somehow still being punished. This. This was the reason his wife now lay in the hospital. Why that crazy Ricky Swain had come into his life, stalking Ruthie in the end. Shit! And maybe poor Lucinda Morgan trampled by the horse— her daddy had loaned him the money to pay back the missing premiums. At least Luci would eventually recover from that accident. But bad luck seemed to touch people Winston had touched. Even the dead goddamn squirrel he'd bartered for with Mrs. Thomas. Winston put his face in his hands.

～

Winston sat by Ruthie's hospital bed, watching light leaving the sky. The shortest day of the year had just passed—daylight was beginning to last longer. This day in their lives, however, had disappeared in a flash.

"The doctor said we could try again . . ."

"Stop talking about it," she said, tears leaking from the corners of her eyes.

"Ruthie, honey, we'll get through this. Little steps, every day . . ."

She turned her head away from the window, away from him.

Chapter 24

Winston stayed home over the Christmas holidays, trying to focus only on family. Except for cooking, he took over all the household duties. Neighbors dropped off unusual casseroles, Jell-O molds that made him gag, and pea salads. Mary Carolyn wrinkled her freckled nose at the odd combinations, but hunger eventually won out.

Ruthie lay in the dark bedroom, getting up only as necessary. She said little, refusing calls and visits from her friends. Most conversations in the house were between Mary Carolyn and the Chatty Cathy doll Santa had left under the tree. Winston wished he could sling that plastic chatterbox into the fireplace.

∽

On Friday, the day after Christmas, A. F. Larkins arrived at the office early. He let himself in and locked the door, then turned up the heat and started the coffee. He shuffled around the room, waiting for it to warm, and smiled to himself—king for a week. Or maybe only a few days. Though business typically slowed to a crawl between Christmas and New Year's, Bayside Life Insurance still needed a presence. That's what Winston had instructed him to do—man the office. Who better to represent the company than himself? Sure wouldn't be that little colored boy. That little brownie. A. F. imagined the KKK might soon set fire to a cross at the office front door. He laughed to himself.

A. F. topped off his first cup of coffee with a generous splash from a small flask. He sipped it slowly, warming his hands around the mug. Then he leaned back against his chair and rested his eyes. A noise at the door roused him, but he kept his eyes closed, knowing who waited on the other side.

At 8:00, opening time, Louis Fisher knocked at the locked glass. He could see A. F. leaning back in his chair, cup resting on that bulging belly. He waited, clutching his new, thin debit book. He knocked again. A. F. didn't move. Louis knew the bastard heard him.

"Hey!" he shouted. "Let me in. It's cold out here."

A. F. startled and snatched up the phone, as though answering a call. No way the phone really rang—Louis would've heard it through the glass. A. F. appeared to talk to someone, mouth moving, face serious. *What a prick!* Louis banged on the door again. The man feigned surprise and raised a finger to wait. The next time Louis saw Winston, he'd be sure to ask about getting a key.

A. F. finally waddled over and unlocked the door, and Louis greeted him like nothing had happened. He wanted to kick the old man in the nuts, put the fat greaser in a choke hold, but anger would get him nowhere. Louis had no room for a screwup. He'd be fired for any conflict, and he knew it. This job was the beginning of his new life in the world of business.

Though Louis already knew about the loss of the Taylor baby, he didn't let on when A. F. briefed him. His inside knowledge would be taken as cockiness, so he only shook his head and listened, offering murmurs of sympathy. The old guy would probably fall into a fit if he knew Miz Ruby had actually dared to visit Winston's house, delivering fried chicken and mashed potatoes to their door. Etta had helped her grandmother prepare it.

A. F. instructed Louis to work on cleaning up the office, starting with the toilet. Said they needed to begin the new year on the bright side. Louis didn't protest, though his thoughts were less than stellar. He found supplies beneath a cabinet and attacked the place with rags and chemicals, even wiping down all three desks. A. F. stood aside to let the boy handle the job. Louis hummed while he worked—old spirituals in the vein of slavery.

Pineville shops were opening for day-after-Christmas sales, and people dotted the sidewalks. A. F.'s plan for their business was to leave Louis in the office to answer phones. The boy didn't have much of a debit route anyway. *Let him put in some desk time,* he smiled, as he buttoned up his coat to leave.

The phone rang, and Louis pounced to answer—the boss was on the line.

"Yessir, we're doing fine," Louis said, glancing up at A. F., who listened from just inside the front door. "Yes, A. F. wants me here today. He's got collections to catch up on."

Louis listened, nodding. A. F. glared at him.

"Okay, I'll do that. I'll let him know. See you soon." Louis clunked the receiver back into its cradle.

"What'd he say?" A. F. wheezed.

"He said lock up the store. Put a sign on the door to call him if anybody happens to come by needing help. You go take care of your business." Louis retrieved his own coat from the stand. "He's waiting on me at his house. Got some clients he wants me to see for him."

A. F. scowled, his eyes disappearing within the folds of flesh. He shook his head and walked out.

﹏

Winston opened the front door before Louis could knock, welcomed him in with a pat on the back. Mary Carolyn hid in her father's shadow, but he pulled her forward for introductions before shooing her off to play. Quietly, he said.

They sat in the living room by the fireplace. Louis looked around. The house was old but inviting. High ceilings and gleaming hardwood floors. The green print couch might be Early American, he thought, but his knowledge of furniture was limited to a twin bed and a nightstand.

Louis was envious—a comfortable home for a nice family. But he knew like in a stage play, cozy settings could fool you. A heavy quiet hung in the air. The Christmas tree, unlit, still stood in a corner. Loose wads of spent wrapping paper littered the tree skirt. Empty stockings drooped from the mantle. The Taylors were suffering from a flown soul, never much more than a dream.

"Boss, I'm so sorry about what happened," Louis said. He hung his head.

"Appreciate it."

Winston opened his debit book, thumbed through the vast tome, choosing clients carefully. Louis wrote quickly on a yellow lined pad, filling pages with scrawled ballpoint notes. Winston finally stopped him.

"No need to write everything I say about these people. Just put down their names and listen carefully. You won't forget what I'm saying, Louis. You're too quick, and your sales instincts are pitch perfect."

Louis nodded, his expression serious, but he couldn't keep the joy from his eyes.

"And besides, I'm going to give you my book to carry. Loan you, I mean," Winston chuckled. "I'll be out of the office at least until after New Year's. After that depends on how Ruthie's doing. But Mary Carolyn will be back in school after the first, so I'm hoping to return by then."

Winston laid out the plan. He warned Louis to expect a few doors closed in his face. Said not to worry. They'd return to those places together after the holidays. Meantime, keep to the plan. Call only on the people he'd written down. After a cursory glance through Louis's own debit book, Winston sent his new agent off to get some real work done.

ᔕᔐ

Several of Winston's clients were clustered in the Spring Lake Heights neighborhood, so those were quick collections. Most were gray-haired women, suspicious of a colored man in their white neighborhood. But he produced his business card, and Winston's too, and delivered the spiel that Winston was home with family until after the holidays. All closed their doors and kept him waiting out in the cold before returning with the money. Winston's book was heavy, but Louis managed to cradle it on one arm as he recorded payments. He wanted the customers to see him write down the collection amount. Back in the car, he zipped the money, mostly cash, into a green Bayside Life Insurance sack.

Edna Williams was a different case. Louis produced his credentials, her door swung open, and he was in. Edna settled him onto her flowered couch, where he was staggered by the smells of old food, grease, and an undercurrent of pine cleaner. He sat very still on her low sofa, mouth-breathing, eyes roving the pictures and bric-a-brac she must have collected over her whole long life.

"Would you care for a cup of coffee, Louis? I just perked it a couple of hours ago."

Louis declined, wondering if she washed her dishes in hot water. He tried to keep his face composed and pleasant. Tried not to show his discomfort in this closed, odorous place. Despite the cold air outside, he wished for a raised window.

As a reminder of why he was there, Louis said, "Let's see now, what does Mr. Taylor normally collect from you . . ." He opened Winston's book to her account page.

Mrs. Williams ignored his prompt and launched into a list of questions about where Louis was from, was he married, and on and on. Jesus. She knew people who worked at Buckhead, so and so related to somebody over off of Green Street. Louis nodded along, no idea who she was talking about. The only people he knew by name at Buckhead were the desperate men like himself who fed the various and hungry machines that turned wood into pulp into paper.

"How did Winston come to hire you, a Nee-gro?" she asked blithely.

Good God, why not me, Louis thought. He straightened himself and allowed that he had met with Winston on several occasions and that Bayside Life thought he was the best candidate.

The old lady leaned forward, squinted her eyes, and lowered her voice. "I'm sure you must have heard about that man who broke into one of the houses out here. Jason Joseph's place. Next street over?"

Louis looked at his watch. "I'm not sure ma'am, but can you save that story for next time? Mr. Taylor's given me marching orders, and I'm running behind schedule. I'm sorry. I'd love to stay and visit."

"Well, I ain't supposed to be telling this, seeing as how this is all still under investigation, but they still got the guy out in the Foley County jail, best as I know, and Winston was the one who helped nab him. Just like that!" She snapped her crooked fingers, startling Louis. Her nails were thick and yellowed.

"No, ma'am, I didn't hear about that." He looked at his watch again. Was this woman making this up?

"I seen the guy myself, prowling around the neighborhood in the daylight. Not many strangers show up here. They brung me into the station, on the hush-hush, and I got a good look at the guy again behind a two-way mirror. Just like in *The Fugitive,* on TV."

Louis stood up to go. "My goodness! I'd love to hear more next time, Mrs. Williams. You gonna be able to make your payment today?"

"Lord yes, I can't get behind on my insurance. I ain't gonna live too much longer, with my crooked back and all. I'll tell you about that another time. Need to make sure one of my kids'll bury me proper." She opened a drawer under the coffee table, pulled out cash, and counted out the exact amount. She handed him the payment, her fingers close to touching his. Too close.

Louis evaporated from the house. He hoped to God Winston didn't give him her account on a full-time basis— the lady probably wasn't leaving this earth for a long time. He left the neighborhood with the car windows down, trying to air out his clothes.

∾

Later, Louis sat in his car, parked at a boat ramp on the Foley River. Picnic tables were scattered around the landing, but the weather was too cold for outside eating. He devoured a sandwich filled with slabs of turkey, cornbread dressing, and cranberry sauce. The food tasted better than it did on Christmas day. The thermos of hot coffee was just what he needed. He licked his fingers, picked crumbs from his trousers, and threw them out the window for the ants.

Beyond the windshield, a movie played out: birds of many varieties flitted from tree to tree or scratched the ground with their beaks, all going somewhere or doing something important. Gray squirrels, less hurried, foraged beneath the trees. A large heron swooped in and landed at the top of the boat ramp. Slender and stoic, surely four feet tall, he commanded respect.

As Winston Taylor commanded respect, Louis thought. And what good fortune: the new guy appointed as keeper of the boss's debit book. All that information. He planned to study it over the weekend. Clean up the notes he'd taken from Winston. He wasn't about to screw this up. He grinned at the thought of A. F.'s face this morning, vicious as a bulldog once he learned Louis had been summoned to Winston's house. Glorious payback for the slave work the bastard had put him through the day before.

Louis finished off the coffee, tightened the thermos top, and put the lunch trappings away. The notes he'd taken at the Taylor house were rough. He squinted at the chicken scratch. He'd been nervous, trying to listen and write, knowing the boss was counting on him. He'd followed the route Winston had outlined this morning. Next on the list was stopping in to see one Deacon Smith. Louis's scribbles said the location was near the township of Iddo, off Highway 19. He studied the North Florida map Winston had given him, then fingered the debit book's S-tab, flipped to find Deacon Smith's page, too far, thumbed backwards. He stopped.

Jackson Smith.

With his brow furrowed, Louis stared at the carefully printed name. He studied the letters, ran his finger beneath each. His mouth and tongue silently formed the words he was afraid to say aloud for fear some terrible spell would be cast . . . or broken.

Head against the seat, he looked out, past the birds and the trees, to the blue beyond. He recalled one of the sayings he'd heard as a child: *Write your wish on the slate of the sky and it just might come true.* His lips moved: "Please, let this not be the same Jackson Smith. Let it not be possible."

Smith was a common surname. Certainly, a number of men in this part of the South were called Jackson. Louis had just let his imagination run crazy. Shake it off. But he couldn't. He studied the page. Tallahassee, but no street. In the margin was a tiny notation: *see M. Griffin.* Bingo! But what had he won?

His fingers traveled backward in the book: Mabel Griffin. Black Acre Court in Hampton Springs. Her page likewise referenced J. Smith. Louis scanned the latest payments on Mabel's account. A catch-up collection notation just before Christmas. He returned to the Jackson Smith page. Same premium collection date. What he had won was a bewildering clue. If he could just decipher it.

Chapter 25

Back downtown by four o'clock, Louis parked on Collins Street, not far from the Bayside Life office. This was his last premium collection on Winston's list. With a loud heart, he entered the very old, very quiet Foley County Library. The hard heels of his new shoes echoed around the lofty room. A young blonde-haired woman at the counter raised her head, eyebrows up. He stepped slower and softer as he approached.

"Can I help you?" she frowned.

"I'm here on business," Louis said, holding all of his five feet and nine inches as erect as possible. He could feel the eyes of a half-dozen patrons swiveling his way.

"I'm so sorry," she drawled in a stage whisper, her ponytail swinging emphatically, "but this is the white liberry. Our colored liberry is only a couple miles from here." She handed him a sheet of mimeographed directions.

Louis took a deep breath. He knew that even though "separate but equal" had long been declared unconstitutional, many public facilities in the South remained segregated. A Southern fact of life.

"Well, thank you, Miss," he smiled. "I didn't come to actually use the library. I'm an agent for Bayside Life Insurance Company. Winston Taylor sent me."

"Ohhh . . ." she drawled. "Then you must be here to see Miss Pierpont." She pulled her yellow sweater tighter around her shoulders, then pointed to the steep stairs. "Her office is up on the next floor, by the reference stacks."

Evelyn Pierpont had served more than seven years as overseer of the County's library system, which included the main facility, one small satellite for colored patrons, and two bookmobiles—one white, one colored. A plain-faced, middle-aged spinster with tight graying curls, she carried herself as straight as the spine of a book, or the ruler she often used to check book alignment on the shelves. More than once each day she'd wander the stacks, auditing the non-fiction decimals, perturbed by even one volume being out of order. What would Mr. Dewey think! The fiction shelves were easier, alphabetical by author's last name, but sometimes her girls mixed those up, too.

Evelyn was born for the written word, for the keeping of information. As a child, she'd clipped every magazine article containing even a single tidbit that piqued her interest. Her substantial childhood book collection was housed on homemade board and block shelves. Fortunately for her parents, most of her reading material was borrowed from the very library system she now managed.

Louis knocked and announced himself at her office door, and she welcomed him in. She'd heard about Winston's new agent, she said, and had seen Louis on the street a few times. She asked for news of Ruthie's recovery, and how well Mary Carolyn and Winston were managing. Winston was well known and well liked in Pineville, and news of the Taylor tragedy had quickly flooded the town.

They chatted about the library building and its long history in Pineville. Before the County's purchase the year prior, the building had originally been owned by The Emporium, a dry goods store; a bank; a dentist; and then for more than forty years housed the *Pineville Times* newspaper. In fact, she said, the third floor still held the newspaper's archives. The paper owners had cut a deal with the County to keep from moving and storing the old issues. A project was underway to convert the deteriorating pages to microfilm, but the process was long and tedious, and Evelyn had a hard time keeping the project staffed. The conversion was jointly funded by the *Times* and the County.

"It'll be so worthwhile to complete the copying," Pierpont sighed. "One little reel of microfilm—you can cup it in the palm of your hand—holds up to 700 documents."

Feigning ignorance of the technology, Louis nodded along. The Carnegie Library on the FAMU campus in Tallahassee already had microfilm back when he was still a student.

"Just to give you a point of comparison," the librarian continued, "a standard archive box to hold the same amount of information takes up about a half cubic foot of shelf space. The newspapers left here aren't even in boxes; they're just stacked everywhere, becoming more brittle by the day. The really old issues are bound between large covers. Newsprint quickly breaks down, but microfilmed stories should last hundreds of years!"

The librarian's face had turned a healthy shade of pink. Louis deduced Miss Pierpont was madly in love with her work.

He kept his face expressionless, but his mind churned. He'd love to get his hands on those old newspapers, especially now, since he'd stumped his toe over a particular name in Winston's debit book. "That's some interesting stuff. I've been wondering where I might go to learn some of the history in this area, to get a real feel for what makes Pineville tick. I'm looking forward to settling down here, but I'd like to know more. I've thought of visiting the newspaper office but sounds like you've got what I need right here."

Pierpont sobered. Louis had put her at ease, but the enchantment was over. She found herself in a bad position, one that required her to do her job, which meant refusing this young man access to information. For no good reason except skin color, and the fact that County statutes still called for separate but equal. This man was a professional, working for a company valued by the leadership of Pineville. Louis was obviously specially chosen and trusted by Winston Taylor. The librarian's complexion was now a mottled crimson.

The silence was stifling, until Louis filled the void between them with a chuckle. "Thank you for the history, Miss Pierpont," he said. "I learned a lot today, listening to you. But I sure did forget what I came here for."

Winston's debit book whooshed open in Louis's hands. He recorded Pierpont's payment and zipped her beautifully penned check into the pouch.

The librarian walked with him to the stairs. Her fingers fluttered at her throat, as if hand-picking the right words.

"I enjoyed meeting you, Louis Fisher. Your hunger for information fills me with hope." She smiled, two pink spots appearing on her cheeks. "I know that what you're after can't be found in our satellite facility. Let me think on this. I want to find a way to meet your needs."

Louis was stunned. "Our meeting was my pleasure, ma'am. I'd be grateful for anything you can offer that would point me in the right direction."

With that, he hurried down the stairs, his sure footsteps making themselves known.

～

Saturday morning, Louis went to work at Abe's car lot. He had a couple of potential buyers on the hook and didn't want to lose them. Abe was happy for Louis's continued part-time help.

An eight-year-old black VW Beetle Louis had been dangling in front of a college student, home for the holidays, was finally a done deal. Louis raked in almost fifty dollars from the sale.

He had promised Etta a New Year's Eve date, and she would have it. On the way back to the boarding house, he stopped at McCrory's department store and bought a red plaid blanket. As he waited in line at the register, he picked up a copy of the new 1964 edition of *The Green Book*. His world was beginning to expand—he might take a trip somewhere, maybe in the spring.

Louis stashed the blanket in the trunk of his car. He and Etta both had fooling around on their minds.

Chapter 26

Winston directed his agents to close the office at noon on New Year's Eve, a Tuesday. They'd reopen on Thursday, January second, when Winston expected to return to his desk. Ruthie was improving, physically and mentally. His time at home had been good for them all.

～

New Year's Eve: Winston called it the Annual Amateur Hour. People trying too hard to chase fun. Bad stuff happened on those evenings before the first of each year, and alcohol was almost always the cause. His last public New Year's Eve celebration, eight years before, ended with his nearly being shot for trying to break up a fight between two drunks.

Ruthie and Winston would celebrate at home with sparklers for Mary Carolyn, steaks on the grill, and strong mixed drinks. They'd send their daughter to bed, put on Dean Martin and Frank Sinatra albums, and dance by the living room fire. They'd say a private goodbye to 1963, to the good and the bad.

Louis and Etta drove to Madison, Florida, for New Year's. He'd made reservations at a fine-dining restaurant listed in his new *Green Book*. The ad touted the proprietor as a retired chef from Jacksonville's Duval Hotel. The couple had their first taste of snails, and Etta couldn't wait to tell her brother, Bubba. He wouldn't believe his prissy sister had eaten anything that nasty.

The waitress kept their wine glasses filled. Louis lost count.

"You 'bout the best-lookin' woman I seen in a long time," Louis said, raising his glass.

Etta, dressed in a red satin shift, touched her glass to his. "You do mean best-lookin' woman you've *ever* seen, don't you?" she laughed. She had only sipped the wine.

"I ain't kiddin', Etta. Ser-ously," he slurred. "I'm a lucky man. Flush enough for fancy . . . 'spensive shit . . . ain't gotta crawl out the bathroom window," he laughed, too loud, tugging his narrow green tie up like a hangman's rope.

Etta shushed him.

"Beautiful girl . . . goddamn lucky man . . . luckiest man . . ." He looked down at the table, shifted his silverware around. "If only you knew . . ."

The whole room swirled. Louis stood, knocking over his nearly empty glass; a small red stain bloomed on the white tablecloth. He pulled Etta to him, a drowning man instead of a lover. Her grandmother's fur-trimmed wrap slipped to the floor as Louis bear-hugged her, then planted his mouth over hers, breathing her in. Applause rippled through the room.

Etta asked the waitress for coffee. And the bill.

The red plaid blanket came in handy . . . situated beneath Etta's bottom . . . rolled up as a booster seat she needed to see over the wheel. She drove them the thirty-eight long miles back home.

～

Cookie's Cocktail Lounge was not a place A. F. Larkins would normally frequent, especially not on New Year's Eve. A serious and secret drinker, A. F. was happier alone. Tonight, though, he needed company. To be sociable, to prove to himself Joanie was wrong. He ordered another Jack Daniels on the rocks. The bartender shoved a bowl of nuts at him.

Last night Joan had called him a drunkard. A sick alcoholic. A weird misfit. He'd gotten his pistol from the car and waved it in the air, just to scare her. He'd never really hurt anyone, he told himself, especially not his wife. Okay, he *had* leveled the .38 at her face, but only because she'd said she was leaving him for good.

Home from work early today, he discovered she'd by-god left his ass. Not a stitch of her clothing in drawers or closets.

A. F. had walked around the house, looking for something that said her departure was temporary. The kitchen looked untouched, except her favorite coffee cup was gone. She didn't cook much anyway; she'd never have taken kitchenware. The bathroom cabinet was cleared of her pills. The vanity's top drawer yawned empty: no cold cream, face powder, or colored pencils she'd relied on for a surprised arch of eyebrows, to transform shriveled lips into a big pink pout.

He'd dropped down into his faded gold, rump-sprung chair, lungs wheezing, and discovered her note on the side table. *Sayonara* was the gist of it. Their son, who lived in Atlanta, had come with a borrowed van to get his mother and her things. A. F. figured she'd phoned him late last night; she always called the boy after they fought. Admittedly, his recall of what happened after he pointed the gun wasn't very clear. Must've been pretty bad for their son to drive from Atlanta, get his mother, and be gone before his father arrived home from work, then almost two o'clock on the eve of a brand-new year, which was apparently going to be a doozie.

Now two hours till midnight, A. F. slumped against Cookie's bar, laughing and laughing, tears rolling down his face. The long ash from his cigarette dropped onto the floor, and he began to swear loudly: "I'm gonna burn up the whole fuckin' place." The bartender motioned for the bouncer, and A. F. found himself on the sidewalk. He wobbled to his car, puzzled over why he had no coat. The night was freezing, but he was afraid to go back inside.

Several customers lined up at the drive-thru window of the JAX liquor store. A. F. didn't mind waiting; at least he was warm inside the car. He leaned down and swept a hand under the front seat, hoping to discover an emergency pint. Came up empty. Who thought that was a good idea, letting the well go dry? Who? His belly shook. Running out of booze wasn't funny, but A. F. couldn't help but laugh. He needed another drink, and soon.

"What we gone do when the cup runs dry, Joan-ie? What we gone do when the bottle runs dry, bay-abe . . ." he sang. "You a funny man, Angus F. Larkins," he said out loud in his hoarse voice. Maybe starting tomorrow he'd ask—no, demand—that people call him Angus. The name A. F. made him sick. Just sick. His whole life was marked with that ugly moniker. The rude nicknames sniggered behind his back: Old Owl. Hootie. Who? Who?

At the liquor store window now, he asked for a setup–no, make that two, and a fifth of Jack. The clerk slid him two small cups of ice with stir sticks and the bottle in a brown bag. He pulled into the parking area and poured the cup almost half full, rattled the ice, and drank the liquor like sweet tea. He threw the ice out onto the ground and poured another drink, this one room temperature. Save the second cup of ice for later in case he wanted a cold one. The liquor warmed him regardless of ice, but he could barely feel his feet. He waited for the alcohol heat to seep all the way through him. The cigarette he sucked kicked up a coughing fit. He soothed his lungs with a slug from the paper cup.

He squinted his eyes and thought about the Smith & Wesson. What had happened to it? After last night? Now the gun was in his hands. He fondled the rough walnut handles, the cold heavy metal.

Was he never going to shoot it? Just protection, he'd said to nobody there to listen. Strange houses; tough customers. Out in the sticks, rutted dirt roads. People as soon shoot you as look at you. *Bayside Life* he'd call out, scared as a girl. Chickens shittin' around your feet or a goddamn mangy dog growling, slobbering, head low, rushing up to tear your leg off. Debit route. Devil's route. Lil' colored boy gonna piss his pants. White people ain't gonna put up with a black boy rapping at their door.

A. F. poured himself another on the rocks. One for the road. The solid-white Ford crept out of the parking lot and onto hardtop. His feet hardly felt the pedals. Main Street, rolling past Henry's Ham House, closed now, lights on a little Christmas tree still burning in the window sad-like. Past the Sheriff's Office, locked and loaded for drunks and fireworks. His own office, Bayside Life, shut tight just like he'd left it.

He pulled to the curb in front of the building. Scrunched up his face, a long sob convulsing in his throat. Goddamn insult, working next to a Negro. Coats hanging on the same rack, side by side. Same shitter. Whole fuckin' world going to hell. Joanie gone. "So goddam screwed," he cried.

The loaded gun, now back in his hand, agreed. In the streetlamp's low light, A. F. examined the dull gray .38 Special. His thumb stroked the hammer: *click click*. He raised the gun to his face, his tongue darting out for a faint taste of lead. Cold, yet comforting. He put his lips around the barrel, then slid it on inside his mouth. His finger assumed its place on the trigger. He waited, scared to move. One quiver of his finger. One tremor. It'd be all she wrote. Sayonara, she'd said.

Joanie. She'd come back. Just quit the liquor. Just quit. His face was an ugly, wet sheet of sorrow crumpled around the gun. He backed the pistol out of his mouth. Released the hammer. Threw the gun onto the seat.

The Ford knew the route; A. F. drank and held the wheel out of downtown and onto U.S. 27, the highway to home.

Nowhere else to go. Joanie. My Joan, be home. His foot grew heavier on the accelerator.

⌒

Charlie Jameson, middle-aged, muscled, and dark as the night, steered with a heavy hand, the log truck grunting and grinding under the full load of pines he'd harvested from a Quitman, Georgia farmer. *Just get 'er home.* His latest woman waited. The road was his own, south on U.S. 221, into Florida, through the ghost towns of Ashville and Greenville.

On the long, moonless stretch from Sirmans to Shady Grove, a sleek Thunderbird flew around from behind him then slowed, too close, beside the straining 18-wheeler. Someone waved and shouted from the car's passenger window. Charlie rolled down the glass, heard: "Taillights out, asshole! Get off the goddamn road!" The car passed, an astral streak, red lights disappearing.

Charlie pulled partly off the pavement and climbed out to check the brake lights. He wiggled the pigtail loose from both the tractor and the trailer, blew the connection points clean, then rejoined the plugs. The trailer's tail end still sat dark as death. The driver shrugged, then hoisted himself back into the cab and kept truckin', on to Lake Bird and Boyd, and into Pineville. He picked up U.S. 27 for Mayo, where he'd then head south for home in Cooks Hammock. The old engine whined when he pushed it to fifty. He slowed the load of timber.

Just shy of Mayo, pandemonium exploded at the rig's rear end, force throwing Charlie's hands loose from the wheel—

168

head snapping, truck lurching, metal screaming. He regained steering, stood on the brakes. He brought the log truck to a standstill and jumped out, expecting to see his load scattered across the highway, but the dark mountain of logs was still secure. In shock, Charlie moved down the side of the long trailer. Dim lights glowed from beneath his rig, then flickered and died. The thick, bitter smell of burned rubber enveloped him.

A car, run up beneath his load, smoked and hissed, the white sedan's front end crunched beneath the trailer's frame and its hanging harvest of trees. Charlie jogged back to his cab, every footfall sending pain shooting through his jarred spine. He returned with a flashlight. The beam quivered over the metal mess, the car's roof reminding him of the rolled-back lid of a sardine can. Light flared over the driver's side and down into the front seat area, now nearly joined with the rear. A lump of something was pressed into the crush of metal and glass, the bloody upholstery. Something with an impossibly angled head told Charlie Jameson the news wasn't good. Neither of them would make it home to see the ball drop.

1964

Chapter 27

Friday after New Year's, A. F.'s cleared desk was now shoved up to the front of Louis's, creating a large temporary workspace for Winston and Louis to wrap their arms around all the customers who'd lost their insurance agent. Together they tore the dead man's debit book apart, talking through every single insured, their locations, and their idiosyncrasies.

Louis made notes as they gradually divided the workload—many of the accounts going to him. Winston also moved some of his own people to Louis in exchange for taking a good number of A. F's troublesome customers.

"These people right here," Winston said, waving his hand over a pile of account pages, "if they saw you at their door, would probably hold you at gunpoint."

Louis widened his eyes, but he knew Winston wasn't kidding. He nodded. "Gotcha, boss."

"We'll work these together, let 'em learn who you are. You'll gradually take over." Winston's face hardened. "But you gotta understand, Louis, I'm gonna need you to carry your share of the load. Once we've called on these people a few times, I can't babysit you anymore. And I can't ride shotgun."

"Yessir, I know," Louis said. He rubbed the top of his head. "It's gonna all work out okay. I ain't gonna let you down."

This was the original plan all along, for Louis to train up and begin taking over, effectively weeding out the weaker agent. Neither had seen this coming, this abrupt loss for them all. But in the end, Winston looked at A. F.'s exit as a cleansing, a purge of negativity from within their workspace, and within their broader customer territory. Though A. F. had caused his own death, Winston still carried a sick spot in his stomach.

Louis hadn't hesitated to ask questions about the green, lined sheets pulled from the debit books. He made good notes of geographical locations—it would be his responsibility to streamline his debit route, minimizing lost time and the expense of gasoline. When the account pages for Mabel Griffin didn't move across the table from Winston's book, Louis was relieved. But extremely puzzled.

It only made sense that he would take Mabel's business. She lived in Hampton Springs, and Winston had just given him all the other Hampton Springs customers. Why not include the Griffin account? And what about the Jackson Smith account? Winston's geographical oversight did not include Tallahassee, which was the address notation on Jackson. Mabel Griffin must be paying that premium. Louis had good reason to ask Winston about the Griffin accounts, but the question hung in his throat. Sweat collected in his armpits.

"I'm gonna make another pot of coffee. You gonna help me drink it?" Winston asked.

Louis looked up from his notes. "I'll make it, boss," he said.

"Nah, I need to get up from here." Winston stretched, walked away from the would-be conference table, swinging his arms.

Ask him now, Louis thought, *while his back is turned.*

"Hey, boss," he called, "I got eighteen accounts in the Hampton Springs area."

"Yeah, so?" Winston said, clattering the aluminum pot.

"When I had your debit book the other day . . . I remember another customer with a Hampton Springs address. Can't exactly call that name, but something with a G—Giddings or Getty—I dunno." Louis waited, tense.

Winston took his time measuring coffee into the urn's metal basket. Mabel Griffin's eyes, magnified by those thick glasses, looked at him: *A good boy, my Jack.*

"What's your question?" Winston asked, turning away from the percolator. He slipped his hand into his pocket, cradled the buckeye.

"Just wondered if you wanted me to take all of those folks. Makes sense to me, since that's probably twenty miles from here." Louis pointed to the partially opened map on the desk, drew an imaginary line from Pineville to Hampton Springs.

"Twenty-one, actually," said Winston, still stalling. He sat back down across from Louis, located Mabel's page. Though he seemed to consider his agent's question, he was instead listening to the interior alarm system he'd built around his own deepest secret. Louis's shoes were stepping softly on its perimeter.

"That's Mabel Griffin you're talking about," he said. "I think I'll just keep her. She's one of my oldest customers, historically and age-wise. I just need to hold onto her." Winston closed the book.

～

Near day's end, with accounts sorted and desks pushed back apart, Winston answered a call from Roger Johns. They talked about the account shuffling and about the Sunday funeral arrangements in Mayo. Winston would represent the company. With the loss of his own baby still weighing on him, attending A. F.'s funeral was too much. But Winston was A. F.'s boss and he would be there.

"Hey, listen . . .," Roger said, "You hear the news about that couple in a storm out on the Gulf? Couple days before Christmas? The woman died?"

"Yeah, I caught part of it on TV. Happened down at Cedar Key. The story struck me as strange that the woman was out fishing, especially so close to Christmas. They're usually in the throes of shopping and baking," Winston laughed, but the joke fell flat. Roger didn't respond.

"Sorry," Winston said, "I just needed a little comic relief." He took a deep breath. "So much death and destruction around here . . . but yeah, I heard about it . . . and wasn't there something about the wife being tied up?"

"That's what I'm talking about," Roger said, excitement in his voice. "Turns out those people are ours. Derek and Pauline Wicks. The husband called here today, ready to cash in on her life policy. She was heavily insured."

"How heavy?"

Roger paused, then: "Let's just say the husband ought to be set for a good while."

"Interesting . . . The news said the Levy County Sheriff's investigating."

"Yep. The whole thing sounds hokey. Bayside Life won't be paying out until they have to. Brian Benson and a couple other big dogs here had a meeting about it. They want somebody on our team to nose around, see what's going on down there."

"Sounds like a good idea. Raymond Tedder's territory, right?"

"Yeah, yeah. But Raymond's up north for the holidays. Seeing his wife's family. Bunch of Yankees anyway. What do they know?" Roger laughed.

"So, who's going?"

"You."

"Me!" Winston looked to the ceiling for a reprieve. "Why me? That's not my territory. I don't know anybody over there."

"Listen, Winston. The shit you uncovered with that Ricky Swain situation was really good. If you hadn't pushed that whole thing, we might've hired him. He'd have kept right on doing what he was doing and next thing you know, Bayside Life would've been held responsible for somebody winding up hurt. Or dead."

Winston tried not to smile, but damn, he still felt good knowing Swain was in jail and should be for a long time. Knowing he, himself, had helped make it happen. Intuition and dumb luck. But talk of Swain also brought up a dark picture of the man approaching Ruthie at the store. Made his blood curdle.

"What you want me to do?" he asked Roger. His own attaboy was over.

"I need you to drive over there tomorrow—"

"It's Saturday," Winton cut in.

"I'll make it up to you, I swear. Can you do it?"

Winston groaned. He'd promised Ruthie they'd do something as a family on Saturday. They could sure as hell use some family time.

"We just need you to poke around. Talk to the Levy Sheriff's Department. Some of the locals. Feel things out. I promise you, Winston, you won't be sorry." Roger dropped his voice: "Your name came up in today's executive pow-wow, about this claim. Brian Benson respects you. That's like money in the piggy bank of your future. In mine, too."

Winston perked up. "When you put it that way, of course I'll do it. But I need some details, like how much we're really about to shell out for the claim. I can't go over there looking like a fool."

"A hundred thousand."

"Seriously? That sounds kinda steep—bunch of poor folks in that area. Wicks must've bought an Accidental Death Rider. A double dip."

"Exactly," Roger said and filled him in with everything he knew.

Winston was now flush with adrenaline. He'd just been hand-picked to help handle an executive problem. Another opportunity to make both himself and the company look good. He didn't want to act *too* eager though. "All right, I'm on it. But Ruthie's not gonna be happy about this."

"Aw, bullcrap. You flatter yourself. She's probably sick of you up her ass, trying to act like her nurse."

Winston laughed. He hoped Roger was right.

Chapter 28

Dan Nettles, off duty on Saturday after New Year's, practically begged Winston to let him ride along to Cedar Key. In the back floorboard, they carried a Styrofoam cooler full of ice, Coca-Cola, and a few Busch Bavarians. Dan's Smith & Wesson service revolver rode holstered on the seat between them. Despite the grim reason for going, the two planned to enjoy the trip.

They'd head first to Bronson, the Levy County seat. Dan knew somebody at the Sheriff's Department there and had wrangled an eleven o'clock appointment for Winston to meet with Lieutenant Archie Riddle. Riddle was in charge of the boating accident investigation.

✑

The day was brilliant, with no clouds and temps in the high sixties. They stopped at Old Town, near where U.S. 19/98 crossed the Suwannee River. The Suwannee Columns diner, right off the highway, was legendary for its fried seafood and frog legs. They bought a takeout frog plate to share and parked at an oak-shaded picnic table on a high bluff. They watched the big river drift, channeling beneath the bridge then momentarily parting around a white sandbar near its middle. The two men sucked the meat off the bones of more than a dozen crispy legs.

"Looks like seven frogs died for us today," Dan sighed, licking his greasy fingers. "You reckon they was run over out there on the pavement?" He kept his face straight. "We need to say a prayer."

"You need to say a prayer," Winston grinned. "You're a lucky man I brought you along for entertainment." He tossed the gnawed bones into a clump of palmettos—a raccoon snack.

Dan nodded. Swallowed. "Thanks, buddy." He wiped his hands with a thin paper napkin. Took a swig of the Busch. "I can already taste them Cedar Key shrimp we gonna get. Dragged straight out of the Gulf. Lord, lord, you know them raw oysters are so good right now. Lil' salty things, with some of that JB's Sopchoppy Sauce dashed on 'em. Mmm-mmm."

"We'll be needin' to stop at every gas station on the road back home. All that grease." Winston laughed. "I ain't sittin' in no stall next to you, though."

"Shit. No stall needed. Got me some toilet paper rolled up here in my pocket," he said, patting his chest. "Just need a bush and I'm good to go."

"A big bush," said Winston, as they got back into the car.

As they drove past the turnoff for Fanning Springs Park, not five miles from where they'd picnicked, Dan broke the after-lunch lull: "Oh, man! I don't think I told you my latest."

Winston glanced at him, seeing the big man's face lit up like a kid's at Christmas. "What now? You gettin' a pony?"

"No, this is for real. The Sheriff's talking about putting together a dive team. We ain't never had one, but there's been times it woulda been helpful. I always wanted to learn how to skin dive anyway."

"Not me," Winston said, shaking his head. "Hell no. You won't catch me under the water where I gotta drag my air out of a tank. Tried it with a buddy a couple years ago in a swimming pool. I couldn't stand it."

"I ain't afraid. And it'd be fun. Might be boring in salt water, though. Nothing but white sand on the bottom. Gotta watch for a shark after your ass, though. I think it'd be neat to dive in a river, find arrow heads and stuff. Or cave diving. Well, maybe not a cave—might get lost, or trapped."

Winston cracked up. He could picture Dan's beer belly in a wet suit looking like a big seal, his stomach stuck in a tight tunnel.

"I ain't kidding," Dan said. "And we got so many sinkholes around here. Probably full of all kinds of crap." He leaned towards Winston. "You 'member a couple years ago, some teenagers come up on a gang of drug runners with a boatload of dope? Late one night, over at Shell Point. They killed them kids, and a snitch said they dumped 'em in a sinkhole off the Aucilla River. They ain't found 'em yet."

Winston's face had sobered. Bodies in sinkholes. How could he possibly be hearing this coming out of his best friend's mouth?

"You got no business being down in a sinkhole, Nettles. Why in hell would anybody wanna go there? You know those places connect to the aquifer, run all over creation

180

underground. You need to stay your ass out of there. Let them young, skinny guys do it."

"Nah, Winston. It ain't that big a deal. You're too damn paranoid. They'll just start us out slow, diving in a pool, like you said. Then move on to something easy to navigate. Like Fanning Springs we just passed. Water clear as gin. Next thing you know, I'll be certified."

"Can't you take a nap? You're wearing me out," Winston joked, but his fingers were white around the wheel.

The Levy County Sheriff's Department was less than impressive. A sand-colored cinderblock building with bars on the windows. A fenced area to one side and back, topped with barbed wire. Inside, Dan elbowed Winston when the duty officer, possibly a first cousin to Barney Fife, asked what he could do for them. Winston introduced himself, and within moments, Archie Riddle opened the security door which led to the inner workings of the operation.

Lt. Riddle was gray-haired with a weather-beaten face. *Fisherman* was Winston's first thought. They all shook hands, and Dan Nettles reiterated he was off duty from Foley County with no official role in Bayside Life's inquiry. Riddle led them to a cramped office and offered seats. Metal chair legs scraped the concrete floor as they sat down.

"Lieutenant Riddle, I just want you to know I'm here under duress," Winston joked. "The boss sent me. Normally our man, Raymond Tedder, would be talking to you. But he's on vacation up north somewhere."

"Yeah, I know Raymond," the lieutenant drawled. "He's an okay guy."

"I was asked to check in with you folks about the death of Pauline Wicks in that boating accident just before Christmas. Our interest, of course, is that both Mrs. Wicks and her husband, Derek, are insured by Bayside Life Insurance Company. The husband's already made a claim on her policy."

Riddle made Winston wait for a response. "Wouldn't that be the thing to do if your wife died? Call up your insurance man and ask for the money?" Riddle smirked.

"Well, sure," said Winston. *Smartass.* "But the beneficiary has to submit a death certificate before any payout takes place. Sounds like in this case the cause of death hasn't been determined." Winston leaned forward in his chair, his eyes hard on the lieutenant's. "It's been almost two weeks since she died. What's the hold-up on the certificate?"

Riddle leaned back and crossed his arms. "Our medical examiner, Gordon Hamilton, just ain't ready to certify cause. He's suspicious, too." Riddle hesitated, then: "There was a nasty laceration to the woman's forehead, but she actually drowned."

"Are you thinking maybe this wasn't an accident?" Winston asked.

Dan Nettles had kept quiet as long as he could. "Hell yes, that's exactly what they're thinking," he said to Winston. "It smells fishy, if you'll pardon my pun." The room was quiet for a moment, then Dan asked, "What's your gut telling you, Lieutenant?"

"I'd say that since the woman was found bound to the front seat of the boat, something ain't quite right." Archie

182

Riddle rose from his chair. "That's why we're investigating. Let's take a ride down to Cedar Key, 'bout thirty miles. Look at the boat. We can talk some more down there." He settled his straw uniform hat on his head.

Riddle led the way in his official blue and gold Ford Galaxie with Winston and Dan trailing. They headed south on State Road 24 through scrub oaks, palmettos, and marshland. Crossing over a short bridge, Winston glimpsed something large scramble from the muddy bank and into the dark water, then the flip of a thick tail. Alligator territory.

"Damn, I'm hungry. Them frog legs done hopped on down the road," Dan grumbled.

Winston burst out laughing. "You are so full of shit," he said.

"Serious. We're gonna have to ask the high and mighty lieutenant to take us somewhere for our seafood lunch. *Before* we go check out that friggin' empty boat." Dan's stomach rumbled. "Seafood's the only reason I agreed to come along."

◆

The two sedans pulled into the unpaved parking lot of Mac's Marina. Winston and Dan followed Riddle around the marina store, down some rickety steps, and out onto a series of docks. Some were covered by metal awnings with electrical outlets for full-time slip rentals. Others were only piers with cleats for mooring, their rubber bumper edgings drooping in disrepair.

The lieutenant led the men to a red and white runabout docked at the end of one long walkout. The craft was a

Glastron Surflite, fifteen or sixteen feet long, powered by a white 35hp Johnson Seahorse. The scene was eerily peaceful, yet a woman had suffered a gruesome death in this very boat. No one spoke.

Winston imagined Pauline Wicks seated in the bow—dirty rope wound around her body, chin resting on chest, hanks of dripping hair. His eyes closed for a moment, and when he opened them, there lay a dead man in the boat's bottom, head poked out from beneath a paint-splattered tarp. *Don't.* He shook his head to erase the image.

"You all right, buddy?" Dan asked. "You lookin' a little peaked."

Winston nodded. He slipped his hand into his pocket, touched the talisman. "It's just a little . . . unsettling."

"That's some scary shit right there," said Dan. "That poor woman trapped underwater." He turned to Riddle: "What you think, Lieutenant? He trying to save her somehow? Or making sure she couldn't get away?"

Lt. Riddle shrugged. "Wicks said he was trying to calm her down by securing her. 'Securing' was his word. He said she was a weak swimmer, and when the weather went bad, she got hysterical."

"Okay if I climb inside?" Winston asked.

Riddle extended his hand to help Winston down into the boat. A couple inches of water pooled in the bottom, wetting the leather on Winston's shoes. The white vinyl seats were in good shape, no obvious damage. He ran his fingers around the windshield trim. Sharp points at the angles. Could have cut deep if her head had slammed against it.

"Wonder why they picked this particular time to fish. Who's thinking about fishing when there's a Christmas tree in the corner? Stockings on the mantle?" Winston asked.

"Wicks said he heard the grouper was biting. He'd planned to go out by himself, but Pauline wouldn't be left behind. Apparently, grouper fishing was something they both enjoyed. This is a great time of year to catch 'em. Gotta go about six or seven miles out, though, to deeper water. He said they was fishing with frozen mackerel off Seahorse Reef."

Winston's eyes roved over the boat. The Surflite was designed more for family recreation. He noticed two rod holders. No live well. All the fishing gear must have been lost in the storm. Wicks had had no way to summon help, either—no onboard radio.

Winston clambered out of the boat. "There's something so weird about this. I mean, surely they wouldn't have launched knowing bad weather was ahead."

"Nah, the weather was supposed to be beautiful. More like late spring than the middle of December. Seventy-eight degrees and no wind. Wicks said the water was smooth as glass when they left the marina and motored out of Crooked Creek and into the Gulf."

Dan Nettles paced back and forth, trying to stay in the background—the case wasn't his. Finally: "Y'all follow up on this rosy picture Wicks painted?"

Riddle's lip curled, "Yes, we did, *Deputy*. Like I said, the forecast was favorable that day. Fishing reports good that whole week. But storms can come up fast on the water. Doesn't even have to be a real storm."

"What do you mean?" Winston asked.

"That wind can get up quick-like, and if you can't get out of it, you're screwed. Especially in a boat like this. Underpowered. The 35-horse couldn't handle it. They would've had a helluva time getting back, just surfing the boat between breaking waves. Or wallowing in the troughs. Just going nowhere fast."

"Hey," said Dan. "How 'bout this. How 'bout we find a nice place to sit down and eat something? We can talk about this some more then. Ain't y'all tired of squinting out here in the sun?"

"Actually, I'm starving," said Lt. Riddle. "There's a little seafood shack one street over. Great grouper fingers."

"Raw oysters?" asked Dan.

⁓

The men got quiet as they dug into lightly battered fried shrimp, grouper, and hushpuppies. Dan had inhaled an appetizer of two dozen raw oysters, some on saltines, all doctored up with JB's Sopchoppy Sauce.

"I'm still a little puzzled," said Winston. "You've given me nothing but bits and pieces. What haven't you told me? Like, what did Wicks say actually killed her?"

Riddle sighed, pushed aside his littered plate. "Here's the long and the short of it . . . Wicks told us the weather went bad, just like I said. The wind turned, coming strong out of the east from shore towards the ocean. The boat couldn't get on plane. The couple was getting swamped, waves crashing over the bow into the boat."

The waitress appeared with a pitcher, filled all three glasses with sweet, iced tea. "How 'bout some key lime pie?" she asked. "Just made this morning."

Dan Nettles raised a finger. The others declined.

"I assume they both wore life jackets," Winston said.

The lieutenant nodded. "But according to her husband, Pauline was still terrified she'd be washed overboard. Then she was thrown into the windshield, head pouring blood, and she went limp. Wicks tied her to the bow seat so she'd be safe. He said his hands were full dealing with her and trying to steer through the waves."

"And then?" Winston probed, tired of the suspense.

"A massive wave slammed them, throwing Derek out into the Gulf. The boat capsized with Pauline still tied in, trapped underneath. He said he tried to swim up under the boat to reach her, but the waves made it impossible. His life jacket kept him afloat, and the fast current carried him away."

"Damn," said Dan, his mouth opening on pie mush. "A day from hell, huh?"

"Wicks was picked up by another fisherman, but they couldn't go back for the wife. Too rough. After the storm subsided, the Coast Guard located the boat, said the hull floated just at the surface. They righted the craft and found Pauline Wicks roped inside."

Winston's food roiled inside his stomach. He called for the tab and paid for all three lunches, on behalf of Bayside Life.

"So, this is an ongoing investigation . . . but what else is there to know?" Winston asked.

"We're trying to track down others who were boating in the area, see if their stories jive with what Wicks said. Did anybody see or hear them arguing that day? We've already talked to the boater who fished Wicks out of the water. He confirmed the really rough seas."

"The issue then, is that she was tied in. It's possible he's telling the truth about doing what he thought was best at the time," said Winston.

Riddle sighed. "Yeah, we're just trying to cover everything. We've talked to their neighbors. And some of the people he works with at Seller's Business Machines. We didn't get a lot out of them. Wicks is a contract employee who travels around fixing mimeograph machines and typewriters. Been with them four or five years." Riddle took the last swallow of his tea. He rattled the ice in the glass. "No reports of the couple fighting. No obvious motive for him to want her dead. We're still running down a few more people. If nothing new surfaces, I guess we'll have to close the case. Personally, though, I'm going to drag it out as long as I can."

Outside the restaurant, Winston said, "I can't say it's been a pleasure, Lieutenant, but thanks for your time." He handed the officer his business card. "If you find out anything new, I'd appreciate hearing from you."

⁓

Dan snored half the way home while Winston turned the Wicks story over and over in his head. Something niggled in the back of his brain, but it would not come forward. Hopefully, he could close the book on Cedar Key.

Chapter 29

Taking advantage of Saturday's balmy weather, Louis and Etta strolled down to Fina Creek. Louis carried two cane poles and worms—Etta refused to fish with crickets. She swung a basket filled with fresh-baked chocolate chip cookies and two bottles of root beer and carried Louis's red plaid blanket beneath her other arm.

They fished from the creek bank, pulling in nice-sized stumpknockers and crappie. Etta brought up a turtle, which let go of the hook just as it breached the surface. Once the fish stringer was full, they sat cross-legged on the blanket, enjoying their snack. They talked about anything and everything, words hushed in the presence of squirrels closing in on cookie crumbs they tossed.

The couple fell silent, opening space for the voices of jays and mockingbirds. The whoosh of something big called their attention to a tall sweetgum. A large Lord God woodpecker landed on the trunk, hopping upward to find a sweet spot. *Tat tat tat tat tat tat tat!* Another flew into the foliage to meet him, both white and black and red beauties.

"That's us, Etta," he whispered. "Two of a kind. Finding our way in the world."

She smiled and said in her slow, sweet way: "Maybe so. We got us a good start, that's for sure. But like you said, ain't no promises between us."

Louis sat up straighter, his brow furrowed. "Whaddaya mean?"

"I'm just going by what you been saying. You got your new job and all. You got a lot going on. We still learning each other's ways. Who each of us really is."

"I think we know pretty good who we are. I sure do know that little half-moon scar on your backside, where you fell off that swing when you were a kid." He wrestled her down onto the blanket, attacking her neck with wet kisses. "Lemme kiss that little scar for you, too."

Etta squealed for him to stop, and they rolled around on the soft wool, knocking an open drink bottle into the dirt. "See what you did!" she wailed.

"Forget that," Louis said, forcing her back down, looking into her sullen face. "I do know you, every inch of you."

"Well, you the lucky one here, because I don't know much about you at all. Hardly anything that matters."

He sat up, grabbed the toppled drink bottle, and threw it into the water. The glass bottle floated until it filled, then sank.

"Baby, what you wanna know? Just ask me." Louis said, his breathing quick.

"What about that man, that Mr. Bevis, come looking for you at Thanksgiving? What about that, Louis?"

"What about it? I told you he had me mixed up with somebody else."

"Ain't good enough, Louis. You acted strange when he showed up. Like you was waiting on something bad to come knocking."

"I'd swear on a stack of bibles I've never seen that woman. Sure as hell never gave her a baby." Louis kept shaking his head.

"You're always so mysterious. You never talk about your family. Where you been. Where you from. You just landed here at the boarding house like a stray cat, and Gramma Ruby give you a big ol' bowl of milk." She stood up and began snatching up the things they'd brought.

Louis rose to help her. His life *was* mysterious—he was bewildered by it himself. Things had happened that he didn't understand. He could not tell her what he wanted to say, for fear the new world he was building in Pineville would disappear. His reality was the present, and he so wanted her in it.

∽

Back at Ruby's Rooms, Louis scaled the fish, then gutted and cleaned them beneath a water hose. He threw the heads and guts out into the dirt for the pack of waiting cats. Etta dropped the fish into a paper sack of cornmeal and flour, shook them to coat, and then fried them in a black skillet fired by a camp stove set up on the back porch. She cooked a nearly-endless plate of hush puppies, and they gladly shared their food with several boarders called by the aroma.

An uneasy truce lay between them.

◡◠

The night was thick with dark, clouds shuttering the moonlight and most of the stars. The day had been clear, the air dry. *Amazing,* Louis thought, *how the good can so easily be obscured.*

His headlights guided him southwest on Highway 98. The confrontation he'd had earlier with Etta had left him unsettled. He longed for answers to questions he could not pose. Just couldn't. He didn't want to mislead people, but did he owe anyone more of himself than he was giving? Really? Bayside Life was getting his best: biggest smile, fanciest dance—his compelling customer hustle. Louis was a good steward of the money he collected—it would be easy to steal, but he had no need or desire. Etta enjoyed his caring and attention. Probably his love. Was it love? He'd also been working hard to earn Miz Ruby's approval.

The Bel Air rolled through the tiny town of Hampton Springs, past a general store, post office, and a small café. Even in daylight, the place was a ghost town. Too bad the legendary resort hadn't survived the long-ago fire. Though he'd heard about the hotel and springs, Louis thought he'd like to know more about the place. Maybe he'd take Etta there and explore the site. He'd been told a deteriorating swimming pool remained, the spring water thick with algae and the odor of sulfur.

Louis shivered and drove on into the dark, anxious to reach his destination. He slowed to watch for the remembered rough road of crushed shells and limestone. He came upon a huddle of small houses, then a few spaced further apart. Shacks, really. A few shed dim light from their windows; most were dark.

He found the mailbox, then turned into a driveway overtaken with dead weeds, his headlights splashing against the house siding. In that moment of illumination, he saw that Mabel Griffin's house was still blue, as blue as he and his friend had once painted it. He cut the lights and turned off the engine and sat watching the front door, the outline of windows. He waited for some faint glimmer of light to appear, perhaps someone flipping on a bathroom switch, or opening the refrigerator for a midnight snack. Nothing.

Louis stepped out of the Chevy, closed the door quietly, and leaned shivering against the car's cold metal. He couldn't see a single house from where he stood. A dog barked in the far distance. He moved toward the dwelling, his footfalls quiet except for the small crack of an occasional stick beneath his shoes. He crept up the steps to the front door and stood there like someone turned to stone. The thumping in his chest should certainly have been heard as a knocking. He waited and waited, then dared to test the knob. The door was locked.

What did he want at this house? Why had he come? Certainly, he wanted to find out if Mabel still lived there. But more than anything, he wanted to know what had happened to Jackson Smith.

Chapter 30

After church, Winston and Ruthie dropped Mary Carolyn off with the neighboring Frazer family and headed to Mayo for A. F.'s funeral.

"You sure you're up for this?" Winston asked, eyes darting from the road to Ruthie's profile.

"It wouldn't look good for you to show up without your wife."

He'd been worried about her sitting today in a church full of grieving people when she herself had not yet healed. In their own case, there'd been no body to speak of, nothing to touch one last time. People didn't talk much about miscarriage.

Winston was sad and disappointed by the loss of their baby, but he hurt more for Ruthie. The miscarriage had hit her hard, emotionally and physically. He hated anything to do with sickness or death. And there'd been enough death in his life, directly or indirectly, to last him a lifetime.

∾

At the end of a long dirt road dotted with ramshackle homesteads of unpainted houses, hog pens, and a few with fenced acreage corralling goats and a cow or two, they found Calvary Baptist, its steeple like a raised finger. The aged place of worship was a white wooden structure with a graveyard off to one side—headstones darkened with age. Only a few cars were parked in the dead-grass lot. Winston and Ruthie entered quietly, their footsteps drowned by the pianist's exuberant pounding of a refrain he recognized: . . . *I am bound, I am bound, I am bound for the promised land.*

As they made their way down the aisle, Winston's eyes locked onto the closed casket at the front, its rounded lid draped in a blanket of blood-red roses. He saw through the oak coffin as though it were made of glass, pictured A. F. like a squashed bug, parts rearranged. *I am bound, I am bound . . .* the dead woman lashed to the boat seat . . . dead man wrapped in a tarp inside his watery grave. Sweat beaded on Winston's upper lip; Ruthie pulled him onto an unpadded pew.

Looking around the sanctuary, Winston could only recognize A. F.'s wife. The young man sitting next to her would be their son. None of the attendees looked like Bayside customers. Not surprising: A.F. had not been popular.

The Baptist preacher droned on about the dead man's life, then kicked into a higher gear of sin and hard-to-reach redemption, hell always dominant in Baptist preaching. Winston could smell flesh burning all around him in the sanctuary. His own pants were hot. He looked at his watch. Twice in church on the same Sunday—enough to last Winston all year.

Ruthie and Winston waited in the churchyard for everyone to trickle out, and for pallbearers to carry the casket to the grave. Winston insisted on standing back from the group, watching from afar as A. F. was lowered into the ground. When the attendees began to scatter, he and Ruthie approached the family, murmuring condolences and shaking hands. The widow invited them for dinner at the house, but Winston quickly declined. He poked a toothpick between his teeth. He and A. F. were done.

Back at the house, Winston changed into denim pants and a plaid flannel shirt. He had wood to split for the fireplace; January and February would bring their coldest days. Chopping was therapeutic—driving the blade into a log, that satisfying *thunk*, that *creak* as the fiber gave way—knowing the wood would have remained stubborn and whole if not for his own strong will, his ability to strike the weakest point. He worked the pile until flannel clung to his wet back, then Ruthie called him in to the phone.

"It's Roger," she whispered and rolled her eyes. She handed him the kitchen extension.

"Hey, man," Winston said, breathing heavily.

"Tell me I didn't interrupt anything serious," Roger said, chuckling.

"Nah, I was just out in the yard working on my wood pile."

Ruthie brought him a glass of iced tea. He sat down at the kitchen table.

"I couldn't wait 'till tomorrow to find out what all's gone on this weekend. Dang if you don't deserve two days of vacation for all this," he said.

Winston snorted. "That's for damn sure. I'm gonna take you up on that, too." He looked around to make sure he was alone. "I'm gonna take off work sometime soon, surprise Ruthie with a little trip. We could use a change of scene."

"Anytime you're ready. Just let me know," Roger said, then cleared his throat. "I'm sure the funeral was the last thing you wanted to do this weekend."

"Yeah . . . can't stand all that sad crap. But I passed along your condolences. Got outta there quick."

"Well, thanks for going," Roger said. He waited a beat, then added "I'm anxious to hear what happened yesterday, too. At Cedar Key."

Winston shut his eyes, re-imagining the Wicks woman upside down beneath the capsized boat, its hull wallowing in the waves.

"Jesus, Roger. That was a helluva thing." He took a swallow of tea.

"You see the boat?"

"Oh, hell yeah. Riddle, from the Sheriff's Department, took us down there—Dan Nettles went with me. The boat was docked at a marina . . . Mac's Marina. Ruined my whole fuckin' day, I gotta tell you." He looked over his shoulder to see if one of the girls had come in behind him; he was trying to clean up his language around them.

"So, what's going on? Why haven't they called it on cause of death?" Roger was insistent.

"Well, the short story's that everything appears accidental. There's no real reason to believe Wicks killed his wife. No proof, anyway." He went on to explain the supposed reason she was tied down.

"You believe that story?" Roger asked.

"You know, I've thought about it a lot. How could he really be guilty of murdering her when most of what happened was just brought on by nature? Wicks couldn't have known the weather was gonna go bad. If he'd tied her to the boat hoping to drown her that way, he had no way of knowing the boat would flip over. He couldn't have flipped it himself."

"What if he threw her in and drowned her first before the weather got bad? Got all remorseful and dragged her back into the boat?" Roger asked.

Winston rubbed his forehead. "Then why would he tie her dead body to the seat, Roger? Remember, he had no way of knowing the boat would capsize. She couldn't have drowned inside the boat and tied to the seat unless the boat sank or flipped over. He'd be nailed for murder as soon as the autopsy was over."

"Mmm . . . You're telling me we're gonna have to ante up on the claim?"

"Yeah, maybe. They got a few more people to talk to, then the Levy cops will probably let it go. He'd be cleared by now if he hadn't tied her into the boat."

"That's just crazy," said Roger. "Can you even imagine?"

Winston could.

Chapter 31

As a result of his creative "Christmas Gift Blitz," Louis had sold four new life insurance policies and coverage increases to three existing customers—all in only six business days leading up to Christmas. Winston was proud, Roger Johns impressed. While the idea of selling life insurance policies as gifts worked, and Louis thought it magical, Winston knew that Louis didn't yet see the magic within himself.

Louis's December efforts jump-started their new year and threw the fledgling agent into the leaders' circle for the sales competition. Bayside Life's Pineville guys had a solid game plan and were working it.

∽

One morning Winton discovered an envelope wedged beneath the office front door, hand-addressed to Louis. The writing looked familiar. He placed the letter on Louis's desk.

After Louis arrived and settled in, he opened the mysterious message:

> *Dear Mr. Fisher: I enjoyed our recent meeting at the library. As I said before you left my office, your interest in looking back at our community's history by perusing old newspapers and historical documents gave me hope for the future. Few people exhibit interest in the past, but your enthusiasm validates my life's work to protect and preserve the written word. As you know, our local government still upholds "separate but equal," thus your patronage and research are limited to our satellite facility. This is unfortunate, and I would like to discuss another option for you. Please stop in to see me as soon as possible. Sincerely, Evelyn Pierpont, Head Librarian.*

Louis folded the letter and slipped it into his shirt pocket.

Winston was more than curious but did not quiz the man. The letter was none of his business.

⌣

The little "liberry" receptionist greeted Louis with a smile. Miss Pierpont had told her to expect him.

"Louis! So good to see you," Pierpont said. "Sit down, please!" Her face glowed.

"Yes, ma'am. I was glad to hear from you. Very curious, too," Louis said.

"I know you're busy working, so I'll get right to the point. I believe I mentioned when you were here before that I have a hard time keeping people on the project to transfer the newspaper archives to microfilm."

"Yessum, you did. I can see why."

"Yes, well, right now we've got nobody working on this. I stay late sometimes, or come in on the weekends, but it's slow going," she said.

He nodded.

Pierpont took a breath through her teeth and let it out. "I'm wondering if you'd be interested in working on this project occasionally—with pay, of course! Minimum wage is all I can offer, though." She rushed on: "It wouldn't be a real commitment . . ."

Louis waited.

"My thought is that you'd have a legitimate reason to be here in the evenings, or weekends if you prefer. Devote maybe half of your time here to the microfilm project, then stay for your own research and reading. You'd have access to everything here, and nobody could say a word about your presence!" Her cheeks flamed.

Louis was dumbstruck. Barring him from utilizing the main library was a crime. Against federal law. He was already employed, and significantly so, especially with the part-time gig with Mr. Abe. A third job was of no interest. Louis didn't know whether he should be furious or grateful. The right words were a struggle, and he searched the floor for them.

"Please forgive me if I've insulted you," she said, her eyelashes fluttering.

"Oh, no ma'am! No! I'm just surprised, that's all. At your kindness. Your willingness to help."

Pierpont dropped her head for a moment, and then she was back in control. "So, what do you think? About helping with the microfilming?"

"I'm not sure," Louis said. "I'm really grateful for your offer, but I need to think on it. Can I give you an answer later this week?"

The librarian agreed and walked Louis to the stairs. She patted him lightly on the back.

∽

Louis Fisher proved his worth every day. At the end of most workdays, his zip-up canvas bag was thick with cash and coin premium payments. He often sold new policies; almost all were to colored customers. And his account collections reconciled on the first pass. As a result of Louis's solid performance, Winston was able to stop putting out fires and ramp up his own sales. The two worked well together.

Winston began moving some of the trickier customers over to Louis. A number of insureds had refused to work with the new agent, left him standing outside while welcoming Winston in. But the team worked together to overcome apathy and rejection.

∽

On a Tuesday in late January, Winston took Louis on a loop around the Cherry Lake area, making introductions and picking up payments. They double-timed a colored couple new to the area and left the house with two new life insurance policies—five thousand dollars on each.

As he drove, Winston told stories about the customers and his time spent in the area. "I tell you, in the spring and fall, might be worth your coming back over this way to fish." He pointed out a sandy, grass-free patch on the lake side of the road, an obvious parking area. "Right there. I caught the biggest damn catfish I've ever seen."

"You eat him?"

"Nah. Those big ones are so old they taste like the bottom of the lake. Mud pumping through 'em for too long. Little ones taste best. You gotta watch out for gators over here, though. Bigger than a grown man."

Rita Owens lived alone at the end of a tree-canopied Madison County dirt road. Her cottage, shaded by moss-covered live oaks, sat at the edge of Cherry Lake, less than a mile from a summer camp for kids. She was a long-time customer in her seventies, and crazy as a bat. Who knew how she'd react to Louis?

"Insurance man!" Winston called as he knocked on Rita's door. He winked at Louis.

Louis circled the brim of his hat with his fingers while he scanned their surroundings. A dog crawled out from beneath an unrecognizable dirt-covered car. The ancient blue-tick hound limped toward them without a fuss.

"Hey, Jingles," Winston called. "How's that good puppy doing?" The dog summoned enough energy to wag its tail, then flopped down onto the ground.

"He don't bite," Winston said. "It's a wonder he's still alive."

Rita opened the door but stood wide-eyed behind the screen. Her yellowed white hair hung in clumps.

"Afternoon, Miss Rita," Winston said. "How're you on such a fine day?"

Rita didn't answer. Her eyes locked on Louis.

"Let me introduce our new agent, Louis Fisher. Louis, this is Mrs. Rita Owens."

She faded back from the doorway.

"So nice to meet you, Mrs. Owens," Louis chirped. "You sure got a nice place here on the lake. My goodness gracious, I bet you can catch some fish! Bet you get a lot of practice too."

"Yeah," she said, her voice hoarse.

"Betcha there's some big ol' bream out there. Granddaddy catfish maybe. Drag them big ol' thangs up from the muddy bottom."

Rita nodded.

"You probably know how to fry 'em up good and crispy, too. You coat 'em in cornmeal or flour?"

"Favor flour for them catfish." She looked and sounded a bit dazed. Then: "Cornmeal for bream."

"Yes, ma'am. Love me some fried fish for sure," Louis said. He looked at Winston.

"Miss Rita, can we come inside? Need to talk to you about something," Winston said.

Rita hesitated, then nudged the screen door open. Louis grabbed it and opened it wide. In that wash of unfiltered light, her pale skin appeared gray as ash. She disappeared into the dark house. Louis shot Winston a questioning look. Winston nodded concern. The two entered, blinking in the dim room.

Winston explained that Louis had been hired to help him, asked if he could count on her to work with the new agent.

"I'll still come around from time to time and visit with you, Miss Rita. But we got so much work these days, and just the two of us to do it. Louis is a good guy, and you can trust him. That all right with you?"

"I reckon so," she said, then fell to the floor with a heavy *thunk*, like somebody cut the strings of a puppet.

Winston dropped his debit book to try to catch her, but she slipped his grasp. Louis knelt, pressed fingers into the side of her neck, then put his ear to her face and chest.

"She's not breathing, and I can't find a pulse. We need help."

Winston hurried to the kitchen wall phone. The line was dead.

"Phone's out. I'm running to a neighbor's."

Louis had already started chest compressions. "Go!" he shouted, then covered the woman's mouth with his. His insides jittered with fear and adrenaline. Though focused on the challenge before him, memories of another still face rose within him, riding on a wave of bile.

The ambulance team loaded a now-breathing, semiconscious Rita Owens onto the stretcher and slid her into the back of the emergency vehicle. Several neighbors huddled in the yard, talking among themselves. Winston walked out of the house and parted the small crowd. He told them the straight story of what had happened and let them know Rita had been resuscitated by his agent, Louis Fisher. He handed out business cards.

"You never know what could happen. If you need some life insurance, hope you'll give us a call. Bayside Life is a company you can count on."

Louis, left behind to wash up, emerged from Rita's house and stopped on the stoop. He looked at the group as he rolled down his sleeves. To his surprise, the people all began clapping.

～

The two agents headed home in silence until Winston finally broke it. "You surprise me nearly every day," he said, glancing across the car. Louis stared out the windshield. "How'd you know how to do that resuscitation thing?"

"High school health class," he replied. "Can you stop the car?"

After retching onto the road's shoulder, Louis slumped back into the Studebaker. Winston handed him his own clean handkerchief.

"Sorry, boss. Tasted like something died inside me." He opened the window and let in the cool, fresh air.

Chapter 32

"Come on, Louis. You saved a woman's life yesterday. I need you to do this. The company needs you to do it," Winston said.

Louis stood up from his desk and headed to the coffeepot. Look, boss, I'm nobody's hero. I'm not looking for a bunch of attention. Just wanna keep moving, doing my job."

"This *is* your job. To uphold and enhance Bayside Life's image in every way possible. What you did for Rita Owens was incredible, and we need some press out of it. And this'll help your career."

Louis walked around the office, feeling eyes on his back. Winston was right; he should do the newspaper interview and be glad for the opportunity. But he knew things Winston didn't: the unsolved store break-in near the FAMU campus . . . he could see the white man on the ground now. And that other thing . . . more terrible than the first. He needed to keep a very low public profile, or the spotlight could turn on him like on an inmate trying to climb the wire.

"Okay, okay! But no pictures. I won't do it if there's pictures. And I sure as hell ain't showing my face on television. No sir."

"You ain't hard on the eyes, Louis," Winston laughed. "What you afraid of?"

"No pictures," Louis repeated. He put on his coat and hat, snatched up his debit book and left.

～

Winston lingered in the office, enjoying the quiet. For the first time in a while, he sensed his rash of trouble was over. The miscarriage. A. F.'s death. The Ricky Swain fiasco. He explored this unexpected peace like a tongue on a newly-filled tooth—solid, but he wasn't yet ready to trust it.

His home life was steadily improving. Ruthie, though not quite her old self, acted happier, and more affectionate. She'd returned to her office job at the elementary school. Laughter was back in their house.

With his personal life on the mend, Winston had high hopes for pulling the Pineville sales office out of its overall flat line by end of first quarter. Louis was an excellent agent, a real asset. The two of them would make the Jacksonville headquarters take notice. Put themselves on the Bayside Life Insurance map.

He opened the phone book, looked up the number for the *Pineville Times* and circled it. He jotted down a couple of points to make his case for a story, then twiddled the pencil between his fingers. This would be great advertising for the company, and he couldn't wait to hand Roger Johns a flattering newspaper article about the Pineville sales team.

The *Pineville Times* receptionist steered him to the local news reporter, Tom Reynolds. Reynolds was definitely interested in the lifesaving story, but timing was important; he wanted it to show up in the next weekly edition, which came out the following morning.

〜

When Louis returned to the office to drop off his daily collections, Winston and the reporter were waiting.

Louis, with a noticeable attitude adjustment, handled the interview like a celebrity, giving the reporter a detailed account of Rita Owens falling to the floor, not breathing, and without a discernable pulse.

"I didn't really have to think about what to do," Louis said. "It was just this feeling of urgency, not fear. In high school we practiced resuscitation with a life-sized doll, Recessi Annie. I hated that thing! It looked like a real dead girl," Louis laughed. "Anyway, I just pumped Mrs. Owens's chest kind of hard, then gave her a good breath. The ambulance took a while to arrive—seemed like forever—but I was able to keep up the breathing repetition."

The reporter said he'd called the Madison County hospital and learned that Rita Owens was still in the intensive care unit, but she was expected to recover. Louis had saved her life.

"Maybe I did," Louis said, ducking his head. "Or maybe her time wasn't up. I was just doing what anyone else would do."

Reynolds plugged a bulb into the camera's flash unit. Louis looked at Winston, then at the camera.

"I thought I made it clear. I'm not having my picture made. This ain't about me. The story ought to focus on people paying attention to signs of a heart attack. You should include that information. And where to go to learn lifesaving."

The reporter snapped several pictures of Winston, one of the Bayside Life logo on the wall, and then talked Louis into an obscure shot, standing at his office desk, hat on head, bent forward as though studying the debit book. Winston stood back against the wall, toothpick in mouth, arms crossed, and observed. Louis was clearly agitated by the camera, a ridiculous reaction. What was the deal?

⁓

After the interview, Louis sprinted from the office to the library, hoping to catch Evelyn Pierpont before she left for the day. She was putting on her coat when he arrived.

"Miss Pierpont! You got a minute?" he asked, his chest heaving.

Louis held his hat in his hands as he asked if the microfilming project was still open. He could only commit to an evening or two each week. And a couple of weeks was all he'd want to do.

Pierpont smiled and agreed to his terms. She'd plan to stay late the next evening to get him started and talk about after-hours access. She'd give him a key. They shook hands, hers damp with perspiration.

⁓

"Lookie here! The Bayside Life superstar arrives!" Winston grinned, waving the latest edition of the *Pineville Times* at Louis as he walked into the office. "Front page of this morning's paper! Bought an extra copy for you."

Louis dropped his book onto his desk and glanced at the newspaper lying there. He unbuttoned his coat. "Well at least it's not my ugly mug staring out at the world," he said.

"The guy did a great job on the story. I'm happy with it! We're gonna get a lot of notice in Jacksonville," Winston said.

The article was well done, maybe overdone, small-town press looking to fill white space. Louis scrutinized the story for racial talk but found nothing obvious. Surprising. Winston's photo, paired with the company logo, was on the third page.

"Nice," Louis said. "You hear any more about her condition?"

"I just called Madison General. She's out of critical care," Winston said. "Could've been otherwise."

Winston was puzzled by Louis's lack of excitement, his shying away from being front and center on the story. The man wasn't bashful. Louis's desire for first place was usually obvious—winning was everything. Getting his name and face on the front page should have been seen as a win.

"Speaking of news," Louis said, "I probably should tell you . . . I've agreed to help out at the library. They're microfilming the newspaper's old issues. Got 'em stacked up everywhere on the third floor. They're paying minimum wage. Dollar twenty-five an hour."

Winston rolled back from his desk. "I know what minimum wage is," he scowled. "Why in hell would you do that? You're already helping out at the car lot . . ."

"Well," Louis cleared his throat, "when I collected Miss Pierpont's premium for you, when you were staying home, we were just talking. She told me all about the history of the place, how they bought the building from the newspaper—"

"All that led to your taking on a third job?"

"I know. I know," Louis said. "She went into this long story about microfilming, and I told her I'd had a little experience with it. She asked me if I'd be willing to help."

Winston stared at him. Hard. The man sounded sheepish. Almost guilty of something.

"Look. Ain't none of my business what you do with your personal time, long as it doesn't interfere with your work here." Winston's mouth was now a tight, thin line.

Louis ducked his head, then raised his eyes to meet Winston's. "Are you unhappy with anything I'm doing for you, boss?" He already knew the answer.

"Three jobs. That's too much for anybody, Louis. I'd think your girlfriend would be needing some of that time."

"It's a temporary thing."

The clock ticked toward a new hour.

Winston got up and straightened his desk. "We better get going. I got a new prospect I'm seeing this morning. Then heading over to Magnolia Place."

"The nursing home? You got some family in there?" Louis dumped his untouched coffee into the bathroom sink, glad the library conversation was over.

"Nah. An insured."

"That the fellow you told me about, the one you said fell off his roof? Taking down Christmas decorations?"

Winston hesitated, his mind still on the library. "My long-time customer, Mabel Griffin. Been out there for months.

Dementia. Broke leg." He put on his coat. "The better answer to your earlier question, Louis, is that I'm thrilled with your performance. Roger's happy. Do what you want with your off hours. Just don't lose sight of your goals here." Halfway outside, he called back: "Lock the door behind you."

Mabel Griffin in a nursing home. Louis was stunned. The rope that had held him fast to the present was beginning to loosen. Fear and excitement stewed inside him.

A nurse waved at Winston as he walked down the long, dim corridor. The odor of pine cleaner and urine was a nauseating mix. He hoped that when his time came, he'd die in his own bed in his sleep.

"Mr. Taylor! Winston," a voice called behind him. He turned to see Dr. Samuels, the nursing home's attending physician. Winston waited for him to catch up. The men shook hands.

"I was just on my way to see Mrs. Griffin," Winston said. "How's she doing today?"

Samuels shook his head. "About the same. She won't cooperate with physical therapy. Dementia's getting worse. She's living more and more in the past."

"I thought y'all were just keeping her sedated so she'd stay off the leg. She's really out of it every time I come."

"We give her a little something to relieve her anxiety, but that's not why she talks crazy. Her brain cells are breaking down from dementia. Sometimes when this happens, the body gets the signal it's time to quit." Dr. Samuels paused, then: "I think we need to locate a next of kin before too long.

I understand her husband and daughter are gone. But she keeps talking about a grandson—Jackson Smith. You got any idea how we might find him?"

A cold chill passed over Winston. Sure, he knew where to find ol' Jax. Down inside a sinkhole. Probably nothing but a pile of bones. Fish food.

He looked down the hall at Mabel's room, then shook his head. "I don't know, Doc. The kid attended Florida A&M a couple years ago. Maybe check there? Mabel says he comes to see her, but I think she's dreaming."

"I just thought since you work in the colored community, you might have heard some talk," the doctor said. "You'd think somebody would know something about her grandson's whereabouts. He couldn't have just disappeared."

He couldn't have just disappeared. Winston weighed the words. Though he didn't have time for it, he thought he'd rather be in the front seat of any potential search for Jackson Smith.

"How about this," Winston said. "I'll ask whoever's in charge at the reception desk to let me know the names of anybody visiting Mrs. Griffin. Maybe I can track down those people to help find him. Just between us boys, Jackson Smith is one of our insureds, and he's also the beneficiary on Mabel's life insurance policy. If something happens to her, Bayside Life's gonna need him, too."

Dr. Samuels liked Winston's idea, but said, "I don't think she gets many visitors other than you and a preacher. And Libby Hart, her social worker. I'll talk to Libby about it again. If the guy doesn't turn up soon, we probably need to ask the Sheriff for help."

∿

Winston found Mabel asleep, her mouth sagged open. He pulled ten ones from his wallet, slid open the drawer of the metal bedside stand, and slipped the money inside.

"Insurance man," he announced, just as always. He took her hand in his. "Good morning, Mrs. Griffin. How you doing on this fine, cold day?"

Mabel's lips came together in an almost-smile. Her cloudy eyes opened.

"You want your glasses?" he asked, lifting them from the stand and guiding them onto her face. He cranked up the head of her hospital bed and dragged the guest chair closer.

"You seen my girl? Suki? She ain't been here for days." The old woman's mouth was dry, her words sticky.

Winston picked up a cup of water from the tray table and held the white paper straw to Mabel's shriveled lips.

"Have I seen Suki . . . no ma'am. Not lately." Winston returned the cup to the tray. "What you been doing since I last saw you?"

"Been shelling them field peas." She pointed to the empty corner of the room, then inspected her thick, yellow nails.

"Must be a bushel there," Winston said. "I'd stay and help you, but I gotta get back to work. I came to collect your insurance premium. Yours and Jackson's."

She nodded.

"You want me to get the money out of your drawer for you? It's $1.76 on yours. $1.25 on Jackson's. How about we go ahead and get you paid up for a couple weeks." He retrieved some of the money he'd just deposited in the drawer, slipped it into his collection pouch, threw in two pennies from his pocket, and recorded the payments in the debit book. Penance toward redemption—he hoped.

He got up to leave and patted her hand.

"My Jack come to see me yesterday."

Winston smiled. His self-inflicted wound called Jackson Smith was still knitting itself together. It began to sting.

Chapter 33

Friday morning Winston and Louis worked together to call their accounts. Between the two of them, they'd sold several new policies, pushing themselves higher on the company's first quarter leaderboard.

Louis left to make another pass at collections. The week had been a long one, and microfilm training at the library was still on his schedule for the evening.

Winston stayed back at the office, tidying up his bank deposit, all the while puzzling over Louis's refusal to show his face in the newspaper. It just didn't make sense. Why shy from positive publicity?

He opened his bottom desk drawer, located Louis' application, and began to study it with new eyes. Employment history on Louis was limited, except for his work in Pineville and his college classes—roughly a two-year gap between education and any specific employment. Louis had mentioned working "odd jobs" while he lived with an aunt somewhere in Georgia. Ruby Wright's endorsement of Louis had been enough for Winston.

He sat back and poked a toothpick into his mouth, rolled it around, pondering Louis's past. He looked up the phone number for Buckhead and gave them a call.

"Good morning! This is Winston Taylor over at Bayside Life Insurance. I'm calling to verify employment on one of your former employees. Could you connect me to the right person?"

"My pleasure," the bright voice chirped.

After several rings, a dull-sounding fellow drawled: "Personnel." He parked Winston on hold while he located Louis's records. Winston inspected the ceiling, wondering how anyone tolerated working in personnel—surely a monotonous job. But wasn't he himself doing the same right now? Yeah . . . mind-numbing. He chuckled into the receiver, enjoying the sound of his own amusement.

The man returned to the line and confirmed past employment for Louis.

"Could you do me a big favor and glance back at his previous work history? I'm interested in jobs before Buckhead." Winston pulled the toothpick out of his mouth and cleaned his fingernails with the unchewed end.

The guy came back with no previous employment listed, but college attendance was noted.

"You mean y'all hired him with no work background?"

"The job we hired him for didn't require any experience. We just needed a warm body to train. Hard work, but not hard to learn," the man replied.

Huh. Winston was still puzzled. Buckhead had no work history on Louis. Bayside Life had no specific work history. Heat crept up his neck; he could have done a more thorough job of vetting the guy. But Winston trusted his own gut. And he trusted Ruby.

Louis was proving himself to be everything Winston had wanted in an agent. Smart and charismatic. An excellent salesman. Was there any reason to worry about Louis's mysterious past if it wasn't impacting the man's success? Or Winston's own success?

But not wanting his face made public. What was that about? Was Louis running from something or somebody? And working three jobs . . . was he carrying a load of debt? Maybe he'd touch base with Ruby anyway. Wouldn't hurt. He found the number and dialed.

"Miz Ruby's Rooms. This is Etta . . ."

Winston hesitated, then hung up.

Louis met Evelyn Pierpont just after five o'clock for microfilm orientation and the first few hours of work. She explained the order of the newspaper stacks, pointed out notes atop each pile that showed issue dates. He'd be recording in the logbook the date of each edition he photographed. Louis flipped backward in the lined book: journal entries indicated that the project was suffering from slow motion, with long gaps in activity. He did not relish the tedious work ahead, but reminded himself it was his only access, with perfect privacy, to search for what he wanted to know.

Pierpont took him through the mechanics of the camera, the changing and saving of film, proper placement of documents on the worktable for best photographs. Louis suffered it in silence—he already knew the basics from his work at FAMU.

"Thank you, Louis, for doing this. I know the pay is hardly worth your while, but I'm glad we could come to this arrangement." She handed him a key to the back door. "I could probably get into some trouble by giving you this, but I know if Winston Taylor trusts you, Foley County can trust you, too. Her feet were not moving. "I feel sure that someday all people, regardless of color, will be able to enjoy this library. Skin color has never been an issue for me...."

Louis was ready for her to leave. "No need to worry about the key, ma'am. I'll be careful to lock the door when I leave. But I better get going on your project or I won't be making much of a dent in what needs doing."

Pierpont took a few steps down the stairs, hesitated, and looked up at Louis. "Please call me Evelyn. 'Ma'am' makes me sound like an old woman, which I'm trying hard not to be."

She finally disappeared down the stairwell, and Louis turned to his newest part-time job.

∽

Working with issues from the early fifties, Louis restricted himself to reading only headlines of every page he prepared for microfilm. County commission news. New city ordinances. Drunk and disorderly arrests. Junior Woman's Club Cotillion. Shriner's fundraiser. What had he signed himself up for?

By 8:30 that evening, Louis was ready to shoot himself. He stopped work and recorded his three hours in the project logbook. Then he performed his best and only magic trick with a peanut butter sandwich pulled from his coat pocket— it disappeared in three big bites. On the hunt for something to drink, Louis located a water fountain on the first floor by the bathrooms. He looked around him. The library appeared empty, except for one old woman behind the checkout desk. She had a direct line of sight to where he stood. He hesitated.

"Mr. Fisher," she called. "We're about to close for the night. Miss Pierpont said you have a key. Are you staying awhile?"

"Just a little longer," he said. "Came to get a drink." He turned the knob and leaned toward the small spout of water.

"Wait! You shouldn't drink without a cup." She waved a white paper cone.

Louis took the cup without comment, filled it, and carried it upstairs. *He didn't want to cause trouble for himself, or Miss Pierpont.*

Excited to start the work he'd really come for, Louis located newspapers from 1961 and 1962 and began scanning. He knew the news report should jump right out at him. Soon, however, he fell into the stories of people he now knew, or knew of, through his work with Bayside Life.

One headline stopped him and his face split into a grin: "Winston Taylor Wins Big." Below it was a grainy picture of Winston in full camouflage, squatting beside a dead deer, holding the buck's head by its massive horns. He read the full story of the newspaper's annual "Biggest Buck Bucks" contest, held on deer season's opening day. Winston's winner scored a 137.2 on the Boone & Crockett system. A national scoring system? Louis had never been a real hunter; his last experience had closed the door forever on that sport. Winston was awarded the $150 prize, but the last line of the article stated that rather than keeping the money for himself, Winston turned the check over to the Children's Home Society, a county orphanage. Louis nodded. He knew he'd been right to take the job with Winston. Right, and very lucky.

Louis read on about local business leaders, high school athletes, and fund-raising efforts. Many named in the articles were Bayside Life Insurance policyholders. Thus far, he'd had no feeling whatsoever for these people—he was only doing his job. But here he saw them as heroes, villains, and victims, integral to the hive of Foley County and its surrounding area.

The research exercise was interesting and amusing, but he hadn't found anything he'd been looking for. He'd be back. He turned off the lights and made his way to the main level. One ceiling light burned over the checkout desk; otherwise, the whole first floor was dark. He bent over and drank directly from the fountain, wiped his chin, and pushed his way through the library's only men's room door.

Chapter 34

Saturday morning at the boarding house, Etta entered Louis's room and knocked on his head with her knuckles.

"What are you doing? What time is it?" he grumbled. He pulled a feather pillow over his face.

"Get up!" she hissed. "That Bevis guy's back. On the front porch, asking for you."

Louis rubbed his eyes. This wasn't good. He pulled on yesterday's clothes and headed downstairs. Ruby and Etta were cooking breakfast for the boarders; the comforting smell of coffee and bacon filled the house. Ruby, wearing a white silk headwrap, looked like a majestic queen. She stared at him as he passed the kitchen.

Reginald Bevis hadn't come alone this time. An older colored man, slightly stooped with drooping red eyes, watched Louis step out of the house. Bevis introduced Moses Nash, the daddy of Lettie, the girl who claimed Louis Fisher fathered her baby.

"Look, man, I ain't got nothing else to tell you," Louis said to Bevis. The three men stood on the porch, breath steaming from their mouths. He turned to Nash: "I'm sorry for your family's trouble, for your girl being sick. But I've never met your daughter. And I sure ain't got any kids scattered around the country."

Louis was furious. He didn't need this crap. His past was nobody's business. He'd buried as much of it as he could, embracing the present, eyes on the future. Etta might be ready to dump him after today. His reputation would be ruined with Ruby. He shouldn't care what those women thought, but he realized he very much did.

Nash looked tired and defeated. He took off his hat and held it against his chest. "I 'preciate that. Mr. Bevis here said you denied knowing Lettie. But I needed to come see for myself. Mind if I set on the swing?" He held onto the chain, lowered himself to the seat.

"I'm sorry, Mr. Nash. Are you okay? Do you need something?" Louis asked. He thought the old man looked ready to collapse.

Nash began a fit of coughing, which ended in an alarming wet gurgle. He shook his head. "Perty soon, Lettie's goin' to meet Jesus. Her young'un needs his daddy. I ain't lasting much longer myself. Just trying ever thing I can to get the baby situated."

The steam left Louis. "I wish I could help. But I can't."

Bevis gave Louis a hard look. "We'll be on our way, then. If you get over your amnesia, give me a call. I sure do hate to get the State involved." He held out a business card.

Louis snatched the card, then hurried back inside—he'd been on the porch without a coat. He stood by the fireplace, shivering with cold, and dread. An uncomfortable conversation was coming with the women in the kitchen.

After breakfast was served and cleaned up, Ruby called Louis to join her and Etta at the kitchen table. He sat down across from the two.

Etta teared up immediately. Ruby's face was calm, though Louis saw a storm brewing behind her eyes.

"This is the last time I'm going to say this," Louis started. "I've never met Lettie Nash. I've never slept with Lettie Nash. I am *not* the father of her baby, or anybody's baby."

"Well, by golly, those men think you are. They must have some reason for that," Ruby said, shaking a crooked finger. "Bevis wouldn't have made a second trip here, dragging the girl's daddy, if something didn't point to you."

Louis pulled the business card out of his pocket and handed it to Ruby. Etta wiped her eyes and leaned over to look.

"So?" Ruby said.

"So, he's being paid by Nash to find that kid's father. He's an investigator. Why wouldn't he come back? He's earning his money!" Louis's voice rose.

"Yes, but it's obvious he believes he's right." Ruby's eyes drilled into him. "Listen, Louis, us colored folks are often wrongly accused. Been happening forever. But these are Negroes after you. That old man probably ain't got a dime to waste on a detective, yet he's hot on your trail anyway. Why? Because he *believes.*"

Louis looked down at the wooden tabletop, scratches etching a history of serving others and solving problems; he knew the table to be just. Reaching over for Etta's hand, he

225

said, "Y'all listen to me. You know me. You know I'm not a bad guy. I wouldn't lie to either of you about this. This is serious."

Etta had quit crying, but she reclaimed her hand. The kitchen was quiet, except for popping noises from the cooling stove and the muffled sound of feet on the floor above.

"I think," Ruby said, "that Bevis, or that family, isn't going to give up easily. They're desperate to find the baby's father." She folded her hands together on the table. "Since you say the child isn't yours, the way I see it, you've got two choices. You can pretend this case of mistaken identity never happened, but you better be looking over your shoulder. Or you can find a way to prove that you're innocent of fathering that child. Which I want to believe you are." Ruby shrugged her narrow shoulders. "What can anyone do to you in this situation anyway? Take you to court?"

Louis took a deep breath and let it out. "Thank you, Miz Ruby," he said.

Ruby raised her hand. "I'm not done." She turned to Etta. "You, missy, need to accept what Louis tells you is true, and stand beside him. Or if you can't believe in him, send the man on his way." With that, she got up and pushed through the kitchen door. It swung back and forth behind her regal exit.

They heard Ruby's car pull out of the parking area, headed to her motor court closer to town, and Louis drew Etta into his room and wrapped her in his arms. "You're my only baby," he whispered. "I swear."

Etta's body was a cold stone. Louis knew it would take time to thaw.

ᔕ

Winston and Ruthie sat in their kitchen, enjoying coffee and catching up on unread newspapers. Mary Carolyn watched *Roadrunner* in the den. The cartoon's sound effects drifted through the doorway, along with Mary Carolyn's laughter. *Beep, Beep!* Ruthie had made cinnamon toast for them all, then left the oven door partly open to help heat the area. The room smelled like a Christmas morning, like the one the Taylors should have had but didn't.

Ruthie discovered herself in the *Times'* community section. She was co-chairman of the upcoming Junior Woman's Club white sale. She and Priscilla Nettles were pictured together, both in button-up blouses with Peter Pan collars. Winston watched her face as she talked about the Club's plans. Someone in the group had a connection to a textile mill in South Carolina—the women were getting a killer deal on sheets and towels and expected to net a bundle to fund their charitable work.

"By the way, honey, I forgot to tell you—" she started.

"And what would that be, madam?" Winston interrupted. "I'm hanging on your every word," he teased, happy that she was happy. Happy she was alive and well and back in his arms. This was a new beginning of sorts. But even so, a part of him wished he could tell her about what he'd done, about what lay at the bottom of Blue Sink. Coming clean would lighten his burden, but he knew the truth would drag her down into that water too. He shook off the selfish longing.

"Thursday night, at our committee meeting, we were having screwdrivers, like we do sometimes," she grinned, "and Millie Meyers got to talking about her sister who lives in Tallahassee . . ."

Winston's eyes drifted down to the sports page. David Morgan's young nephew had killed an eight-point buck last weekend. The photo showed the boy holding up the deer's head, the rack wider than the kid's shoulders. Maybe the size of that deer he'd never found . . .

"Millie's family is from Branford, or Bronson, or whatever that town is near where you went. You know, to see about that woman who died in that accident?"

Winston raised his head. "Hold it. Hold it," he said, squinting at her. "You talking about that boat accident at Cedar Key?"

"I'm getting around to it, if you'll pay attention," she said, making a face at him. "So anyway, Millie's sister, Michelle, told her about a girl she works with in Tallahassee, but who is also from Bronson, who's seeing the guy whose wife drowned in that storm."

Winston, eyes still narrowed, mouth turned down, said: "Seeing . . . you mean Derek Wicks is dating a woman in Tallahassee? How could you forget to tell me that?"

"The meeting was only two nights ago! Good grief. I've hardly seen you all week," she said. "And all I said was that she was *seeing* the husband of the dead woman, not that she *killed* the woman."

Winston closed the newspaper and put it on the table. "I can't believe Wicks already has another woman. His wife only died a month ago. Some grieving husband, huh?" he said. His mind raced, recalling the particulars. "I doubt seriously he started up a new relationship with the accident investigation going on. This girl must be somebody he's known awhile."

Ruthie shrugged. Got up and cleared the table, putting dirty dishes into the sink. She turned on the hot water and squirted Joy into the faucet stream.

Winston began drying the clean, rinsed dishes Ruthie stacked in the dishrack.

"That whole investigation just petered out," he said. "They couldn't find any evidence that Wicks killed her. The M.E. just recently declared cause as 'accidental drowning.' Wicks is waiting on Bayside to pay up, a whopping hundred thousand. A double indemnity policy." Winston shoved the dry plates into the cabinet and began wiping the cups with enough force to crush them. "I tell you, I haven't stopped thinking about this case since I saw that boat tied to the dock. Floating like a ghost. Something inside me says he killed her. Sure as shit."

"Well . . . you want me to talk to Millie about it again?"

"Wouldn't be a bad idea—if she can keep her mouth shut. I'd like to know her sister's name and phone number, and the name of the woman who's supposedly seeing Wicks. You think you could get that?"

"I can't say for certain she'd keep her mouth shut. Especially if I'm obviously asking for contact information." Ruthie rolled her eyes. "She'd be too curious. Maybe I'll just casually bring up the conversation again when I see her. Tell her I had too many drinks that night and the story's fuzzy. I might fish for names that way."

"That's my girl! Go get 'em!" Winston popped Ruthie's rear with the towel. "Beep, Beep!"

Chapter 35

Louis and Etta took a long Sunday drive, a nearly seventy-mile trip to Quincy. They followed Reginald Bevis's directions to the small hospital. The private investigator was waiting for them at the entrance, along with Moses Nash.

"I 'preciate you letting me come here, Mr. Nash. You sure it's okay for me to see her?"

Nash nodded. "I told her you was coming."

Louis held Etta's hand as they followed Nash into the lobby, with Bevis at their backs. Several visitors were scattered around the room, immersed in television or reading magazines. The voice of a small child erupted as they passed: "Papa! Papa!" A chubby toddler, dressed in red corduroy pants and a striped tee shirt, stood with his arms raised toward Nash, a big grin on his face. The woman in charge of the boy shushed him. Nash glanced toward the woman but kept the group moving.

They took a left past a nurse's station and followed the colorless corridor to its end. The patient room was small, with two beds—one stood empty. Lettie Nash lay in a wash of light filtering through Venetian blinds. She was all but a skeleton, bones prominent beneath the shriveled ash of her skin. Her head was almost completely bald. Louis knew the look of someone dead, and she was not far from it. His insides trembled.

"Lettie, girl, you got you some company," Nash said gently.

Lettie's milky eyes opened—eyes too big for her face.

Louis moved closer as Nash stepped back. He kept his voice low: "Hello, Lettie. My name's Louis Fisher. I'm pleased to meet you," he said. His memory rolled up a black and white photo of a pretty young girl, slender, with a playful expression on her face. The girl that lay here today bore no resemblance to his mental picture.

The hint of a smile surfaced at the sound of his voice. Her full gaze fell upon him, roved the shape of his face, the set of his ears, the slope of his shoulder. Louis gripped the bedrail to steady himself beneath the horror of her inspection.

Lettie looked at the ceiling, or beyond, whispered something unintelligible. Moses Nash moved closer to catch the words. He took her hand: "What, baby, what you saying?"

"Nuh uh. Not him." She closed her eyes.

Back in the lobby, Louis faced Moses Nash. "I can't tell you how sorry I am for you, Mr. Nash. I know this identity mix-up's caused you even more grief. I wish I could do something . . ."

"No, no," Nash said. He tried to stifle a cough; his eyes ran and he dabbed his face with his handkerchief. "You tried to tell me true," he said, glancing at Bevis. "I'm the one's sorry, sorry for dragging you into this. I shore do hate it, you come all the way over here. But kinda glad, too. We just gonna keep on lookin' for the baby's daddy."

The squirming little boy broke free from his caregiver and waddled toward his grandfather. Nash bent and picked up the chunky baby, nearly losing his balance in the process.

Louis was quick to steady the old man.

"And here's our lil' fellow what's caused you all this trouble today. Our Louie," Nash said with a smile that did not match his watery eyes.

A large rock of regret dropped to the bottom of Louis's stomach. A very real reminder of the poor choices he'd made in his life. He reached out for the little one's hand and squeezed it.

"How you doin' there, Mr. Louie?" Louis's calm voice masked his feelings. He searched the child's features, looking for something familiar, but in truth, all little kids looked pretty much alike to him.

The baby raised his eyes to Nash for reassurance, then hid his face against the old man's chest.

"He ain't usually this shy," Nash said.

Etta watched the interaction without comment. The boy was precious, but the situation pitiful. After hearing the baby's mother today, she believed Louis had been telling the truth all along. The boy wasn't his. But she also recognized that Louis was deeply touched by the situation. Her man was a good man, yet she still had much to learn about him.

⌒

Leaving Quincy, Louis and Etta talked about anything and everything except Lettie Nash. Relief was in the air, yet the suffering they'd witnessed was overwhelming. Instead of driving straight back to Pineville, Louis toured Etta around Tallahassee's points of interest. First stop was the airport, where they got out of the car and watched a plane take off.

"That's gonna be us someday," said Louis. "When I get enough money saved, we're gonna take us a big trip."

"Oh! New York City! The World's Fair opens there in April!" Etta hopped up and down like a little girl.

Louis drew back, wide-eyed, but laughing: "Ain't no way I can save up that quick!"

"Well, the fair runs a whole year," she argued.

They drove into a park at nearby Lake Bradford. The pavilion and concession stand were closed for the winter. They got out and walked beneath the oaks, acorns crunching under their shoes. Bright sunshine sparkled off the water.

"Could we swim here in the summer?" Etta asked, shading her eyes with her hand.

"Not here we couldn't. This park belongs to Florida State University. Whites only. But there's a private area owned by an old colored man. He opens his shoreline every summer. Sells drinks out of coolers. Snacks and stuff. I've been there a time or two. Met a cute girl there once," he winked.

"I bet she liked you a lot. You're a good-looking guy," she grinned, hugging his arm.

"She was a FAMU student, too. But she wasn't poor like me. She wouldn't have nothing to do with me after she found out I was on government assistance. Her daddy was some bigwig in Philadelphia."

"Oh, baby. It's hell to be needy, huh?" she poked at him.

"Nah, it's fine, Etta. We all got our problems and our pasts. Our ghosts and skeletons. It's what we make of 'em that counts." He pulled her by the hand back to the car.

～

On Tennessee Street, near Florida State University, they spotted the golden arches of a McDonalds, one of those new "fast food" places they'd only heard about. Louis pulled into the parking lot and observed the customers standing in line at both service windows; all were white. Soon two Negroes fell in line with the rest. Louis and Etta held hands and waited behind the colored couple. Hamburgers and chocolate shakes. And French fries! They ate their feast in the car.

Louis drove them slowly around the FAMU campus, pointing out the various buildings, especially the library, trying to explain his euphoria at all the information found within. He told her he'd barely scraped by financially, but many of the students came from affluent families. His education had been funded through a pittance of government assistance, odd jobs for the university, and a rare envelope of cash from his aunt in Georgia. A time or two, he'd gotten a letter from his grandmother with a ten-dollar bill tucked inside; he'd only seen her a few times in his life.

At a filling station on Monroe Street, an attendant pumped gas while Louis bought Coca-Colas and sleeves of peanuts. As an afterthought, he pushed a coin into the newspaper box and took the last copy of the *Capital Democrat*. Etta thumbed through it on the way home and read him a funny letter in the Ann Landers column. She scooted up next to him and drifted off to sleep with her head on his shoulder. Louis's sense of relief and well-being fairly lifted the wheels off the road—the Bel Air was almost flying.

∽

That same Sunday evening, while Etta and Ruby worked in the kitchen, cleaning up from dinner and prepping breakfast for the boarders, Louis sat in the small parlor by the fireplace, scanning the newspaper he'd bought in Tallahassee. He perused a section dedicated to the upcoming March legislative session and the bills up for consideration. Road work was high on the docket, with proposed support of the future extension of Interstate 10 from Jacksonville to Tallahassee—currently only a small section of that road moved west from the east coast. A prison improvement bill was on the list as well . . . Louis frowned—good thing he hadn't landed there . . . yet.

A recap of the latest Florida Cabinet meeting was a snoozer. The current administration showed concern for the environment, authorizing the Department of Natural Resources to set up a committee to explore protection of the spiny lobster, and another group to study water quality. Louis yawned and turned the page mid-sentence. No way the State could pay for all that. Bunch of officials busy dreaming.

"Mind sharing your newspaper?" asked one of the new boarders who'd just wandered in.

"Sure, sure," Louis said, handing over the first section. He propped his feet back up on the ottoman, eyes roving the community news.

Count Basie Refused Food Service. Louis wasn't surprised at that headline. The Negro musician had recently performed at FSU, then crossed the road to a student eatery just outside the university's front gates. After being refused service, the jazz pianist joined protestors at the restaurant. The demonstrations were ongoing. Louis smirked. Basie was good enough to entertain the white folks, but not good enough to eat beside them. He hoped to God that someday the world would be different.

Then, a ghost from his past. He sat up, moved his feet to the floor. The newspaper trembled:

```
G&W Store Owner Dies
Tallahassee, FL

A shot rang out more than two years ago
on the night of September 6, 1961, not
far from the Capitol and just off the
campus of the all-Negro Florida A&M
University. Fred Graham, 78, a white
man and owner of the popular G&W
vegetable stand, was defending his
place of business when he pulled the
trigger of a 12-gauge shotgun, pointing
the barrel at the night sky, meaning to
scare away three thieves who'd broken
into his store. One of the colored men
attacked Mr. Graham, rendering him
unconscious when his head hit the
concrete sidewalk. The beloved
proprietor was diagnosed with a serious
concussion. Though he eventually
regained consciousness, he was never
able to resume working and his son
stepped in to manage the store. City
and campus police investigated and a
year later arrested a FAMU student, but
the suspect was eventually cleared.
Other suspects were never identified
and the case remains open. Anyone with
information should contact Tallahassee
```

Police. A reward is being offered. Fred
Graham passed away yesterday. See
Obituaries for funeral details.

Without a word to anyone, Louis hurried from the
boarding house, cranked his Chevy, and drove as far as his
headlights could see.

The *Democrat* article circled inside his head like a noose.
He, Louis Fisher, was one of the perpetrators the police had
never identified. Likely under pressure and desperate, the
cops had rounded up an innocent student to charge with the
crime. The terror that guy must have endured—all because
of Louis and his so-called friends: roommates Rascal and
Moby. What had become of them? Had they gone into hiding,
too?

An indistinct image appeared in the back of Louis's head,
a picture he struggled to sharpen. Suddenly it rushed
forward, fully fleshed in the form of Moby. Big Mo? Shit, Mo
would have been a highly visible suspect, just on size alone.
Had Moby been the one in the jail-cell hot seat, covering for
Louis and Rascal? A bitter taste flooded Louis's mouth.

"What a goddamn coward!" he screamed at himself and
beat his hands against the Chevy's wheel. Where would he
be now had he never gotten drunk and rambled those
campus streets that dark night with those guys? Never
tagged along, laughing and cutting the fool. Whose idea had
it been to break into the store? Louis knew he'd never have
trespassed on his own. But he'd been a follower back then,
with a sickening need to belong somewhere, to somebody.

He remembered police had crawled the campus for days,
rousting students, looking for perpetrators of what they
thought was a racially-motivated crime. But race had

nothing to do with it, and the store owner's injury was more accident than crime. Tallahassee had loved the old white man, Fred Graham. Shit, he'd liked him, too. Now today Graham was dead. If the police were able to find the attackers, even this long after the event, surely they'd be charged with murder. Someone would pay.

Louis had left school immediately after the incident—the beginning of his junior year. He'd simply disappeared. He'd found what he thought was safety in the company of an unlikely friend. And that had led to his second major mistake . . ..

"Shake it off. You're a leader now, man. Not a follower," Louis said aloud to himself, his Bayside Life selling voice almost echoing inside the big Bel Air. "You ain't even the same person you used to be." He swallowed that line again, a lie big enough to strangle him. His eyes watered, and he beat the wheel again. "You going places. You gonna be okay," he preached, his words cracking.

But somewhere within Louis, his small self still lived, the boy whose drug-addicted mother had left him alone, scared and hungry, in cold, shithole rooms. He could see that child, blinking in the dark, waiting for someone to come get him, to tell him he was safe.

↝

On the same Sunday evening, Winston, too, perused the *Capital Democrat*. He scanned the Governor and Cabinet initiatives, and the creation of a water quality task force caught his attention. He was all for the government's proactive stance on protecting Florida's natural resources.

Winston read on about some of Florida's freshwater issues, including the negative impact of toxic chemicals dumped by industry or agriculture into the karst system. Karst, the article explained, was a geology term for landscapes that formed in areas where limestone was near the surface and had undergone dissolution.

He re-read the section with a closer focus. Dissolution was chemical weathering of limestone from naturally acidic rainfall. Caves, springs, and natural bridges were created in the process. And wet sinkholes . . . like his very own Blue Sink.

Oh, hell no! He didn't need anybody poking around in that hole. What were they gonna do, pull out all the old shit that was probably down there? Find the Ford wagon, Jackson's casket? Winston's heart began to trot. How many sinkholes were there in Florida? Where would they start? Maybe close to the capital city, Tallahassee . . . and Blue Sink was only a stone's throw from there.

Surely Jackson's identification papers had dissolved by now. But the car...its VIN number and the tag. If the station wagon was registered in Jackson's name, well, here we go . . . investigators would eventually discover that the dead man was a Bayside Life insured. Winston had rectified the "special policy." He'd backdated the policy application to a time prior to Jackson's death; the life insurance actually existed. Hell, he'd even been paying the premiums out of his own pocket—a year, maybe?

So, what had he been afraid of for the past two-plus years? He thought about it some more, his hand creeping for the buckeye. He actually had much to fear.

For starters, his imagination said that if Jackson Smith was discovered in the sinkhole, somehow, some way, he, Winston Taylor, would be found out. Bayside Life Insurance would need to honor the terms of the burial policy and pay out. What if, say, Bayside Life decided to investigate the Jackson Smith death, just like in the Pauline Wicks case? Shit, what if Roger decided to drag Winston into the investigation of Jackson's death, too. That would be another new nightmare, working on his own insurance fraud case. Jesus, he might as well check himself into the nuthouse in Chattahoochee.

What if Bayside Life discovered that right after Jackson Smith disappeared, Winston had borrowed a sizeable amount from David Morgan at Foley Savings & Loan. David didn't know what the money was for, but Winston had helped the banker believe it was a gambling debt. Oh, it was a gambling debt all right, just not from cards at the Starlight Motel. What if Ruthie was asked about it? Roger was no dumbass; he'd want to get to the bottom of what happened.

Winston just couldn't afford for Jackson Smith to be found. His intestines rumbled agreement. He closed his eyes. Enough. Nobody would find Jackson. If the bureaucrats did decide on sinkhole cleanup, it would be a long time before the government quit fiddle-fartin' around and took action. Maybe not in his own lifetime. Probably not.

With the funny papers folded under his arm, he hustled to the hall bathroom.

Chapter 36

The following week, Ruthie returned home from the Woman's Club meeting with the inside scoop on Derek Wicks.

She had taken wine and cheese for the girls. Four of the seven members showed up. At agenda's end, they ate and drank and gossiped.

Winston's ears were rattling from Ruthie's in-depth, buzzed discussion on her evening. "Sounds like a good time for a good cause, honey. But what about Millie?"

"Oh! Right." She fanned the alcohol heat in her face with a magazine. "Whew! I'm too young for hot flashes!"

Winston could read her level of indulgence by the redness of her nose. He steered her to the sofa and brought her a glass of iced tea. Tomorrow they'd have a serious discussion.

"Millie Meyers?"

"Right, right . . . somehow or 'nother we got around to talking about her sister. Michelle Doss. She lives in Tallahassee."

"You get that phone number?"

"Of course not. Millie'd think I was crazy. Like why would I even want her sister's number?"

241

"Okay, you're right. Maybe Information's got it. Y'all talk about the woman dating Derek Wicks?"

"A little. She lives in Tallahassee. Works for the State with Michelle. Department of Commerce, I think."

"Interesting . . . Michelle is Millie's sister, right? All those M's . . ."

"Winston! Pay attention," she said, narrowing her eyes. "So, the guy, Wicks, fixes the duplicating machines and typewriters. His company's got some contracts with the State, and he travels around doing that. He must've been messing around with the woman for a while because guess what?"

"Uh . . . she's pregnant?"

"No . . . she's got a big ol' diamond on her hand!"

Winston's eyes widened appropriately.

"Yeah, this is really good," Ruthie nodded with a lopsided smile. "The woman told Michelle the engagement was a secret. At least for a little while, because his wife just died in that awful accident." Ruthie yawned then and slumped over onto the couch pillows. "I'm so tired."

"Did you hear the woman's name?"

Ruthie's eyes were closed. "Veronica. Cirsey. No . . . something foreign, like Ciresi. Veronica Ciresi."

∾

Winston had a difficult night. His mind flashed up pictures like a slide show. The imagined face of Pauline Wicks, bloated and deathly white. Her hair, matted to her head and neck. The gash on her forehead. And, of course, his memory threw in a few frames of Jackson Smith, dead in the dirt. Wrapped in a paint tarp. Nothing but bones in that deep watery grave.

But I wasn't the one who killed him, Winston reassured himself, trying to shake off his own corpse story. He needed to focus on what mattered right now—the Wicks case, and the possibility that Derek *did* kill his wife.

Wicks was a low-rent bastard. If the women had all been telling the truth, that Derek had another woman, maybe before Pauline died, a possible motive for murder had just materialized. Right in his own living room. Winston couldn't believe his good fortune—this information could possibly stop a killer from receiving a big payout from Bayside Life and help send that killer to prison. At three a.m., he was perking coffee and making notes. He watched the clock. At seven, he picked up the extension in the den, dialed Roger's home number, and told him Ruthie's story.

Roger was stunned. He let out a torrent of profanity about Wicks. About murder. About insurance fraud. When he calmed down, he said he'd head straight to the office. Talk to Brian Benson. See if the check for Wicks had been cut or mailed. Probably have to get outside law enforcement involved, but that would be in the hands of Bayside Life investigators. "Holy crap, Winston, you can't make this shit up."

∽

As they did every Friday, Winston and Louis reconciled their accounts. Winston stumbled through his and couldn't balance the money with the debit book. On edge, he was waiting to hear from Roger, anxious to find out what would happen next. Also dying to talk about the case, but afraid to tell anyone. Louis took Winston's book and collections to his own desk and worked through it. Everything balanced.

"You go ahead and knock off early," Winston said.

"A whole half a day early?" Louis was suspicious.

"Yeah, you go ahead. You deserve it. I'm gonna make the deposit and then grab lunch. Waiting on a big call from Roger."

"Everything okay, boss?"

"Oh yeah. Just a lot of stuff going on in Jacksonville. I'll tell you later."

⌒

Back at the office with a BLT and a Coca-Cola, Winston waited. His hand crept to the phone, thinking to go ahead and call Roger, but talked himself out of it. His insides jittered with anticipation and the exhilaration of following his instincts, of not "letting things go." This was the good stuff, the big challenges that made his pulse race: investigations. Like Roger had suggested not long ago, he had a nose for getting to the bottom of things. Maybe he'd someday move into that arena. Move away from Pineville. A worthy goal. But his hopes fell, remembering that Ruthie was the one who'd teased out the critical information. But no . . . originally, she'd had no understanding of the significance of her conversation with Millie Meyers. He, Winston, had known in a flash that the nugget of information was a meteor streaking across the sky—it would hit the earth, and when it did, he'd be the witness who'd predicted it.

The phone jolted him out of his reverie. He scrambled for a toothpick and stuck it in the corner of his mouth. Wished for a cigarette.

"I gotta tell you, Winston, this has been some kind of day. You started it off with a bang," Roger chuckled.

"Do tell." Winston shut his eyes, concentrating on every word Roger uttered.

A half hour later, Winston had settled down, though his jaw was still tight from chewing the wooden pick, his hand numb from gripping the receiver. "So just to make sure I got all this...." he said, drawing lines under notes he'd scribbled on a tablet, "I'll be hearing from Wally Sears, our own investigator—never met him. Probably have the Levy County cops involved, maybe their medical examiner. Maybe State cops. What about Raymond Tedder? It's his territory. Wicks is his customer."

"Nah, he hasn't done shit to help figure this out. A hundred-thousand-dollar loss hurts, even for a company our size. Screw him. I'll give him a call, let him know we got a tip and we're running with it."

"I guess this'll crank up on Monday?"

"Oh hell no. It's already moving. Wally should be calling you shortly."

Chapter 37

Saturday morning, Winston welcomed Wally Sears into the Pineville office. Short and chunky, Wally reminded Winston of Mary Carolyn's well-loved teddy bear. The man's dark eyes were round and shiny as buttons; he wore an almost-constant smile on his chubby pink face. His thick brown hair glinted with hints of silver and sprang from his head in tight spirals. Winston liked him immediately.

"You've got quite a reputation around the home office," Sears grinned as they shook hands.

"You didn't say what kind, but I hope it's all good."

"Oh yeah. The Ricky Swain story was unforgettable. What a coup!"

"Wouldn't have happened without Roger and Brian. I guess I was more the instigator," Winston chuckled.

"Now you done brought us on a mission to debunk Derek, the wicked Wicks." He slapped Winston on the shoulder, laughing.

Twenty minutes later, Levy County's Lieutenant Archie Riddle arrived in his patrol car. Winston figured all the store owners just opening for the morning were craning their necks, wondering what was going down at Bayside Life. Out-of-town law enforcement was unusual.

The three men reviewed the day's agenda. They'd all meet first with Ruthie's friend, Millie Meyers, in Pineville. Then Sears and Riddle would drive to Tallahassee and pick up Leon County Sheriff's Deputy Bill Wayne. The three investigators would then call on Millie's sister, Michelle Doss, to talk about her coworker, Veronica Ciresi. Based on that interview, they'd bring Veronica in for questioning.

Winston wasn't happy that the plan excluded him from the trip to Tallahassee, where the exciting action might happen. Wally explained that Winston had already helped immensely, but he had no official investigative authority, thus no need to go with them to the capital.

"I understand where you're coming from, but I disagree. This *is* part of my job." Winston poked at his own chest. "I was the one Roger sent to Cedar Key to begin with. He trusted *me*. I should be included in the Tallahassee investigations. I'm the one who brought this potential motive to light."

Wally relented. "This wasn't in my marching orders, but I tend to agree with you. Just keep your lips zipped; I'll talk for the company."

Winston alerted Ruthie that he'd soon be heading to Tallahassee for the day. The three men took off in his Studebaker to visit Ruthie's friend, Millie Meyers. Millie didn't disappoint—she confirmed everything she'd told Ruthie about Derek Wicks, all learned from her sister, Michelle Doss. The men were quickly on their way to the capital city where Michelle was expecting them.

In Tallahassee, the original posse of three became four with the addition of Leon County's Detective Bill Wayne. They all loaded into his official sedan and descended upon Michelle Doss's residence in an upscale Tallahassee neighborhood.

Michelle was eager to help. She said she knew Derek Wicks from school but didn't move in his circle. She also remembered his wife, Pauline, though the women had not graduated from the same class. Michelle's blue-green eyes watered when she talked of the woman's death. She felt sure Derek was somehow the cause. Riddle asked her to explain her suspicions.

"I work in the same office with another girl from Bronson, Veronica Ciresi. I found out last year that she and Derek were having an affair," Michelle said. "They still are."

"How do you know this?" Riddle asked.

"Veronica told me. We're work friends, but not close friends. We go on break together sometimes, down in the cafeteria. I've kept her secret to myself. It wasn't my story to tell." Michelle's mesmerizing eyes misted again. "I keep thinking that if I'd said something sooner, maybe Pauline wouldn't be dead. But who knows? Anyway, Veronica told me that after he settles Pauline's affairs, she and Derek are planning to get married." Michelle's eyes widened. "I was shocked! And a little bit afraid. I didn't know what to do with the information, so I talked to Millie, my sister. And here we are now . . ."

The investigators thanked Michelle for her cooperation. Said they might need her help again soon.

〜

During lunch at a small College Avenue café, which was Bill Wayne's recommendation for authentic Cuban sandwiches, the men hashed over the conversations they'd had with sisters Millie and Michelle. The interviews had confirmed critical information—the Derek Wicks case was beginning to unravel.

Through the restaurant's front window, the Capitol's dome was visible in the near distance. The men watched as a steeplejack, who from their perspective was the size of an ant, clung to the building's crowning flagpole.

"He's paintin' it," Bill Wayne mumbled, his mouth full of fried pickles. "No way I'd climb that high."

"Who'd even know the pole needed painting," Winston commented. "Nobody'd be able to tell the difference." The Cuban was memorable; he talked while he chewed. "I do know, though, that we ain't hanging by a thread anymore like that guy up there. I'm no investigator here, as my friend Wally pointed out earlier," he elbowed Sears, "but I think this case has moved to more solid ground."

All agreed.

"Very interesting that all the people we're questioning went to Levy High School together," Lt. Riddle said.

"So, in your investigations around the death of Pauline Wicks, y'all never came across even a hint of this connection?" Wally asked.

"No. We'd have no way of knowing anything about the sisters. One living in Pineville. One in Tallahassee. Veronica and Michelle working together. They all know Derick Wicks. What're the odds?" Riddle's fur was standing up just a little.

Winston brushed crumbs from his starched shirt, then looked around the table. "I'm the rookie here, so just humor me a second." He cleared a corner of the table and picked up the four unused spoons. "The death of Pauline Wicks appears accidental, an 'act of nature' as we say in the insurance business. Suspicious, but no evidence of wrongdoing. No motive." He laid one spoon down, horizontally. "Now, just a month after the accident, we hear from reputable people that Derek Wicks, Pauline's grieving husband, is already engaged to be married." He placed another spoon at right angles with the first. "According to Michelle Doss, her co-worker, Veronica Ciresi, is the secret fiancé of Derek Wicks." The third spoon formed a stainless-steel U. "When we find and question Veronica," Winston said, "and if she admits this, we have a plausible motive, and we nail Derek." The last spoon became a lid on a box.

"That's the simple diagram to make a case against him," admitted Riddle. "It's way more than we had before. But Veronica might duck and cover. Stand by your man and all that happy crap. Let's don't get too far ahead of ourselves."

The men were quiet. The waitress brought the check. Wally glanced at it, then put a twenty on the table.

"Here's what I'm wondering," Winston said. "Wicks is a traveling man. Anybody know how many State agencies he services? I mean, what if he's dippin' his wick in more than one place?"

The men broke into laughter.

"I may have heard the number of Tallahassee accounts when I talked to Wicks's company, but if I did, I can't recall," Archie Riddle said. "It wouldn't have been important to me at the time I interviewed them."

Wally, still grinning, said: "What if we make up a story for Veronica that Wicks *may* be seeing other women who work for the State. I've always heard a bunch of lonely women live here. Good lookin' ones, too." Wally's eyes crinkled at the corners.

"Can we do that?" Winston asked.

"I dunno...." Bill Wayne said, then mumbled something about ethics.

"Screw ethics!" Winston said. "Pauline Wicks is dead and my gut says that asshole killed her. And Bayside Life Insurance is gonna be funding the whole fuckin' fiasco."

Wally Sears made a motion for Winston to zip it.

After lunch, Bill Wayne turned off the one-way Bronough Street into a narrow concrete driveway buckled by the roots of abundant live oaks. He parked the unmarked car behind a pale blue, late-model Buick. The house was a cottage of faded green asbestos siding, its windows protected by wrought-iron ivy-embellished bars. The formidable-looking group—one uniformed officer wearing a gun, along with three men in suits—proceeded to the house and waited at the stoop for Veronica Ciresi to answer their knocking. Any neighbors able to see through the overgrown azaleas would have been more than curious.

Veronica was unprepared for company. Her blonde hair was tangled, the back flat as though she'd slept in one position all night. She wore a man's flannel shirt, a pair of wrinkled pedal-pushers, and dirty pink slippers. Winston's eyebrow went up at the sight of a sizeable marquis-cut diamond on her ring finger. His Ruthie would love a stone that large.

Acting only a little surprised, the woman let the group in without issue. Detective Wayne made introductions and explained the reason for their visit, asked if she'd mind answering a few questions.

"Not at all," Veronica said, but excused herself for a moment. She returned with bright pink lips; the ring had moved to her right hand.

Levy County's Lt. Riddle led the conversation. His tone was friendly—after all, she'd grown up in his domain. They talked a little about her background in Bronson, the way the town had changed over her thirty-two years. Veronica said her mother still lived out in the county. She visited there often.

Riddle steered Veronica around to the subject of Derek Wicks. Yes, she and Derek were friends. She'd met Pauline once, maybe. Such a tragedy! Everyone knew about her death, though. At least everyone back home. Most people in Tallahassee had never even heard of Bronson, Florida. She twisted the ring. Twisted the ring and chattered. And poor Derek. Some thought he might have been responsible. But Derek's real friends agreed he'd never hurt anyone. She knew for a fact that Derek was wrecked by what had happened to Pauline.

"When was the last time you saw or spoke to Derek Wicks?" Riddle asked.

Veronica hesitated. Closed her eyes and shook her head, trying to remember. "I saw him just this past week. Up at the Larson Building, where I work. He fixes a bunch of equipment for the State. Our bureau's duplicating machine needs replacing; we have to keep calling for service." She twirled a piece of hair around her finger: "I took my break and we talked for a little bit. He got very upset. He's having a real hard time."

"It sounds like you and Derek are close," Lt. Riddle said.

"We've known each other for a long time. Why are you asking me all this?" Her neck pinked.

"As Detective Wayne said, we're trying to close the official investigation into Pauline's death. This is nothing out of the ordinary," Riddle said.

Wally Sears, who'd kept silent, stepped in with his teddy bear smile. "This investigation *is* going on a little long. Part of the reason is that there's a rather large insurance policy on Pauline's life. Our company just needs to dot a few more i's before we write the check."

Riddle picked back up: "Sounds like you'd be a great character witness for Derek. Would you mind going with us to the Sheriff's Department? We could get an official statement from you there."

"In Bronson?" she asked.

"No, here in town," said Detective Wayne.

Veronica scanned the four faces. She twisted the ring. "I guess I should go. If it'll help Derek."

Chapter 38

At the Sheriff's Office, Detective Wayne set up an interrogation room, testing the recorder and taking orders for water and coffee. Riddle chatted with Veronica, keeping the conversation light. Next door, Winston and Wally watched and listened through a surveillance window.

Lt. Riddle began the session, asking Veronica to once again explain, for the official record, her relationship with Derek Wicks.

"For your records," she said, "Derek and I are old friends. We went to school together in Bronson." Then she meekly raised her hand. "I thought I was just giving a character reference. That we were just talking about Derek. Not about me. Why are you asking about our relationship again?"

"Well, we need to establish how you know Derek," Riddle said. "A little history that makes you qualified to speak on his behalf. You couldn't provide a character reference for someone you just met on the street. Right?"

Veronica nodded. Riddle led her gently back in time, back to Bronson, to the good old days. Then his questioning grew tougher.

"Isn't it true that you and Derek had a relationship of sorts when you were young?"

"Who told you that?" Veronica asked, a puzzled look on her face.

"We've interviewed a number of people during the course of this investigation," Riddle said.

"A bunch of us were just friends. Just hanging around together. You know, Friday night football games. Drive-in movies. Derek wasn't my boyfriend, if that's what you mean."

"Not what I heard. I heard you and Derek were having sex long before you were legal."

Veronica's face caught fire. "That's a lie, whoever said that."

"Also heard you're *still* having sex with Derek, maybe even earlier this week." Riddle crossed his arms.

"That's just jealous bullshit. People in Bronson can't stand the idea that I got a good-paying job. That I can afford nice clothes. Drive a new car."

"Would you put your hands on the table, please?" Riddle asked.

Her eyes narrowed.

"On the table."

Detective Wayne lifted her right hand. "Beautiful ring you got there."

Veronica snatched her hand away. Tucked them both between her thighs.

"What's your point?" she asked. Body language said she already knew. Loose lips . . ..

"Yeah . . ." Riddle said. "Got it on a good source that you and Derek are planning to get married. Better do it quick before Pauline's side of the bed gets too cold."

And there it went . . . Riddle drilled into a sobbing Veronica and her story was soon in his hands. She and Derek were in love. He'd told her he'd always loved her, since high school. The ring came from Tallahassee's Moonstone Jewelers on Monroe Street, less than a month earlier. Bill Wayne left the interrogation room to call the jeweler and confirm the purchase date, which turned out to be back in November. Another strike for Veronica.

Riddle threatened to arrest her for being an accessory in the murder of Pauline Wicks. She squalled a denial. Then he planted a seed with the notion that she, Veronica, might not be the only woman Derek was crazy about. The repairman had ample opportunity to meet women everywhere he went. In Tallahassee. Pineville. Madison. Derek Wicks was a man who got around. Did Veronica believe she was Derek's only mistress? Sellers Business Machines had provided them with Derek's key customer names. Other women might soon be sitting in her current seat.

With Wally's approval, Winston left the room to phone Michelle Doss. He asked her if she had any other friends in Tallahassee who might also be "friendly" with Derek Wicks, through his repair work. Maybe in another State agency? She thought about it, and said she'd make a call or two. Winston said she'd be able to reach him at the Leon County Sheriff's Department.

Veronica asked for a break. The day was wearing on. A lady from the records department escorted her to the women's restroom, then returned her to her seat. A young deputy brought her an icy bottle of Coke and a pack of cheese crackers and sat with her while Riddle and Wayne talked with Wally Sears and Winston in the adjoining room. They couldn't hold Veronica forever, and they didn't have a solid reason to arrest her. But the officers didn't believe they were getting the full story.

A deputy stuck his head inside the doorway: "There's a Miss Doss on the phone, asking for Winston Taylor." Winston jumped up and followed him to a desk. The deputy pointed out the correct flashing line.

Michelle Doss did indeed know someone else who knew Derek Wicks: her friend, Linda Flowers, out at the Department of Transportation. She gave Winston Linda's phone number.

Linda Flowers answered Winston's call on the first ring. She confirmed a guy named Derek serviced their office equipment. She called him "Derek the Dinker" because he dropped in often to check their equipment—too often in her opinion. Linda said that another employee at the end of her hall, Sharon Freed, was rumored to be very friendly with the man. Gossip was that Sharon had moved from long lunches with Derek to drinks after work, sometimes at the swanky Governor's Lounge. Whatever happened after those evenings, Sharon Freed either wasn't telling, or the rumors just hadn't filtered back to Linda's end of the hall. Winston thanked her for her help.

In the Tallahassee phone book, Winston located a Sharon Freed on Park Avenue. He wrote down the address and phone number and returned to the observation room. After he shared what he'd learned, Leon County's Bill Wayne took the contact information and headed off to call the woman. He returned with news that Freed was amenable to talking and was already on the way to the station. He moved the group to a small conference room, in agreement with Lt. Riddle that Winston and Wally could sit in on the interview.

As they waited for the woman's arrival, Winston paced with anticipation. Wally's eyes twinkled, watching him. Bill Wayne set up a tape recorder while Riddle checked back on Veronica, next door with the babysitting deputy. He assured her they only had a few more questions and would begin again shortly. The young officer had given her permission to smoke and she'd bathed the room with her exhaled haze. So far, she'd made no request for an attorney.

～

Sharon Freed was a striking redhead put together in a tight wool skirt and cashmere sweater. A simple strand of pearls lay against her ample, pointed breasts. She slid onto the metal conference room chair and tugged her skirt down. Detective Wayne thanked her for coming in and let her know their conversation would be recorded.

"Fine with me," she said. Her sideways smile revealed a slight gap between her front teeth.

Detective Wayne pressed the start button and Lt. Riddle began the interview.

Yes, she knew Derek Wicks. Knew him well, she said. The nature of their relationship? "Let's just say we enjoy each other's company."

"You're saying the relationship was sexual?" Lt. Riddle asked.

"I'm saying it *is* sexual."

Winston's eyebrows went up. Did she just wink?

"How long have you been 'enjoying' Derek's company?" Riddle asked.

Sharon looked up at the ceiling for an answer. "Almost a year?"

Riddle clarified: "Maybe since February or March of last year—1963?"

"That's about right," she smiled. "I don't keep a calendar."

"When you began your relationship, did you know Derek Wicks was a married man?"

"Not at first. But the deeper we got, he had to fess up. Derek wasn't happy in the marriage. They just got married too young. He's told me he missed out on too much."

"You do know that Derek's wife, Pauline, was killed last month?" Lt. Riddle asked.

"Yeah. That was a terrible thing for Derek. He told me they went fishing and a storm came up. She drowned."

"Have you thought that her drowning might not have been accidental? That maybe Derek was responsible for his wife's death?"

Sharon shrugged. "He's a nice guy. I can't see him doing anything to hurt a woman." She chewed her lip for a moment. Then: "No. He wouldn't do it."

"How soon after that accident did you see Derek again?"

Sharon shut one eye and screwed up her face. "I think maybe four or five days later? He came to see me. We had supper at a spaghetti place, then went to my house. He was pretty upset."

"Did you sleep together that night?" Riddle probed.

Sharon didn't hesitate: "Oh, yeah. He said he felt a little better when he left."

All four of the men exchanged glances.

"Are you aware that Derek is seeing at least one other woman besides his wife? And you, of course," Riddle said.

"He's a cute guy. He travels around. I always knew it was possible, but it doesn't matter to me. We're just having fun."

"Has Derek ever proposed marriage to you?" the lieutenant asked.

Sharon chuckled. "He's talked all around it, but he knows I'm not interested in being tied down. I like my single life. For some reason, he thinks every woman is just dying to get married. I don't need a ring."

Lieutenant Riddle smiled with her. "Do you think if Derek were to remarry, say, in the near future, the two of you would continue your relationship?"

"I think so. I mean, why not?"

"Has Derek told you that he is, in fact, engaged to another woman?"

She laughed. "You're relentless! Do I have to tell you all the pillow talk?"

Riddle waited.

"Okay, yes. I know he's been involved with a girl he knew back in high school. Veronica something. They've been a thing forever. He says he just can't let her go. He gave her a ring, but he won't ever marry her. He's kept her dangling all these years. His favorite saying is the one about free milk." Her expression was serious, but her eyes smiled.

After Detective Wayne escorted Sharon out, the room filled with big sighs, and a "whew" or two.

"She's hot to trot, now, ain't she?" Winston laughed.

The men all agreed. Wally Sears mopped his brow with a handkerchief.

Archie Riddle rewound the tape. Moments later, Riddle carried the recorder, like a ticking bomb, into the interrogation room where Veronica Ciresi still waited. Winston and Wally Sears returned to their post at the glass to observe.

∽

Veronica was agitated and complained about the hard chair. She had things to do and her weekend was evaporating. Riddle promised only one point of discussion remained. He switched on the recorder to add to Veronica's earlier questioning.

"Veronica, you've been good to share details of your relationship with Derek. Because you've been so honest, we think you deserve to know a truth about him that you might not be aware of," Riddle said gently. Then, on the second machine, he played the tape of Sharon Freed's questioning.

Veronica cocked her head, listening. She looked confused. As the voice of Sharon Freed continued, Veronica shook her head back and forth, then shot up from her chair: "No! No! She made this up!"

Bill Wayne put his arm around her shoulder. She shook him off. He settled her back into her seat.

"That lying mother *fucker*," she cried. "He's always been a liar! Since we were kids." She wiped her nose on the back of her hand. She accepted Bill Wayne's handkerchief. "I thought he'd outgrown it. I believed what he said—he only wanted me."

Riddle maintained a solemn face, kept the recorder running through her crying, and the tapering into silence.

Then he said quietly: "Veronica, we need you to help us. Pauline is dead, and we don't believe it was an accident. We're trying to find out the truth. Anything you can tell us about this . . ."

"I can't. Derek would go crazy. I just can't." Her body visibly shook.

"Don't be afraid," Detective Wayne said. "We can protect you. Don't you worry."

Minutes passed in silence.

Veronica spoke quietly. "I hate him. I hate his lying, fuckin' guts."

Riddle picked up the questioning again. "Did Derek ever talk about killing Pauline?"

Winston put his hand on his stomach to quieten its angry roil.

Another long silence, then: "He talked about it a million times. How to get rid of her."

"What did he tell you he was planning to do?"

Veronica sniveled and wiped her eyes with the detective's now-soggy cotton handkerchief. "Crazy stuff. He actually did something to her brakes one time, hoping she'd have a wreck. But nothing happened. She ran through a stop sign. She didn't even hit anything."

"What else?"

"I can't remember . . .," she whispered. Then her breath hitched: "He wanted to pay somebody to shoot her. But he couldn't find anybody who'd do it. Anybody he'd trust anyway."

Veronica's face was pale, eyes swollen.

"Did he plan to kill her on the day they went fishing, the day she died?"

She looked long at Riddle, maybe considering the cost of her words. "Pauline wanted a baby. Kept pushing him. But Derek didn't want it. He never wanted any kids. What he wanted was for us to be together," she said with fresh tears running down her face. She looked at the second recorder. "At least that's what he made me believe . . . He said he couldn't bring himself to tell her, though. He'd been with her for so long. He couldn't hurt her feelings like that."

Veronica put her fingers over her closed eyes. Her words had flattened into a monotone. "She didn't want to go fishing. She liked to fish, but she didn't want to go. He talked her into it anyway. He'd had enough. He said it was time he did something about her."

Winston bent his head and shut his eyes. The murder he'd imagined was real: the terrified woman tied to the boat. Her head bashed in. The Glastron tossed upside down. His own lungs struggled for air.

"Did Derek tell you how he killed her?"

"No." Veronica stared at the wall beyond the two officers. "Not exactly. I told him I didn't want to hear any details, or I'd never be able to live with him. He said that what he started, the storm finished."

Riddle let that statement sit while the tape recorder continued to roll. Then: "How do you feel now, knowing he's responsible?"

Veronica took time with the question, then said: "I feel dead inside . . . and I'm afraid that when he knows I told you, he might try to kill me, too."

∽

Just before nine, Winston called Ruthie from Tallahassee. He gave her a quick summary of what had happened. The Leon County Sheriff's Department was "providing protection" for Veronica until Derek Wicks was located and arrested for murder.

"He killed his own wife," Ruthie said. "That poor, poor woman."

"It's looking like it. I can't quite understand all this legal talk. But they have Veronica's statement that he did it—I mean he took her out in the Gulf to kill her, but he had the help of the storm. And Veronica said he'd tried a couple of times before." Winston heard Mary Carolyn chirping like a bird in the background. "I don't think they're done with Veronica either; she might be an accessory or something. I'm not sure."

Ruthie yawned into the phone. "Sorry . . . I'm tired. I let Mary Carolyn have Angela here all day to play. They wore me out with all the noise."

He smiled. "Tell her I'll sneak in and give her a kiss when I get home. Leave a light on for me."

Chapter 39

While the majority of Pineville was in church, the sinners and the saved, Louis entered the library's back door using his officially issued key. How strange to be the only soul in the building; the library wouldn't open until two o'clock.

Not a bad gig, he thought, roaming around in the stacks, the smell of paper and glue and floor wax enough to make a person high. No wonder Evelyn Pierpont was always so animated.

Louis lost himself for almost an hour on the main floor in the local history section, flipping through pages of the past. He knew the local economy had long relied upon forestry for lumber and paper products. But he'd never heard about the once-lucrative turpentine business. Long ago the sticky resin was used for boatbuilding. Growers slashed the pines to induce the ooze of turpentine, which was the tree's way of healing its wounds.

Huh . . . you cut; you bleed; you clot. Nature's way. A good analogy for how he'd survived two life-altering traumas. His wounds were healing nicely.

✍

The story of Hampton Springs drew him in. A few locals had mentioned the legendary resort, but the past came alive in grainy photographs he found of a grand 1908 hotel flanked by palms, palmettos, and majestic oaks wrapped in Spanish moss. Even that long ago, the property had its own power and water plant. The sulphur spring water was said to be a cure for rheumatism. Visitors came by train from North Florida and South Georgia. Legislators from Tallahassee congregated there to settle political issues. Over time, the resort deteriorated and was destroyed by fire in 1954.

Louis shut the book; he'd read more another time. History this old was not what he needed. He hustled up the stairs to the newspapers.

✍

The microfilming process was tedious and unrewarding. What the hell was he thinking? He shouldn't have to trade work for the chance to put his hands on public information. Two hours at the camera flew by while he griped to himself about equality. But until he was willing to *do* something about it, to help bring change, he had no room to complain. Now was just not the right time. He needed first to establish himself, his credibility, and his new life in Pineville.

Louis logged his time, then fell to work on his own project scanning *Pineville Times* headlines. Somewhere, there had to be *something* on what he wanted. Where? He went back to all issues of October 1961. He'd already been through these same pages on his last trip, but maybe he'd been tired and just missed it.

Nothing.

Finally, in a late-November paper, his roving eyes landed on the bolded words: MISSING MAN. He took a deep breath and read . . . about a man reported missing from a nursing home over in Madison. Damn it. He laid the paper on the worktable and looked at his watch. The library would be opening soon. One more issue . . . and he stumbled over DEAD MAN: *The Foley County Sheriff's Department was called to the scene of a house near Buckhead mill, where a neighbor noticed a bad smell coming from the house next door—*

Something touched his shoulder.

Startled, Louis whirled from the worktable, almost knocking Evelyn Pierpont onto the floor. "I'm so sorry!" they both said, and she stooped to pick up the pages he'd dropped, which lay like the spread wings of a great bird.

"Lordy, you scared me," he breathed. His forehead glistened despite the room's chill.

"I didn't mean to," she said. "I thought you heard me come up the stairs." She studied the bold dead-man headlines in her hands. "You looked very intent . . ."

"No, no," he said, running a hand across the top of his head. "I was finishing up my work. Just reading some stuff that caught my eye."

The story of the missing man lay open on the table. She moved closer to it, put a finger on the caption.

"Louis, what is it you're after here? It must be something important." Her eyes narrowed as she studied his face, as if she could see into his thoughts.

"I don't know what you mean," he said, glancing toward the stairs. She had hemmed him in.

"I've thought a lot about this, about your working on this dreadfully dull project for almost no money, just to have access to local history." She cocked her head. "The librarian in me wants to believe it . . ."

The table was at his back; he didn't know what to do with his hands.

"If you'd just tell me what you want to know, I could probably help you find the answers. Are you in some kind of trouble, Louis? Is that it?"

The noise in his ears could be a jail cell door clanging shut. "No ma'am! No disrespect, Miss Pierpont, but you've got me all wrong. I apologize if I've caused you to worry. I'm gonna go ahead and clean up all these papers. I've been here way too long." He turned his back and began straightening the worktable, folding the yellowing issues. In a moment, he heard her shoes clacking down the wooden stairs.

✍

When Louis had screwed up the courage to enter her office, Pierpont acted as though nothing out of the ordinary had happened on the floor above.

"You calling it quits?" she asked, shuffling papers on her desk. Her neck was splotched. She opened her desk drawer and stirred the contents, then shut it.

Louis shrugged, following her act. "Yessum. I've read a lot about Pineville and Foley County. I think the past is always interesting," he said. "I've learned that community volunteers made a big difference in quality of life, for the county as a whole and for individuals needing help. They still do. I think that's what I've been feeling about this place, why I like this town. People care."

"Oh, yes . . .," she said, smoothing her graying hair, glancing at him and then away. "Kiwanis, Lions Club . . . people are very civic minded."

Louis cleared his throat. "Look, Miss Pierpont, I just want to thank you again for the chance to come in here. For your trust in me. I hope I helped make some progress on the microfilming project, but I know I gained much more than you did during my time here." He pulled the library door key off his keyring and laid it on her desk.

"As a newcomer who's been helped by people like you, and in the spirit of community service that makes Pineville tick, I'm donating my hours of work here. Please don't send me a check."

On the way out the front door, he waved goodbye to the "liberry" girl.

Louis sat in his car. Didn't see that coming, he thought, wiping his hands down his dark pants. What a waste of time, too. The answer to his most haunting question was still out of reach.

Sure, he'd learned enough to rock his world in just that one newspaper he'd carried back from Tallahassee last week:

Fred Graham dead. The law would be back on that assault case like somebody'd bumped a hive of bees. He imagined they'd reclassify it from assault to murder. Maybe he needed a lawyer. But a lawyer in this town would be sure to spread the news at supper club and BAM: Winston Taylor would be one of the first to know.

But what about the rest of what he'd been searching for? How could someone just disappear into thin air?

What had happened to Jackson Smith?

Late that evening, the parking lot at Magnolia Place was brightly lit. Louis was cheered by the building's nice exterior. Winston had said she suffered from dementia . . . would she even remember him? He was taking a huge risk with this visit. He pushed through the front entrance and headed for the registration desk.

"Evening," he said, addressing the attendant. "Could you point me to Mabel Griffin's room?"

The white-uniformed receptionist told him visiting hours were long over. Residents needed their rest. She resumed her crossword puzzle.

"If you'd just let me see her a few minutes, I promise I won't wake her if she's asleep. You'd be doing me a big favor." He gave her his best earnest look.

She eyed him for a moment, then told him to sign in. "Room 112."

Louis made his way down a poorly lit corridor that smelled of decay, mixed with a pine-scented coverup. The muffled noise of coughs and TV's canned laughter leaked from the rooms.

Mabel's door stood ajar, and Louis looked through the opening. The room was dark except for the glow of equipment lights on the wall behind the metal headboards of two single beds. The bed nearest him was filled with a large lump of cover, the one by the window stood empty. His eyes adjusted to the gloom, and he saw her dark face. She snored softly. Her hair was a halo of snow.

He stepped inside.

What was he doing here? Winston had told him Mabel Griffin's mind was a mess, that she had no idea where she was living. She sometimes thought she was cooking in her own kitchen, or she was tracking down her long-dead daughter. She often talked to her grandson that nobody'd seen in several years. Chances were slim that she'd ever return to her home. Louis had to see for himself.

He moved close to the bed, his insides quivering. His last glimpse of her was when he and his friend had painted her house. She'd picked the color: robin's-egg blue. Had it been almost three years? She'd made them buttermilk cornbread and pork chops with rice and lima beans. He could taste the bacon seasoning on his tongue even now.

Mabel Griffin was his one last hope for finding out what had happened. And here she lay, corpse-like, supposedly without a lick of sense. Squeezing her for information would be cruel . . . but what if Winston was wrong? What if she knew more than anyone realized?

He put his hand on her warm arm, but she didn't stir. He squeezed it gently, and she sputtered and rolled her head toward him. Were her eyelids cracked open?

"Hello," Louis whispered, leaning closer.

Mabel's eyes popped open, startling him. She raised her head, then slumped back into the pillow. "Where've you been?" she asked, her tone accusing.

His mouth curled up at the corners. "I been off to see the world. But now I come to see you. Find you here in this fancy hotel, people waitin' on you, feedin' you. Goodness gracious, you got it made." He stroked her hand.

"Food's terrible," she grimaced.

Louis pulled a misshapen peanut butter sandwich from his coat pocket and unwrapped the waxed paper. He pinched off a piece of the bread and held it beneath her nose to smell. "Try this."

Mabel stuck out her tongue in acceptance. She rolled the food around in her toothless mouth, smacking. Louis offered her water from a cup on her nightstand and helped her sip it. He put the cup back, next to a glass holding a set of dentures.

"Good?"

"Uh-huh." She opened her mouth for more, and he stood there and fed her—a baby bird—until the sandwich was gone.

She shut her eyes, and soon she breathed through her mouth again.

Louis leaned against the bedrail and stared at her. His face was wet.

"Can I ask you a question before I go?"

She looked at him.

"Where is Jackson Smith?"

Mabel studied his face. "My Jack," she said, then smiled. "A smart boy . . . gone off to school. But he always comes back to see his granny."

Louis pulled the blanket up beneath her chin. He patted her shoulder. "Sweet dreams, sweet lady. I'll be back soon."

He wiped his nose on his sleeve and left.

Chapter 40

February ended, and Mother Nature closed the door on North Florida's coldest days. The sun shone bright and the days warmed, though spring weather was often unpredictable. People sported shorts and sandals but knew better than to mothball the sweaters.

On the first Monday in March, Roger Johns called Winston with the December through February sales competition results.

"You did it! You and Louis friggin' did it!" Roger said. "And, well, we have to add in the couple of new accounts A. F. opened, but those were minimal. You both won the fishing trip!"

The boss's voice was so enthusiastic, Winston could hear dollar signs rolling like a Jersey slot machine. He reared back in his chair and grinned: "Hot damn!" He shot Louis a thumbs-up and watched his agent beam. "Hold on, Roger," he said, covering the mouthpiece. "Get your glad rags on! We're going deep-sea fishing," Winston announced to Louis, who hopped up and danced around the room.

Winston listened, nodding and making notes. "Yep, yep. It's gonna be a great time. What's even greater is what we're taking to the bank."

Louis's eyes were riveted on Winston's face. The call ended. The two men sat and stared at each other, then burst into laughter.

"I tell you, Louis, I thought I had a winner when I found you. Today the proof is in the puddin'—you're a superstar."

Louis ducked his head, accepting the tribute.

"You and I both had the top sales in our region. In the whole damn region, Louis. We beat 'em all. I'm so proud of you, buddy. Hell, I'm proud of us both," Winston said.

"What about the money? I mean, the trip is nice and all, but it's the money I care about," said Louis.

"Of course! We're each gonna get a fifteen percent bonus, coming next week. It'll be a separate check, not in your regular pay."

Louis thought about it, then: "What if I didn't want to take the trip. Could I cash in the value of that and add it to my bonus check?"

"Why wouldn't you take the trip? You deserve a little R&R. You've been working your ass off."

"I know, but I could use the money. I'm trying to build up some cash, give myself a cushion. Save for my own place to live. The boarding house is nice, but I'm tired of not having any privacy. And then there's Etta . . ."

"Well, the short answer is NO. The company never lets us do that. They encourage getting to know other salespeople, sharing knowledge, all that. It'll be good for you," Winston smiled. "You need a chance to see that Bayside Life is a company bigger than just the two of us in this little bitty office. And you and I'll get to know each other a little better. Talk about stuff not related to work."

⌒

Winston and Dan Nettles met up for lunch at the Ham House. They hadn't seen each other in weeks. Though Dan knew Derek Wicks had been arrested for murder, he hung on Winston's every word about what had happened in Tallahassee.

"Oh man, I wish I'd been there to watch that show unfold," Dan said. "It sure was fun, that trip we took to Cedar Key. Not ha-ha fun, of course; you had a bad situation to deal with. But just fun being on the road with you, watching you work. Nice that it wasn't my ass on the line for a change," he chuckled.

"Yeah, I was glad you went along. You, but mostly your service weapon," Winston grinned.

"I knew damn well I smelled a skunk in that woodpile— Wicks is crazy," Dan said, slathering butter on his last chunk of cornbread. "There's lots of normal-looking people out there, capable of horrible things. And you'd never even know it to look at 'em, or to hear 'em talk. Somebody like you, for instance," he said, crumbling the bread into the small bowl of collard greens.

Winston swallowed his food, looking at him. "Not somebody like me."

"Oh yeah, somebody like you—a nice-looking, well-dressed, family man. Somebody lots of people know and like. You coulda killed somebody and buried 'em in your back yard, and nobody'd ever guess you did it."

Winston covered the rest of his food with his napkin. "Jesus, man. Pick somebody else for your hypotheticals. You're giving me the willies."

Dan laughed. "Just joshing you . . . but, hey . . . remember what I was telling you about the skin diving? I'm really doin' it. Priscilla ain't happy about it, but what the hay. Our team's going on a trip to Wakulla Springs, south of Tallahassee. We're gonna dive down there where they made Tarzan movies. Back in the 30s. That's gonna be crazy."

"I hear you," Winston said. "And I still think *you're* crazy. If man was meant to breathe under water, we'd have been born with gills."

Winston made a mental note to get Ruthie to talk to Priscilla. Somebody needed to pull the plug on Dan's latest adventure. Hell, the man might be diving Blue Sink before long, find himself nose to nose with the remains of one Jackson Smith. Dark dread filled him.

Back at the office, he fretted over the slim possibility of the car and the body being discovered by the Sheriff's amateur dive team—no better than a bunch of Cub Scouts. The Sheriff didn't need his own damn divers. Good god, they weren't but a stone's throw from multiple state law enforcement teams in Tallahassee. Let those guys come if a need arose to hunt for bodies under water. Old Ramsey was just wasting taxpayer money. Building his kingdom. Dive trips—what a bunch of hooey.

Winston looked up the number for the *Pineville Times.* He hesitated, then called the reporter he'd worked with before, Tom Reynolds. The guy's article about Louis saving their customer, Rita Owens, had been accurate and professional.

"Hey, Winston! Good to hear from you," said Reynolds. "What's happening in the world of insurance?"

"Nothing exciting. But I was just wondering . . . if I were to give you an idea for a local story, would you keep my name out of it? You know, like an anonymous tip or something. You'd have to do some research, but I think readers might be interested in how the Sheriff spends our money . . . and the new underwater diving team he's putting together."

Reynolds laughed. "A diving team? What in the world brought this to your attention? And why would you even care? I mean, it sounds pretty neat to me."

Winston was startled by the reporter's response and felt his neck prickle. "I just heard it on the street. I thought it sounded risky. Taking inexperienced deputies and training 'em to dive for bodies, when there's surely experts not fifty miles from here with the Florida Law Enforcement Department who have their own equipment. Is our Sheriff's Department flush with cash? I'd think diving gear is expensive. And really, how often do we have drowning victims around here?"

"Huh. I didn't think about it like that. I'll be sure to check it out. But keep in mind, this is a small town with small-town politics. Our editor may not be keen on unnecessarily raising the ire of Sheriff Ramsey. And aside from the potential budget questions, it really doesn't sound like a bad move on Ramsey's part. I think this could make for a good read. Thanks for the tip, Winston."

"Hey, don't forget . . . I don't want my name mentioned. I'm just a *concerned citizen.*"

When they hung up, Winston's face felt hot. His call to the newspaper had likely just backfired. He avoided local politics for good reason, but this was a little different. This was personal. He hated the idea of his best friend underwater, dragging his every breath from a can strapped to his back. And he sure as hell didn't want anyone rooting around in the bottom of Blue Sink. Though there wasn't much he could do to stop either from happening, he owed it to himself to at least try.

A couple of days after the winners of the sales competition were announced, Roger called with details of the fishing trip. March 13th, a Friday. They'd be staying two nights at the elite El Camino hotel on Jacksonville Beach. Their charter boat would depart from a nearby marina at six on Saturday morning for a full day of fishing. Let the alcohol flow!

"Man, I'm really looking forward to this," Winston told Roger. "I've lived my whole life close to the coast, but I've never been deep sea fishing. I know Louis's never done anything like that either. I think he's a little apprehensive for some reason."

"He already out on his route?"

"Yeah, been gone a little while. The guy doesn't need a boss. He's self-policing," Winston laughed.

Roger cleared his throat. "We've, uh, run into a little problem with the trip planning. Just a logistical issue . . . but something we think we've settled to everybody's satisfaction."

While he listened for Roger to spit it out, he sketched a boat on the corner of his desk blotter, with waves lapping against its hull.

"Turns out the owners of the El Camino don't cotton to coloreds," Roger said.

Winston put down his pencil. "What? What does that mean?"

"Means we had to find another place for Louis to sleep. We've located a nice little motor court about three miles down the beach. They'll be glad to take him."

Winston was stunned. This was his agent Roger was talking about, his agent who'd won the trip. This was Louis. Winston's stomach began to burn like someone had given it a squirt of lighter fluid, then struck a match.

"You're saying we're just gonna dump the man off down the road. At a fleabag motel. While the rest of us assholes live it up?" Winston's steam was building, a train about to leave the station. "What, we're gonna feed him leftovers from our table? Let him on the boat, but he's gotta bait all the hooks?" Winston's voice rose. "Roger, I can't believe you're even considering this. I can't fuckin' believe it." Winston choked the receiver. "This is one of your top salespeople. In the whole goddamn state. And you're going to lay down and let this happen?" His last words drew blood.

"Simmer down! We've worked out the kinks with El Camino for him to join all the activities. They just wouldn't make an exception for him to sleep there. That's the only difference."

"That's just fuckin' dandy."

"Winston, look. Bayside signed a contract with the El Camino several months ago for this event. We're past the cancellation period; we can't up and move to another site. Our legal guys looked into it. It'd be too expensive for us to get out of the arrangement."

"That's a piss-poor excuse and I'm calling bullshit. The fix is unacceptable in my book. I'm embarrassed for the whole damn company."

Roger's voice was an octave higher: "Let me remind you who you're talking to. We might be friends, but I, by God, am your boss. I've done my best to remedy this. I agree it's a screwup, but this is the way the event's gonna work. The way it *has* to work."

"Well, we aren't fuckin' going."

Winston put the phone down with a firm click. He snatched his center drawer open and rummaged for an old pack of stale cigarettes. Bitter smoke rose.

Chapter 41

Winston held firm on his refusal to participate in the Jacksonville fishing trip. He didn't care if he got fired over it. Well . . . he cared, but he knew the disagreement wouldn't come to that. He and Louis were too valuable to Bayside Life Insurance. He tried to talk Roger into giving them the cash equivalent of the trip, but Brian Benson wouldn't approve it. If management made that exception, and other agents found out, they'd want the cash too. Stalemate.

As much as he hated it, Winston shared the situation with Louis: the event hotel didn't allow colored people and Winston had therefore cancelled his and Louis's participation in the whole corporate celebration.

"I'll tell you, Louis, if I were you, I'd pack my shit and move up north. I've heard colored people aren't treated like this up there. Seriously, if I were a Negro, I'd be in jail. I'd have killed somebody by now. I'd be the meanest man that walked."

"It's okay, boss. Just another example of racial divide," Louis said, trying to shrug it off. "Trust me, there's lots of men in jail right now for what you just said." He managed a chuckle. "But it doesn't get you anywhere. That's why Dr. King preaches peace. Violence doesn't produce positive change."

"You're an outstanding salesman, Louis. You could sell anything. But if you really like insurance, you could think about working for one of the Negro-owned companies. There's Supreme Life Insurance, up in Chicago. Hell, there's even one in North Carolina, in Durham, I think. Of course, the white people there might be as bad or worse than here in Florida. Who knows?"

"I hear what you're saying," Louis said, "and I appreciate it. But I'm just starting to make a life here. I got people around me now who care. I'm crazy over Etta." He looked down for a moment, then met Winston's eyes. "I think I'm gonna marry her. She's got deep roots here, and someday Miz Ruby's gonna hand down her businesses to Etta and Bubba. Their mama's been gone a long time, and there ain't nobody else but Ruby's brother, Jimps. He's about worthless."

Winston nodded, a lump in his throat. The idea of Louis and Etta building a life together was satisfying but bittersweet: Jackson Smith had hoped for a future, too. Winston had to settle for knowing he had at least been instrumental in helping this young man who was standing here in the flesh.

"Maybe we ought to go on over to Jacksonville. Play nice. Ain't no big deal, boss. Save you from being on the hot seat. I'll be just fine."

"Nuh uh. I've already decided. I registered my protest. I ain't backin' down."

∽

Four days before the scheduled Jacksonville event, Roger called with an olive branch.

"I hate it that you and Louis aren't joining us in Jacksonville. I do understand, Winston, and I respect your decision. But I've got another option for you . . ."

Roger had rented a two-bedroom house for Winston and Louis to share on Dekle Beach, not more than twenty-five miles from Pineville. He'd also arranged a charter boat with a guide for a private fishing expedition. The dates matched the Jacksonville event. Skin color was not a problem—Roger had been sure to check.

"Please say yes, Winston. You and Louis both need a break, and this will give y'all time to get to know one another on a different level. Whaddaya say?"

Winston didn't hesitate. "Thank you, Roger. We'll take it."

∽

On Friday, Winston and Louis called their accounts early and hung a "closed" sign on the door. Louis left for a previously scheduled appointment, trying to close another new policy sale before they left for their weekend trip. Winston hung back, tidying up the bank deposit he'd make on the way out of town.

"Bayside Life Insurance, Winston Taylor," he said, catching a call on the second ring.

"Good morning, Mr. Taylor. This is Dorothy Halston. I'm calling from Magnolia Place. I'm sorry—"

"Is this about Mabel Griffin? Is she okay?" He rubbed his forehead.

"Oh, yessir! Mrs. Griffin is fine, far as I know. I didn't mean to worry you. As I was saying, I'm sorry it's taken me so long to call. I understand you asked for her visitor report."

"Yeah, Dr. Samuels and I talked about that recently. But since I hadn't heard anything from y'all, I assumed nobody'd been there to see her."

"It's true, she doesn't get many visitors. In the past three weeks, only a few people have signed in to see her."

"Go ahead," Winston said. He grabbed a scratch pad but didn't expect anything worth writing down.

"Yessir. These are mostly just the same people: Libby Hart, her social worker; Dr. Reynolds, the orthopedic specialist; and Reverend Canton from Hampton Springs AME. He visits all the colored patients about once a month, whether he's invited or not," she giggled. "We've got you on the list, of course."

"That it?"

"No sir. Mrs. Griffin had a new visitor just recently. A Mr. Louis Fisher."

Winston stiffened. "When?"

"Uh . . . it was on a Sunday evening, after visiting hours. A couple weeks ago. Do you need the date?"

"No, that's okay. Just please keep me posted on anybody new." He thanked her and hung up.

Why in hell would Louis visit Mabel? She wasn't his customer. He had no business there. A worm of concern writhed within Winston. He leaned back in his chair, trying to make sense of it.

Louis was a smart man. He apparently hadn't believed Winston's reason for keeping Mabel's accounts for himself. Especially not when he, Louis, had been assigned all the other customers near where Mabel lived. But why would he *not* believe it? Why would he even care? That was probably the most important question.

Louis helped Winston reconcile accounts on Fridays. He saw the regular payments Winston collected on Mabel and on her grandson Jackson's policy. He had no idea that Winston was actually making both of those premium payments out of his own pocket. To the naked eye, none of it was suspicious. Not now anyway . . ..

Almost three years ago, though, Jackson Smith's life insurance was a "special policy." Nobody knew anything about that. Winston had fixed it. He'd fixed all his special policies. He'd paid back what he'd taken. His face went hot at the thought of it. God, what a mistake he'd made.

But what if—back when Roger had been in charge of the office—he'd been suspicious of Winston's premium collections? His ethics? Maybe Roger was suspicious even now.

Winston squeezed his forehead and talked to the empty room: "Is Roger using Louis to help investigate *me*? *Me*?" He looked around his office. *His* domain. "No fuckin' way." Couldn't be . . . could it?

Winston got up and headed to the back, where all customer records were housed in a tall cabinet. He alone was responsible for those documents, he kept them neatly in alphabetical order. He opened the top drawer and checked the files on three insureds that were once "special policies." Today, of course, they were real policyholders, properly insured and alive and well. Their files looked fine. In the second drawer, he located Mabel's file in the G's, just where it should be. But right behind it, completely out of order, was the file on Jackson Smith. He pulled both folders and examined the contents. Nothing appeared to be missing. But someone had definitely been nosing around in those folders. Louis? Or Roger Johns? Why?

Winston's heart was a bird in a cage.

The beach house directions took the two prize-winning agents close to the end of a point jutting out into the Gulf. Winston steered the Studebaker down the paved road until the asphalt dwindled into hardpacked limestone and crushed oyster shells. They passed a string of pastel houses, then located their rental by its numbered pink mailbox. Winston turned into a rough driveway bordered by palmettos and tall palms. The pink cottage sat high on stilts as slender as flamingo legs. They parked the car and climbed the steep wooden steps, ten or twelve feet up, to a small front deck. Winston let them in with the key he'd picked up at the marina store.

They stepped into a kitchen and living room combination with pebble-patterned linoleum, furnished with a beige corduroy couch, navy blue butterfly chairs, and a coffee table covered with a partially finished jigsaw puzzle of what appeared to be the prow of a fishing trawler. The name, *Dream Boat*, was just visible in the puzzle.

The common room then opened onto a covered screened porch that ran the length of the house, with white swings at both ends and an oversized picnic table in the middle. Beyond the porch, a wooden deck waited with chairs for soaking up the sun or enjoying a mesmerizing view of the Gulf of Mexico. This outside living area was the real reason to stay.

The wind gusted through the screens, rattling the loose-fitting screen door. Big-breasted waves waltzed toward land, rose with curled white lips, then crashed into the sand. Down the beach, a spot of black pepper moved—a dog chasing seagulls.

"Too bad we're not going surfing," Louis said, studying the scene.

"You ever been?" Winston asked. Louis seemed too buttoned-up to waste time on a frivolous activity like surfing, but anything was possible. After almost four months together, Winston felt he should know much more about the guy's past. And after today's phone call from the nursing home, he needed to fast-track his Louis Fisher education.

"I was joking you," Louis said. "But nah, I've never been surfing and don't plan to start now. Looks a little rough for fishing, boss." His brow furrowed.

Though Winston laughed at Louis, he thought the man could be right—the Gulf was usually much more placid. "It's gonna be fine. Whitey said there's some system out in the Gulf kicking up the wind and waves, but he's following the weather. Might get a little rain tonight. Prediction is this'll move north PDQ and be calm by morning." He knew Louis had been skittish about the trip since he'd first heard about it.

"Channel Six said it's going to be a great weekend. I know you're not into television, but you ought to at least watch the morning weather. Know how to dress yourself," he said with a smirk. When Louis didn't play along, he added: "Whitey's a professional guide, and we're gonna catch us some fish tomorrow."

Louis ran his hand over the top of his head. "We done caught us some fish for the last three months, and I still got a few potential customers on the line. Ain't we 'bout caught our limit?" He gave Winston a sideways grin.

"Exactly why we deserve this trip, a little R&R. We are *good,* man. Just enjoy the hell out of this," Winston said, turning from the scene. "Let's get our gear and groceries, then we're gonna have a few beers, maybe make us a toddy, and sit right out here till we can't stay upright no more," he grinned.

Ruthie had cooked and packed all their food. Baked ham and potato salad. Ham biscuits for breakfast. Thick slabs of sour cream pound cake. Sleeves of peanuts to pair with their bottled Budweiser. Winston had hidden a new bottle of Jack Daniels in his duffel bag—didn't want Ruthie to think the two men were going on a drunk. But he planned to let loose. Maybe even get tight-lipped Louis's tongue to wag.

Winston had promised himself that he wouldn't attack Louis about visiting Mabel. He was desperate for the reason why but knew if he lost control of his temper, he'd only come across as paranoid and suspicious. Winston fully expected, however, to go home with a firm understanding of what, or who, sent Louis to Mabel's bedside.

They sat in the deck chairs awhile, drinking ice-cold Bud, absorbing heat from the afternoon sun. Louis wore long cotton pants, a light-weight long-sleeved shirt, and a wide-brimmed canvas hat with the string tied under his chin to keep from losing it. Winston was bare headed, his recent crew-cut glistening with tiny beads of sweat. He'd pulled off his shirt and sat just in khaki shorts, bare legs stretched out in front of him. Dark hair matted his chest; his skin carried the remains of last summer's tan.

A screen door slammed at the house next door. A small blonde girl with her doll appeared at her deck railing. She waved at them. They waved back. Winston thought the girl looked younger than Mary Carolyn. Maybe four or thereabouts. She navigated the steep steps one at a time until she reached the sand, maybe to come over for a visit. A young woman, likely her mother, hurried out the door, called the child back up the steps and into the house.

The more beers they killed the more Winston craved a cigarette. He'd already decimated a number of toothpicks. On his last bathroom break, he'd brought back a pack of Camels and his lighter. "You can't have a beer, you can't have a beer, you can't have a beer without the other . . ." he sang, then took a big drag. "I shoulda been a singer instead of a salesman."

Louis shook his head.

They talked about work. Both were obsessed with it. Winston tried to steer the conversation toward Louis's private life by talking about his own world. About his father, a strict man who'd taught him discipline, how to hunt and fish. How to never give up on anything he wanted, once he figured out what that thing was.

"Never do anything half-assed," Winston said and lit another cigarette. He snapped his lighter shut and slid it into his pocket. "He must've told me that a million times." His dad, dead almost ten years now.

Winston switched gears, entertaining Louis with his often-told stories of living with two females, how toilet paper was in great demand. About his hunting trips. About his friendship with Dan Nettles, who always made him laugh.

Louis spoke of the here and now. About Etta. His friendship with her brother. His respect for and adoration of Miz Ruby, who had basically adopted him.

Winston tolerated it, barely listening. He was waiting for Louis to offer up some connection to Mabel Griffin. Emboldened by alcohol, he wanted to jump up and seize Louis, shake it out of him. But he didn't want to ruin the whole trip. And the truth was, he was afraid of the answer.

"That's some boring shit, Louis," Winston said suddenly. "You're putting me to sleep." He drained the bottle in his hand.

Louis laughed, uncomfortable with this side of Winston. "What? I got a nice life. Nothing to complain about."

"I already know all that crap. We been sitting out here all afternoon, and I've told you about my whole damn life. You ain't said shit about anything that happened before you hit Pineville." Winston opened another beer. Lit up again. He gave Louis a one-eyed squint. "What you got going on that's such a fuckin' secret?"

Louis straightened. "Are we on *To Tell the Truth*?" He looked around. "I don't see any cameras." He wasn't smiling.

Winston didn't respond. He understood too late that he'd nearly lost control of himself. He had vowed not to make accusations about Louis visiting Mabel, wouldn't voice his fears aloud. But he had crossed a line with Louis. The man was a hard nut to crack. Winston touched his pocket, feeling for the lucky buckeye.

∽

They sat without speaking, watching the sky, lit with orange from the west. The surf's symphony continued. The wind blew cooler.

"I'm starving," Winston said. "Let's eat."

Louis agreed.

They moved into the house to consume Ruthie's feast. Winston brought out the bottle of Jack, found jelly glasses, and poured them both two inches of amber.

"To Bayside Life!" they toasted, clinking glasses and tossing down the contents. Winston looked Louis straight in the eyes and poured them another. They toasted their own individual success, then their teamwork. The puzzle caught their attention for a time, Louis on the couch and Winston on the sandy floor. They toasted every time one of them found a piece of the puzzle that fit. Louis snapped the last shape into place that added a white life ring to the still-incomplete scene.

"Going to bed," Winston mumbled, hefting himself up from the floor, losing his balance, regaining it, then weaving toward his bedroom. "Up early, man. Sis . . . shit." He took a breath. "*Six* ah'clock," he said, holding onto the wall.

The lump of Louis slumped further into the couch. His head rested against the furniture's arm. His eyes followed Winston down the hallway that might have been ten miles long.

Chapter 42

Winston's eyes cracked open to nothing; his mind worked to get his bearings. The cottage. The bed beneath him moved like a living thing and the room chattered. Rain beat against the house. A helluva storm, he thought, running his swollen tongue over dry teeth. Too much booze.

Something on the bedside table clattered and crashed to the floor. The walls, the floor pop-pop-popped. Winston jumped up, feet landing on a floor slick with water. He called out for Louis as he felt for the light switch—no power. He made his way down the pitch-black hallway, like walking the wet deck of a ship, arms sweeping for the unseen.

"Louis," he called again, louder. He stopped at the open doorway of the second bedroom. He ran his hands over empty beds.

A map of the house was fixed in his mind. They'd gone to sleep with the door to the porch still open; the wind swung it back and forth on its hinges. The sound of water was everywhere: hard rain drummed the roof, the windows, and the sides of the house.

"Louis!" he yelled, and by touch found the man still on the couch, which had walked itself close to the stove. Winston's toes caught on something, a chair leg, and he winced and swore. "Louis, goddamnit. Wake up!"

Winston groped for him, grabbed him by the shirt, and shook him. "Get your ass up! We gotta get outta here."

"What? What!"

"Get up! The house is coming apart. We gotta get to the car before the whole damn place falls in."

The wind roared and delivered another blow to the wooden structure. Kitchen windows shattered. Louis, who had slept in his shoes, stood and steadied himself against the kitchen counter. Winston's next two steps buckled him— bare feet on broken glass.

Where the hell were the car keys? Somewhere here in the kitchen . . . he'd tossed them onto the counter. He felt for the ring of keys, fingers brushing shards of glass. His hand closed around them, nestled in the sink drain. He dropped the keys into his pocket and touched the buckeye still there. Surreal.

Louis navigated to the kitchen door and turned the knob. Wind seized the heavy panel, tearing it off its hinges, slamming it into Louis's head.

Sensing a commotion, Winston hobbled to the open doorway. Water rushed over his feet. He leaned into a torrent of wind and stinging sprays of cold rain. He dropped down at the threshold to crawl out of the kitchen and onto the raised front deck. Then he understood.

The deck, at least ten feet above the ground, was already underwater. The Gulf poured into the house through the funnel of the kitchen doorway. A flood. A tidal wave. Water surged everywhere. The Studebaker must be gone, the roads too. Stilts holding the house must have shifted and were sinking into the tide. The whole structure would soon be gone.

Winston crawled back into the house, calling for Louis. He located the door lying on the linoleum, pulled it back, and found Louis, face up on the floor. Oh, shit. He lifted Louis's head from the water and examined it with his fingers, tracing a deep gash just above the temple that traveled up the skull. He put his hand on Louis's chest—was it moving? Hard to tell. The whole world roared.

They had to get out of the house, but they needed flotation. Louis had told Winston that he wasn't much of a swimmer; he'd drown immediately in his current condition. If he was even still alive. Winston stood up, pain shooting through his feet, and dragged Louis up onto the couch.

The wind seemed to whip from all directions, buffeting the whole house. He expected the structure to just explode, or implode, with the opposing pressures. He hobbled to the back porch, dropped to his knees in the face of the wind, and crawled to a remembered wooden dock box. When he managed to open the lid, the wind ripped it off the box. Winston pounced on the contents, finding canvas-covered life jackets. He threaded an arm through the straps of three vests, but the fourth was snatched away. Plunging a hand back inside, he scored a coil of limber dock line. He looped that over his head and around his neck for safekeeping.

Back at the couch, Louis had not moved. Winston tried to listen for breathing but couldn't hear over the noise. He couldn't tell if the man's chest even moved. He slipped a life jacket over the limp head, wrangled the waist strap around Louis's torso, tightened it, and snapped it securely.

Winston protected himself next and held onto the third vest. He wished he had on a shirt, he was so cold, but the thought streamed away.

Winston worried about Louis's blood loss, but he couldn't see anything. He couldn't see his own hands. He could only trust his instincts.

He pulled a couch cushion from beneath Louis's legs, dropped it on the floor to protect his own feet from further cuts, and stood on it to graze the kitchen counter surfaces with his fingers, searching for whatever he could find to help the situation. He located two long, thin dish towels. His mind's eye saw them as cheery blue and yellow stripes. He knotted them together, forming a crude bandage, and wrapped and tied the rags around Louis's head. No medic, Winston could only hope the pressure would help stop any bleeding and keep debris from the wound.

The couch cushion still beneath his feet wanted to float away in water now more than knee deep inside the house. Foam . . . mattresses were made of foam. Would a mattress float? He stepped off the cushion, trying to ignore the stabbing pain in his feet. He waded back to the nearest bedroom, the room with the twin beds—Louis's room he'd never used. He yanked one of the mattresses from the bed frame, stuffed it through the doorway and shoved it into the cave of the living area. The mattress floated beneath his hands.

That was it. They had to get out. No question the house was going down. He got in Louis's face and tried to talk to him above the roar. He put his ear to the man's mouth.

Jostled him. The wind stole any whisper. He slipped a hand beneath Louis's life jacket, against his chest again. Thought he detected a slight rising and falling. He put his lips to Louis's ear and shouted, "Louis! We gotta get out of the house. Water's everywhere. You got on a life jacket. Don't worry, I'll take care of you."

With that, he rolled the helpless man off the couch, dragged him almost to the front door, and propped him against the wall. He wedged the mattress into the doorway, half in, half out, the exposed end bucking in the waves. He removed the salvaged rope from around his neck, shook out the line, and tied it around his own waist. He wove the rope through Louis's lifejacket, threaded on the extra vest, and secured it all with a slip knot. Who knew what faced them out there?

On the deck now, in waist-deep water with Louis on the mattress, Winston steered the would-be raft in the general direction of the stairs. They pushed through the opening to the steps, and rather than descending them like in the real world, both free-floated.

The beach house shuddered and groaned and tore loose from its foundation. The structure was now a houseboat bound for nowhere, seawater swallowing it by the second. The mattress whirled and soaked up water like a sponge. The more saturated it became, the lower the mattress, and Louis, dipped. Winston held onto the rope tying the two of them together. Soon Louis was floating in the water, face up, head resting on the collar of the life vest. The mattress was gone.

A mountain of water rose above them, sensed rather than seen, then crashed over the two, dragging them both down deep and deeper, tumbling and twisting them like the flotsam they'd become. Winston thought his lungs would burst, and when he'd accepted the need to breathe in the salt water, it released him. He gasped and sputtered. The Gulf lifted and dropped them again and again, the rope that bound them tightening, loosening, tightening.

Winston tugged his partner close and grabbed him by the vest. Louis was lifeless, but he suddenly vomited into the few inches between them. Dead people didn't puke.

Dead people . . . Winston's mind was playing tricks. For a moment, his arms held the body of Jackson Smith, wrapped in a canvas tarp, the very fabric that held Louis Fisher right now. Louis Fisher, who, in his mind's eye, appeared every bit as dead as Jackson Smith. He'd not been able to save Jackson. But maybe there was hope for this one, this promising young man.

The Gulf of Mexico reclaimed them, smothering and tumbling them within its dark belly. Something large and sharp sliced Winston's thigh; the pain was far away. Like two corks, they rose and fell into unseen troughs, sucked down, then spit out. Over and over. How long could they last? Winston thought of Ruthie. Of Mary Carolyn. Would they be okay without him?

Ocean and sky were still indistinguishable.

Winton could not see the series of coming waves. The new surge slammed them into something solid, sucked them away, and smashed them again against the unmovable object. The monster tide swirled the roped tangle of men, in effect lashing them to what couldn't be, but was, a tree trunk. A palm? Trees did not grow in the middle of the Gulf—dry land was near.

Winston perceived that as knotted around the tree as they were, they could drown with the next big wave. Operating with a heightened sense of touch, without benefit of light, he freed them. He searched the trunk for handholds, anything to elevate or stabilize the singular mass that he and Louis had become.

Louis made a gargling noise and threw up.

"You still with me? Talk to me, Louis." Were his eyes open?

"There's a tree here. Feels like it's leaning. Gonna try to climb up a couple feet."

Was Louis listening?

"If I get up there, I'm gonna pull you. Help yourself along. Can't lift you all the way."

Winston lengthened the expanse of rope between them. He gripped the trunk with his legs and shimmied himself up just above the water. Then higher, trying to make room for Louis. But with Louis like an anchor below him, he could go no further.

"Climb up, Louis," he shouted. "Can you try?"

No help. What did he expect? The guy was half dead. He clutched the tree, muscles trembling with shock and fatigue. No way he'd ever get both of them out of the water. If he tied the two of them to the trunk again, they'd drown under another siege of waves. He dropped back into the Gulf, dragging Louis beneath the surface with him.

A hole opened in the dense cloud cover, letting in a hint of light from the sparks of tiny stars. The moon appeared, briefly—a pale crescent thumbnail. In his cold and somewhat confused state, Winston felt the world being twirled by something unseen. A new day was coming. He knew for sure it would look very different.

∽

The sky grew lighter, and Winston could make out the outlines of Louis's face. He pulled him closer, wishing he'd raise his head and say something smart or clever. In that moment, Louis had become colorless to him, the man's skin a blend of water and sky, and Winston saw him, maybe for the first time, from the inside out—a man the same as himself. Both fighting for survival.

The wind and waves were subsiding. They bobbed and bumped into one another. Winston frowned at the gash in Louis's head—a wonder they were both still alive. He rested his head against his life jacket's collar and dozed.

Daylight . . . a noise. Something black moved through the water, heading their way. A dog. A damn dog. Way the hell out here.

"Come on, pooch," he called. "Here, boy. Here, Blackie boy." The dog chuffed toward them and began to claw at Winston, toenails scraping skin for purchase.

Winston caught the dog and turned it around to avoid the flailing paws. He wrestled the extra life vest to sit beneath the heaving belly and secured the straps over its back. Little by little, the dog began to trust its new safety net—the paddling stopped. Winston rubbed the wet, furry head.

"Aren't you a lucky puppy? Yes, you are. I saw you chasing those seagulls yesterday. I know it was you." The black dog, a lab mix, rolled its eyes at Winston.

Winston looked at Louis's slack face raised to the sky. "We're all gonna be okay," he murmured, then shut his eyes.

Chapter 43

Though the air was very cold, the sea had settled and the sun was out when Winston and Louis were spotted by officers of Florida's Department of Fish and Game. With two pairs of helping hands and a long-handled gaff, the survivors, along with the dog, were hauled into the boat. Once onboard, Winston's feet screamed from imbedded glass; his legs gave out and his body shook violently.

The officers cut off Louis's wet clothes, bundled him in a thermal blanket and administered basic first aid, wrapping his head like a mummy's. Louis, in and out of consciousness, was secured inside the cuddy cabin.

Winston refused to give up his shorts but was grateful for the warm blanket. They wrapped his feet and the gash on his thigh; he'd need stitches.

As they worked on their passengers, the Fish and Game guys tried to answer Winston's questions about what had happened.

The older officer, Bradley, spoke: "They're already calling it The Storm of the Century. The weathermen were surprised by it, that's for sure."

Winston blamed himself for what had happened to Louis Fisher. He had put the man in harm's way. His feelings of guilt were not relieved by the news that even weather experts had been caught off guard.

The other officer, Wilkins, said, "What we was told, when they called us to work about two this morning, was the national weather people knew a big ol' low was moving east." He poured water from a jug into a paper cup and handed it to Winston. "That system was gonna collide with a high coming in from the north. Somebody screwed up though, those local guys, I guess. They thought it was gonna skip on past us here."

Officer Bradley offered a wry chuckle. "Yeah, they didn't even issue any warnings for the coast until about five this morning. Shit, we were already in the boat looking for survivors by then."

With his blanket a barrier against the wind, Winston rode outside with the officers. The dog, unwilling to leave him, lay at his feet. As a precaution against objects floating just below the surface, the boat moved barely on plane.

Winston watched the water. The all-night black nightmare had become smooth blue-green swells. But scattered debris marred the Gulf's surface—pieces and parts of houses and their contents, sheet metal, shoes, coolers and kitchen containers, paddles, an upright eerily-empty kayak. The scene looked like the site of an airplane crash.

The boat neared land where the silhouette had changed. Gone were the raised homes on the spit of land where

Winston and Louis had started their get-away weekend. Just gone. Homes torn from their foundations—the stilts built to keep them high and dry had snapped or collapsed, feeding the houses to the sea. A few structures appeared intact but sitting flat on the sand. Others were a child's game of pick-up sticks, tossed from a can.

"I assume we had fatalities . . ." Winston said.

"Oh yeah," Officer Bradley said. "Hearing on our radio they've found maybe eight so far, just right around Keaton and Dekle beaches. Some people got lucky like you two. Some of 'em picked out of trees. Coast Guard's out here, too. And local volunteers."

Winston nodded. He worried about the safety of the little girl next door to his rented cottage. And what about her mother? Could have been his own wife and daughter. Did Ruthie even know what had happened? Or were she and Mary Carolyn still dreaming in their warm beds?

﹋

Rescue teams were staged at the Dekle Beach marina, which had flooded during the night. But the water had subsided enough that boat ramps were again accessible. The Fish and Game boat arrived with Winston and Louis, and emergency personnel took over. Against Winston's wishes, a crew of local firemen whisked both men on stretchers to an assessment tent. Medics made the decision to move them to the hospital in Pineville.

Louis was stuporous with signs of a serious head injury. Winston, showing obvious symptoms of both hypothermia and dehydration, as well as multiple lacerations needing attention, insisted on sharing an ambulance with Louis. Someone strapped him onto a narrow bench beside Louis's stretcher.

A short, pudgy guy climbed into the back with them, introduced himself as Chunk, and began working on Louis, checking vitals and inserting an IV needle. The ambulance took off, full lights and siren.

"Can you talk to me, sir?"

Louis's eyes rolled open. Stared at the ceiling.

"What's your name?" Chunk asked as he shined a small light into Louis's eyes.

"He's Louis Fisher," Winston said. "He works for me. Bayside Life Insurance. In Pineville."

The medic ignored Winston and tried again: "Sir, can you tell me your name?" He leaned in closer to the stretcher.

Winston heard a mumble but couldn't make it out over the noise of the ambulance. "What'd he say?"

"Jackson Smith is what I got," Chunk said, scribbling on his clipboard.

"Jackson Smith?" Winston screwed up his face. "No. Hold it, hold it," he said. "Don't write that down. It's not right. For heaven's sake, the man's brains must be scrambled. Jackson Smith is one of our customers." He felt a wave of dizziness, and looked at the back door of the ambulance, wishing he could open it for more air.

"Huh," Chunk said, eyeing Winston. "You could be right."

"I am right," Winston huffed. "Check his ID."

"Nothing on him. They must've cut his wet clothes off after they pulled him out of the water. Belongings might be bagged, up in the front seat. Didn't they strip you, too?"

Recollection of the water rescue was already vague. Winston touched the wet shorts underneath his blanket, then shook his head. He explored the rough outline of car keys still in his right pocket and the curve of the buckeye. Amazing. He had no memory of what might have happened to his wallet. Or his lighter.

"Taking you both to Foley General. Once they've assessed Mr. Smith in the ER, they may move him to Tallahassee."

"Look, Chunk, he's Louis Fisher. Get it straight. You've no reason to dispute that. And if he's going to Tallahassee, I'm going with him. We need to stay together," Winston said, his sharp bottom incisor showing.

"Like I said, he may be transferred to Tallahassee. He's in way worse shape than you. It's not your decision."

The medic busied himself with the riggings for a new IV. "We're just gonna give you a little hydration, a little go-go juice," he said to Winston. "Oughta help you feel better, a little less cranky."

Winston pulled the blanket tighter. His teeth chattered and his body shivered. *Jackson Smith . . .* where the hell did that come from?

～

At the Foley County ER, the admitting physician decided to keep Louis in Pineville. His head injury received immediate attention.

Medical personnel stitched up the cut on Winston's thigh and administered a tetanus shot. He, too, was admitted for further stabilization and observation. Picking the glass fragments from his feet would take some time, but Foley

General was about to drown with storm casualties. Winston was old news.

An ER orderly rolled Winston out of his curtained cubicle and parked him next to a nurse's station, making way for a gurney bearing a small girl with blond hair. Winston raised his head for a better look: was it the neighbor kid from the beach? What happened to her mother?

"Mr. Taylor," a nurse called, "we reached your wife. She should be here pretty quick."

"Thank you," he said. "Can you locate Ruby . . . uh . . . you know, the colored lady who owns Miz Ruby's Rooms . . . It's Wright. Ruby Wright. She'll send somebody here to see about Louis."

Winston watched a cluster of starched white medics rush a gurney past him. Then another.

An old woman's face poked out above a blood-stained blanket. "Critical!" someone shouted.

A very large man nearly spilled over the rails of his cot. He moaned like a whale, clutching his thigh just above a bloody calf pierced through by a length of something like a splintered door frame.

Winston shut his eyes and waited for Ruthie. He heard the nurses talking about room assignments. Sounded like he and Louis would be on different floors. He raised his head above the bedrail: "Hey. I wanna share a room with Louis. We need to stay together. Can you make that happen?"

One of the nurses frowned. "We'd usually put you in *different* departments," she said.

Winston scowled at her. He knew what she meant.

The woman blushed. "We are filling up, though, with more injuries coming in from the storm. I could talk to someone . . ."

"How 'bout you do that. Louis works for me. We've been through a helluva lot."

~

The hospital room was crowded. Winston's bed was jammed against the window, Louis by the door. Ruthie sat in a wooden chair wedged against Winston's IV pole. Etta, Ruby, and Bubba surrounded Louis's bed. They kept their voices low, in deference to Louis, who slept and slept.

Roger Johns called and spoke briefly with Winston, offering sympathy and support. He promised to call again when Winston was back home. Said he had something important to discuss. Winston listened and responded appropriately. But he felt an invisible wall now stood between them—a wall he himself had built. A barricade against any "special policies" investigation Roger might be conducting against him. Since he'd found his client files in disarray, and learned that Louis had visited Mabel Griffin, his paranoia had grown. Would this be the subject of Roger's next call?

Ruthie hung up the phone for him, then laced her fingers through his. She was the calm in his every storm. He felt himself relax. At her urging, he shared highlights of the storm experience with his small audience. All but the part about Louis calling himself Jackson Smith.

Chapter 44

On Sunday morning, Foley County was on the CBS national news. The Weather Service admitted they had known for a couple of days about a gigantic low-pressure system lumbering eastward, but it had increased in speed and intensity by Friday evening. The system was on a collision course for a strong cold front coming from the north. One prediction was for the storm to become the worst of the decade. Most meteorologists predicted Georgia and the Carolinas would get the brunt of it. General consensus was that the Panhandle area and Florida counties north and east of the Gulf of Mexico would be unscathed. As a result, no warnings were issued for low-lying areas in that region until after the storm's hurricane-force winds and tidal surges began devastating Florida's coastal communities in Foley, Dixie, and Levy Counties. The storm was currently ravaging Wilmington, North Carolina. Thus far, 120 people had lost their lives.

From his hospital bed, Winston watched a CBS News reporter interview a couple from Alabama who had been vacationing at Keaton Beach, Florida. They told of being shaken from their beds in the early morning hours, forced to jump from their rental house as it collapsed into the storm's turbulent tidal surge. The two had held onto several pieces of buoyant lumber to keep themselves afloat in the inky dark until the Coast Guard plucked them from the water.

"Channel Six oughta send somebody over here to talk to us," Winston said to his roommate. "We could tell a helluva lot better story than that, don't you think?"

Louis declined to respond.

~

By the time church let out Sunday, Winston was ready for discharge. Louis would stay another couple of days. He'd shaken the worst of the head injury but was still battling headaches, dizziness, and forgetfulness. Doctors were also treating him for a mild lung infection.

Louis had said very little during the time he and Winston had shared a hospital room. His responses to Winston's questions had been limited to two or three words. Eye contact with anyone was minimal. He either slept or stared off into space. Winston was not satisfied that Louis's strange behavior was all related to the injury.

Winston shed his pajamas and dressed in a pair of sharply creased khakis and a blue plaid button-up, paired with his loose bedroom slippers. His feet were still bandaged and tender. He packed his duffel bag with all his belongings, along with a box of chocolates he'd bought from the candy striper's cart for Mary Carolyn.

He limped over to Louis's side of the room and sat down in the bedside chair.

"How you gonna survive here without me?" Winston joked. "I've watched over your ass for days now."

Louis turned his head and gave Winston his full attention. "You saved my life, boss. I'm all torn up about that." His eyes watered.

Winston was shocked. Louis was talking again.

"Aw, bullshit," he said. "I'd a done that for anybody. I hope you'd have done the same for me."

"You don't understand," Louis said. "I didn't deserve to be saved. And I don't deserve anything you've done for me, since the day we met."

Winston made a sour face. "What the hell are you talking about? I thought you were gettin' over that knock on your head, but I guess not. Besides, anything I might have done for you was self-serving. You've been my prize guy. You've brought us both nothing but success." He patted Louis on the leg. "You're gonna be okay, Louis. We're both gonna be okay. You just need to get well so we can get our insurance show back on the road. We're a dynamic duo."

Louis reached out and grabbed Winston by the arm. "Listen, I need to talk to you. Private. Close the door."

Winston shut out the world and sat, leaning forward, hands clasped between his knees.

"Something happened in college. My junior year. First couple days. Something bad. I ain't never told but one person, and he's gone." His voice cracked, and he coughed and coughed, as though still bringing up water from the Gulf. "All that time out there in the storm, floatin' in hell, I swore to God if he'd let us live, I'd try to make up for what I've done. And I'd tell you the truth. You deserve to know."

Winston glanced away and scooted his chair back a bit. "Ah . . . I'm not sure I wanna hear this, Louis. This sounds like something you need to tell your preacher-man."

"You gotta hear me. It's important." Louis fidgeted. "Can you crank up the head of my bed a little?"

Once he could see over the rails, Louis continued. "What I did was serious, back at FAMU. There was me and my two roommates since freshman year, Samuel and Albert. Samuel stayed in some kind of trouble—we named him Rascal. Albert was a big ol' heavy, slow guy. He was Moby, like the whale. Everybody loved Mo." He swallowed hard and his eyes glistened.

"What about you?" Winston asked, breaking the emotion.

"Ace. I was Ace because I made good grades and helped save their failing asses." Louis offered a half smile. "Anyways, we got drunk one night . . . lotsa nights, actually. But this one time, walking around the campus, just laughing and shit, somebody said 'hungry.' One of us was always hungry . . ." Louis stared at the wall behind Winston, conjuring up the past.

The boys tried to be quiet, but Rascal kept laughing, falling all over the other two, stumbling over the cracked sidewalk leading to the G&W vegetable stand, which also sold milk and bread, cheese, and peanut butter—survival food for students.

The store was closed. It was the middle of the night. But the liquor made them reckless, stupid. The three huddled at the padlock preventing their entrance. Big Mo lumbered around the building and returned with a piece of discarded pipe. He beat the lock until it surrendered. Ace picked a laughing Rascal off the ground, shushing him like a baby, and the three squeezed through the door as one.

Ace had a pack of matches, and struck them one by one, shedding light on items they grabbed, filling their pockets and arms. Ace snatched a whole cabbage, which prompted Moby to keep repeating, "Why you got that stinkin' cabbage?" Rascal fell into fresh hysterics.

The alcohol haze kept Ace rooted in indecision. What was the right choice? Apples? He should have taken cheese and apples, but Moby was dragging them to the front. As they all tried to squeeze back out the door, Ace dropped the cabbage with a thunk, and they watched the pale green spectral head roll in slow motion over the sidewalk to a pair of boots, and when they thought to look up, there stood the store owner, Mr. Graham, with his white hair and beard making him look like a ghost. Except the apparition was holding a shotgun. He fired it into the night sky, terrifying the students who tumbled over one another, causing Mo, who was like a tree trunk, to fall over the sidewalk and onto the boots, which knocked the old man down. The storeowner's head struck the street like the cabbage had and blood darkened his hair, pooling on the pavement and running like shiny ribbons into the cracks, visible in the light of the stars.

"He looked like he was dead, Winston. And you know what we did?" He stared at Winston, his body trembling. "We fuckin' ran."

Winston let out some of the air he'd been holding in his chest. This didn't sound too bad. Not too bad at all, considering . . . "Was the man seriously hurt?"

"Head busted open." He touched his own bandage and grunted, "What goes around comes around, huh? But yeah, he was knocked out cold. And what made it worse was he was a white man, boss. And people loved that old guy and his store. Hell, we loved him, too. A nice old fellow. And here we were, three drunk, colored boys. College boys. And all we could think to do was run."

Winston nodded. "I woulda probably done the same . . . What happened to him?"

"They put him in the hospital and he stayed in a coma. Long time. And the police turned Tallahassee upside down, looking for whoever was responsible. There was a reward, too. If they found the people who might've done it, and it turned out three Negroes had attacked a white man, somebody was gonna swing."

Louis got quiet. His lower lip quivered, and he moved his jaw from side to side. Then: "So, guess what I did? Your superstar Bayside Life agent?"

Winston waited.

"I made myself disappear."

᠃

Winston got up and filled Louis's water glass. Louis gulped it and choked and fell into a coughing frenzy. Winston brought him a wet cloth.

"Maybe we should talk about this another time. You're 'bout to make yourself sick remembering all this stuff. And I don't think I need to know any of this anyway, Louis. What's past is past. It's nothing horrible. It doesn't change the way I see you today."

314

"No. I got to get this out. You need to know who you got working for you."

"Okay." Winston sighed.

"When I say disappeared, I mean *poof!* I was gone. I left campus with nothing but my wallet and a few clothes. I didn't tell my roommates or teachers or anybody. I was fuckin' terrified of going to jail for Old Man Graham's injury. And that ridiculous robbery."

"Where'd you go?"

"There was this guy who worked on campus, doing painting and odd jobs. I was assigned to help him in exchange for campus room and board. I needed all the assistance I could get. He was only a couple of years older than me, and we got close, all those nights we worked together. Good friends. For some reason, I just spilled my guts and he took me in. I didn't know what else to do but stay invisible until the smoke cleared."

Winston felt sick, thinking of Louis's desperation and fear. Thinking of the injustice. All because the man's skin was darker than his own.

"I stayed with him in his off-campus efficiency. Since I couldn't be seen on school grounds, we came up with a plan to make money painting for local businesses instead of campus buildings. He got us a couple of State building contracts and we hired extra hands to meet deadlines. We didn't have a car, so we traveled by city bus, hauling our supplies in two rolling carts. We looked like most all the other street people.

"It wasn't long before we pooled our money and bought us a used car. I mean in a matter of *weeks*," he said. "When we were more mobile, he got us a job at a legislator's country mansion near Hampton Springs. It was empty and under restoration. The bigwig had bought it to turn into his private hunting lodge. We worked our rear ends off in the daytime and slept on the marble floors at night. Sometimes we burned a fire out back, drank whiskey, and told all about our lives and what we would do when we decided to grow up."

"So did the whole store break-in just die down? Weren't you tired of hiding?"

"Lord, I was still scared. I guess the police didn't find any suspects, but I don't really know for sure. I read the news when I could get a paper. What I did know was racial protests were really heating up. I wasn't about to go poking around town, gettin' caught like a rabbit in a trap. I'd uh never again seen daylight if I got jailed for the attack on a white man. And if the man had maybe died . . . well . . . that was an even worse nightmare."

"This is hard to hear, Louis. But I'd like to think that the scales of justice would have balanced out just fine." He fidgeted in his seat, wanting to go home. "So, I guess sooner or later you two just parted ways, because you're here now, safe and sound and successful." Winston cocked his head. "Right?"

"Would you do me a favor and open those blinds so the sun can come in?"

When the light poured through the slats, Louis stared into it until water ran from his eyes, then he shut them tight and waited for that one certain memory to come forward, the one he kept buried far back in his head. The final Chapter that had almost made him give up during the storm.

It was fall. The day was warm and sunny. The legislator kept a couple of guns and hunting gear in the soon-to-be lodge.

316

The painting partners borrowed a shotgun, a rifle, and some camo, and went for a ride in their Ford. They had the windows down, and the dry air cooled the car. They traveled down a dirt road, dust flying behind them, and wound up on Buckhead Paper Company's logging property.

Doves were flying, jockeying for a spot on the overhead power lines along one particular stretch of road. The car stopped and the men got out and stood near each other, squinting into the sun to observe the fluttering birds.

The younger man had the shotgun. He knew how to shoot.

The other had no experience with guns. He watched his friend load the weapon, then turned his gaze to the gray doves swarming the line. "Shoot us some supper!" he laughed, shading his eyes.

The shooter, though his vision was still slightly blurred from staring into the sun, said "Watch this," as he began to raise the gun, stepping forward to take the shot. But his weight shifted in the deep sand, twisting his ankle so that a pain tore through his foot, and he uttered a loud gasp, causing his partner to turn to see what was wrong, just as the shooter began falling. The gun fired. The man who had come only to watch was knocked backwards, his chest blooming with blood.

He was dead. Dead in the fine, white Foley County sand.

"I killed him," Louis said.

Images of Winston's own dead man in the dirt flared like flashbulbs from a crime scene camera.

"I didn't mean to," Louis continued. "And I didn't know what to do. I held his hand and I told him it was an accident. That I was sorry. He'd taken me in, fed me. Gave me a job.

Helped me believe I had a future." He bent his head and sobbed.

Winston sat, unmoving, trying to understand what was happening. Why the images Louis painted for this story were so eerily familiar. He finally offered an "I'm so sorry, Louis." But he was rooted to the chair, waiting for the rest of it. And afraid he knew what was coming.

Louis said he walked the road, thinking about taking the car and finding help. Help for what? The man was dead; nobody could fix that. He considered scooping up the body and taking it back to Tallahassee. But if he arrived there with a dead man, where would he go? The hospital? The police station? He'd try to explain, but the authorities would be suspicious and have to investigate. Then they'd check his own background and Bingo!—they'd discover he'd been a student at FAMU. And maybe they already had a lead on him as a suspect in the storeowner attack. They'd have him. He'd be putting the noose around his own neck.

How was he ever going to shake his past, growing darker and darker with the death of his friend? He'd been enjoying a brand-new start with the painting business, but now his partner was gone.

"I got his wallet from underneath him. I looked for family information, phone numbers, somebody I could call to tell the bad news. But he was a loner; he never talked about any family. I found nothing but a picture of a pretty girl. On the back it said 'I love you—Lettie.' That's when I decided."

"Decided what? What did you do?" Winston asked, drawing back in the chair as if to put distance between himself and the scene. But it was too late. He'd been sucked into that story a long time before.

"I swapped our social security cards, our licenses. I gave him my student I.D." Louis's words and tears flowed. "The first time I ever even knew his whole name was when I read his drivers' license. His middle name was Earl. Louis Earl Fisher . . . my only friend . . . dead because of me. Man, I was so torn up."

Louis covered his wet eyes with a hand, took a deep breath, then looked straight at Winston. "Before I stuck my own license in his wallet, I read my name out loud—Jackson Alan Smith. I always liked my name. It was a good name. But I never really belonged anywhere, to anybody. And now I was giving my own self away. I didn't have a choice."

Jackson Smith was gone for good.

Winston pulled a shredded toothpick from his mouth and tossed it into the trash. His insides felt as ragged as the wooden pick. He stared into the space between his feet.

The sound of a rattling food cart grew closer. In a moment, an aide delivered two lunch trays and shut the door on the silent room. Odors of broccoli and gravy-covered chicken steamed up from the plates.

Winston hurried into their small, shared bathroom and closed himself in. His pale reflection floated in the mirror. His stomach churned. The story was almost inconceivable . . . Jackson Smith had just been resurrected in name and flesh. What a fuckin' mess. He was mortified. And afraid. He gripped the sink, staring into the reflection of his own wild eyes. "It's okay," he whispered. "It's all going to be okay." Then he bent over the basin and washed his face in cold water. When he looked up into the mirror again, he was back in control. The face of fear was gone.

∽

"You want your food?" Winston asked.

Tears trickling down Louis's face said no. Winston handed him the napkins, then put the lunch trays on the floor outside the room.

Winston looked into Louis's reddened eyes. "The shooting was an accident, Louis. You didn't do anything wrong. You could have just taken the guy to town. *Why* in God's name did you run?" But Winston knew why. Hadn't he stood in Louis's same shoes? "Yeah, the cops would've asked a lot of questions. But you had no reason to kill the man."

"I was scared, and I guess I was in shock. It wasn't so much I was afraid of being accused of shooting my friend. I think I coulda talked my way out of that. Maybe. The cops don't go crazy when it's a colored man dead. That's kinda the way the white world works . . ."

"That's bullshit, Louis. The police would've done an investigation. They'd have made sure the death was accidental. They wouldn't have let it go because you were *both colored.*"

Louis grabbed the bedrail and leaned toward Winston. "You think you know everything, don't you Winston?" The words hissed from between his teeth. "You ain't lived in my world . . . I saw that *noose*, hanging back in Tallahassee, from a big ol' oak tree in front of the G&W vegetable stand. That's where my black neck would've snapped for a white-sheeted mob. *That's* what I was afraid of. If I was being investigated

320

for the hunting accident, they might come around to linking me to the attack on the storeowner. A white man. And I was—and still am—damn sure guilty of being a part of what happened that night."

Winston shook his head, exasperated.

"I had no way of knowing if the law in Tallahassee had a lead on me for the assault. If they'd questioned my roommates. If somebody'd told. No way to find out if the storeowner was even still alive. I read the papers dammit, and listened to the news when and where I could. I didn't always have a goddamn TV like you. Staying invisible was my best protection." Louis sought and held Winston's eyes. "And now I've found out that the old man, Fred Graham, just died. Because of that attack two years ago! Maybe now they'd try to link me to murder."

"Then why did you say your real name in the ambulance?"

Louis looked puzzled. "Maybe I was delirious. I don't remember saying it, but I heard you arguing with the ambulance guy. I do remember that."

Winston studied Louis's face, the white bandage still around the man's fractured skull. "Why are you telling me all this, Louis? Are you planning to turn yourself in? Is that it?"

Never surrender. The idea of Louis giving up made Winston almost wish the man had not survived the storm. He didn't bring Louis back to have him implicate them both. Like Louis, Winston worried the police might link *him* to the body in the sinkhole. Irrational. Nobody knew he'd dumped that body. Nobody knew a thing.

"I haven't figured out what I'm gonna do next," Louis said. He wadded up the wet napkins. "Like I said, I swore I'd tell you the truth if we got back home alive."

He said he was tired of carrying the secret. Tired of living in fear. He wanted a clean life, and he wanted it with Etta. He thought maybe he should tell her the truth. What did Winston think?

Winston shook his head. "Slow down, Louis. Just slow down. Let this sit awhile . . . Tell me about you and Mabel Griffin."

"Mabel is my mother's mother. My mother's name was Suki Lee. She got pregnant and ran off with my daddy, the very married Baptist preacher, Percy Smith. They disappeared into the hills of North Georgia and lived with Daddy's sister, Annie. My parents both dead now. I guess I learned how to disappear from them," Louis shrugged. "My mama was always trouble. Drugs and alcohol. And men. So restless. I was bounced from place to place and sometimes wound up again at Aunt Annie's."

Louis said he'd only seen his grandmother a few times in his life. They stayed in touch by mail. Now and then she sent him a little money. "She's always been special to me," Louis said. "She's one of the reasons I moved from Georgia to Pineville. To get closer to her. But I've been afraid to make myself known. I could screw up everything."

Winston nodded, rolled another pick around in his mouth. Though he knew Louis had been to see Mabel at the nursing home, he let that little lie go. So much was becoming clear. He crossed his arms, tucked his hands into his damp armpits and sat in silence, looking at Louis lying against white sheets, at the way the sun filtered through window blinds and locked the young man behind the bars of a gray cage made of shadow.

322

"You aren't afraid of someone around here recognizing you?" Winston asked.

"Nobody really knows me from the past. I wasn't at Mabel's place enough for anyone to remember me. I mighta been two years old on one visit, five the next." Louis touched the bandage on his head. "Last time I was at Mabel's was when we painted her house. But I'm still on guard anytime I'm over near Hampton Springs."

Silence settled between them.

Over the past two years, Winston had become a professional secret keeper. He knew it took practice, learning to say all the right things, words that didn't cast the slightest amount of doubt. The dreams were the worst, sometimes swallowing screams in the middle of the night, watching bodies pop up when least expected. Bodies bloated, swollen out of their shoes. His secret was a stone he held under his tongue, unable to swallow it—afraid if he opened his mouth at the wrong time, it would roll out on its own.

Finally, leaning forward from the chair and locking eyes with Louis, Winston said in a voice like the first rattle of a snake: "Tell me your name."

Louis frowned. "Which name?"

"Your real one."

"My real name is Jackson Smith. Jackson Alan Smith."

"Say it again."

"Jackson Alan Smith."

"You like the sound of it?" Winston asked.

Louis nodded. "It kinda feels good to say it again, out loud."

"Then once more."

Louis made a face. "What are you doing?"

Winston didn't speak but held Louis's gaze.

"Jackson Smith."

Winston stood up, pressed against the bedrail with his face inches from Louis. "That's the last time you're gonna say that name out loud. You hear me?" His voice was low but fierce. "If you say it again, you're done. Jackson Smith is dead and gone. And if you want to be accused of killing him, and killing that storekeeper in Tallahassee, and you're prepared to live the rest of your natural life in a jail cell–if they don't execute you first–then say it again," he hissed, and spit flew from his mouth. "If you dare to bring Jackson Smith back to life, he may be the one who kills *you*. And dangling from a rope would be a fuckin' luxury—they fry 'em up in the electric chair now." Then finally: "I'm not shittin' you man. It's over."

Neither man blinked.

Then Louis ducked his head. "There's just one more thing . . ."

Winston pushed away from the bed, his face a red scowl.

"I went back, boss, to the road where Louis died. The next morning. I'd decided to bring him back to town. Turn myself in. But Louis was gone. The body and the car. Just gone. I've been looking for him ever since."

A small puff of air came from Winston's mouth. It sounded like the word *don't*.

The hospital room door opened.

"Excuse me," a nurse sang, bustling in. "Mr. Taylor, the doctor's released you to go home." Her smile showed deep dimples in both cheeks. "I just need to remove that needle in your arm and give you a few discharge instructions. You might want to go ahead and call that pretty wife of yours to come get you."

As she stood close, removing the needle and covering the hole with gauze and tape, Winston breathed in her clean, cosmetic scent. She smelled like Ruthie's Jergens lotion, a cherry-almond smell. He closed his eyes a moment and saw his wife smoothing cream over her neck and arms, and he was suddenly sick. Homesick.

An x-ray orderly, tall and ebony, poked his head through the doorway: "Mr. Fisher, we gotta go for a ride," he grinned. He rolled a wheelchair up to the bedside and locked the wheels.

"I can walk," Louis said.

"Oh, no siree. You going in *style*. They's wanting a few more pictures of you today."

"Hey, Louis Fisher," Winston called, "I'll catch you maybe tomorrow. We got a few business items to talk about." He winked, but his countenance was grim.

Louis threw up his hand as the technician rolled him out the door.

Chapter 45

Back on High Street, Winston lay on the living room couch, drowsy and drifting in the safe sounds of home. Ruthie had built a respectable fire, one of their last for the season. Its gold, hypnotic flame danced low over a bank of glowing coal.

Mary Carolyn hadn't left his side. She'd played doctor, listening to his chest with her plastic stethoscope and sticking Band-Aids onto his gauze-wrapped feet. Now she entertained herself on the floor near him with a tangled pile of Barbies. Her dolls held long conversations filled with the drama of a storm. Ruthie rattled kitchen pans, and the aroma of his favorite dish—stewed beef with tomatoes and rice—floated his way. He closed his eyes and his thoughts wandered.

Jackson Smith, Mabel Griffin's grandson, was alive. The sum of Winston's guilt—writing the "special policies," pocketing the money, hiding the corpse in the sinkhole—had been embodied in Jackson Smith. For more than two years he'd carried the secret, afraid if anyone found out, his life would be wrecked. He'd lose his job, maybe his family, and possibly even his freedom. He believed any of this could have happened even if he had taken Jackson's body back to town.

Now that Jackson Smith was no longer dead, shouldn't that somehow release Winston from guilt? From any responsibility? Maybe the time was right to talk to someone about what had happened at the sinkhole . . . Ruthie? Louis? He took a deep breath, then let it out slowly.

Winston had saved him, the real Jackson Smith; secured him in a canvas life vest and watched over him through a treacherous storm until rescuers arrived. Now he was still watching over Jackson Smith, guiding and advising and sustaining. Without question, he would keep Jackson's secret safe. Louis Fisher's secret, he should say.

He'd advised Louis to never reveal his true identity. Advised? Shit, he'd *ordered* him to keep quiet. Wasn't his warning to Louis self-serving, another way of protecting his own hide? What was right about that? Subjecting Louis, a very young man, to a lifetime of secrecy was as bad as consigning the dead man to the sinkhole. Did Winston want this on his conscience?

Though it was clear to him now that Roger had never suspected him of pocketing premium payments, he still wondered if he'd ever redeemed himself for what he'd done. He'd paid back the money he'd taken. He'd activated all formerly non-existent policies. He'd continued to make reparations, too—guardianship of Mabel Griffin and her policies, his support and hiring of Louis Fisher. Could he stop punishing himself?

He'd learned his lesson, and he had little doubt that someone or something had called him to accountability. The voice spoke from anywhere and everywhere—in the whisper of trees, in the whoosh of a book's pages, in the whistling of wind. Even through the eyes of an animal . . . .

Winston's own eyes flew open. Had he actually been *called* to shoot that deer, on the day Jackson Smith had died?

He tried to reason through his actions again. He'd only been out looking for deer tracks. But the buck had appeared suddenly, had stared into him, and he'd involuntarily pulled the trigger. The search for the dying animal had led him to the dead man in the logging road, which steered him to the crazy decision to get rid of the body, something he ordinarily would never have considered. Never.

Could it be true that he'd been led—no, directed—to *find* the dead man? To hide the body? For what purpose? His thoughts tumbled. Was he sent to protect Jackson Smith? Protect him from being accused of a murder that was nothing more than a hunting accident? An arrest for that could have very well pointed to Jackson in the Tallahassee store-owner's injury, too. The way Winston saw it, Jackson Smith, aka Louis Fisher, was just in the wrong place at the wrong time in both cases.

"Who appointed *you* God?" Winston asked himself. But he couldn't shake the idea that the chain of events tying him to Louis, to Jackson, was Fortune at its finest, somehow linked through a ten-point buck. He had looked into that buck's eye and felt a primal but silent communication he might never decipher. The buck's eye . . . say it, Winston: "Buckeye."

Winston pulled the dark nut from his pocket and examined its smooth, polished surface, the shallow indentation on one side. He'd found the buckeye at the sinkhole that day he'd almost fallen in. Right at his feet, in a circle of sand. A mystical message that he'd done the right thing? Despite all the hell he'd been through, including the proverbial high water, he still carried the talisman. He stroked the buckeye with his thumb. You are certifiable, he thought, then smiled. Who else might he tell? *Nobody.* Nobody else would understand or believe this in a million years. But he, Winston Taylor, did.

～

Ruthie woke him for dinner. Dan Nettles, who'd been working storm control down by the coast, had called earlier—Winston's Studebaker had washed up in a swampy area almost two miles from the beach house. The storm had swallowed then regurgitated numerous vehicles along the Foley County coast. Dan said Winston's would be towed to the junkyard out by the drive-in theater on Highway 19.

"Dan also said that the dog you rescued is sitting at the Foley County pound. Nobody's claimed him. He just thought you'd want to know," she said with a wink.

Mary Carolyn flung herself across Winston's middle. "Can't we keep him, Daddy? He doesn't have a home. Please?"

Winston rolled his eyes. "Are y'all ganging up on me? Two girls against one old, crippled man?"

They all laughed, and Winston promised they'd talk about the dog later. He figured he owed Mary Carolyn something after the dead squirrel fiasco.

At supper, Winston cleaned his plate, then rested his elbows on the table. "I've been thinking," he said, "we should find you a new car. I can drive the Comet. It's still a good car. I've got that bonus check coming in, and if I put that with insurance money from the Studebaker, we can afford to buy something you want." He reached for Ruthie's hand and grinned. "Even a station wagon, if that's what you're still thinking."

"Boy, that storm sure sweetened you up. And loosened your wallet," she grinned back.

"Had a lot of time to think about you and that car you want, while I was floating out there in the Gulf with nothing to do. Thought about that, and a lot of other things, if you know what I mean." He wiggled his eyebrows.

"You did not," she laughed.

"Oh yeah, I did. Still thinking 'bout those other things."

"But you haven't fully recovered, and your poor feet are still healing," she said, poking out her lip in mock concern.

Winston looked down into his lap. "I don't think I need my feet for that."

〜

It was Tuesday morning when Roger phoned. Winston tried to act casual through the pleasantries, but his stomach was in a knot. They joked around a bit, then Roger got serious.

"Winston, I've just gotta tell you that what happened to you and Louis has shaken up our company. From the secretaries to the CEO. And not just about the storm you two endured, but also what caused two of our best agents to be there in that beach house, separate from the rest of the event participants. Top management has had several meetings about this, talking about our company's values, our ethics, and our policies on race and hiring. I thought for a while that Brian and I might lose our jobs over this, us and part of the legal team that advised us and even the event planners who made the arrangements that excluded Louis."

When Roger paused for a breath, Winston lightened the conversation: "I'm stunned. There are actually real people running this company?"

"Yeah, buddy, a bunch of us have taken a beating. With real sticks. Things are about to change around here, and for the better."

"In all seriousness, I'm glad, Roger. Changes have been needed. It's a shame, though, that it took a freak storm to enlighten a big company like Bayside Life."

"Yeah, and most importantly, we realize how crucial both you and Louis are to what we do. You are so damn talented, Winston...multi-talented I should say. As a salesman, as a leader, and as an investigator."

"As an investigator?"

"You heard me. Rather than just talking about it, you've *shown* me your affinity for investigative work. I recognized it, but your sales success made me want to ignore it. That Ricky Swain thing, and that case with Derek Wicks—you gained some fame with those, but you were never properly recognized or compensated. I blame myself for that, and I'm sorry."

"It's okay, Roger. I get it. I appreciate what you just said."

"It's not okay, Winston. But it's *going to be* okay. Very soon."

"Meaning?"

"You are still extremely critical to our success in the Pineville-Foley County area. But we're working up a plan that I hope you'll be interested in. You and Louis."

"Tell me." Winston's smile was obvious over the phone.

"We'd like to keep you in your current position until next spring, while Louis gains greater experience and acceptance by our customers and the business community. What Brian and I want, *if you agree*, is for you to train him to take over your management responsibilities. We'd have to hire another agent, of course. This is still in the planning stages, and not to be discussed with Louis for the time being."

"And where am I going?"

Roger chuckled. "I was saving the best part for last. You're gonna love this, I hope. As soon as you've recovered from that catastrophe at the coast, we'd like to schedule you for regular investigation training sessions here in Jacksonville. Wally Sears will take you under his wing—he loves you, by the way—and you'll shadow him on some of his cases. Then, about this time next year, you should be ready to move into a position as a full-fledged insurance investigator."

Winston took a deep breath, then: "Holy crap. This is just unreal, Roger." He could not stop smiling. "I can't believe this!" Ruthie would be thrilled.

"It's real, and you can take it to the bank. Oh, I forgot to say, Bayside will generously compensate you and Louis for what you endured—that settlement number is still being sorted out. And of course, you'll both be getting significant raises next spring with your new positions. Again, we can't tell Louis just yet. And you should keep your deal quiet for now. Except for telling Ruthie, of course."

Winston was without words. He finally uttered a choked "thank you" at the end of their call.

〜

Wednesday morning, Winston had Ruthie drive him back to the hospital. He asked her to wait in the car. "I won't be long," he said, squeezing her hand. She seemed afraid for him to be out of her sight. He had still not told her about the investigations job. She'd had enough excitement. And until he saw it in writing, he would consider it just a dream.

Winston rapped on the open door of the hospital room he and Louis had shared. Louis was just tucking a new shirt into a pair of casual black pants.

"Hey, man, you're looking good!" Winston said.

Louis offered a half smile. "Thanks. Feeling pretty good. Etta's coming to get me after lunch." He sat on the edge of the bed. "I'm ready to get back to business."

"You still need a few days, Louis. You can't come bounding back that quick. You still got some things to think about."

"I've already thought about what all you said before you checked out of here. I'm done with that. I need to get back to selling insurance. I gotta get on with my life."

"Listen, Louis," Winston said, hands in his pockets. "I've been thinking hard myself since I got home. About everything that happened, about things I said—"

"There's nothing else to say, Winston. I heard you loud and clear."

"No, listen . . . I might've told you the wrong thing to do. I still wasn't thinking straight myself when I got discharged.

And I was so shocked by what you told me." He took a deep breath. "To be honest, I think I was thinking more about myself."

Louis scowled. "I don't understand that," he said. "You were trying to protect me, to make me see I needed to protect myself. Always. You weren't thinking of yourself at all, Winston. You've been trying to help me since the day we met."

Winston studied his slippers. "Yeah, that's one way to look at it," he mumbled. "But Louis, you've got a very long life ahead of you. Do you really want to carry such dark secrets through the only life you have? It's hell . . . I mean I think it would be hell." He pulled the buckeye from his pocket and rolled it between his palms while he talked. "My advice was selfish because I don't want to lose you. Your ability to sell equals, maybe exceeds, mine. Together we can make our office one of the best in the state."

Winston crossed the room to the hospital bed that had been his. He sat on the edge. "The odds of finding success by myself are pretty good but pretty good isn't enough. I want you to help me climb to the top of the Bayside Life ladder. You lift me, Louis, and I'll lift you. Teamwork. That's the ticket."

Louis stared at Winston, listening.

"So even though that's what I want, I'm here to tell you I think you should disregard what I said previously about keeping your mouth shut. About never claiming your own real name. Louis, this is your life. Not a game. And if you want to turn yourself in for leaving the scene of that accident, and even for your involvement in the death of the old guy in Tallahassee, I'll stand up for you. So will Miz Ruby. You know you got Etta. We'll all do whatever to help you. You'd have your own name back. And most of all a clear conscience."

Louis's eyebrows arched. "Do you really think I should come clean with the law?"

"I didn't say that exactly. I just think you should disregard my earlier advice and make your own decision. But no matter what, your secret is safe with me. I'll never tell a soul what you told me. Unless you want me to."

Louis stood up to face Winston. Their eyes met and held. They shook hands, and Winston left.

That afternoon, Etta picked Louis up from the hospital in his Bel Air. She drove them to the Dixie Drive-In and ordered chocolate milkshakes. They sat in the car, sucking on straws, and talked.

"I hate to bring this up on such a happy day . . . but there's something I need to tell you," Louis said.

"What's wrong?" Etta set her cup on the tray hooked over the car window.

"I called Moses Nash yesterday. Something just told me to. I found out Lettie died last weekend."

Etta moaned. "That's so sad, Louis. I'm so sorry for that poor woman. And her little boy. It's a shame they couldn't find that baby's daddy."

"I'm going to the funeral on Saturday, over in Quincy. And I'm gonna see her boy, Louie. Feels like the right thing to do. I mean, we got the same name. That ought to mean something. Would you be willing to go with me?"

"Of course. I wouldn't let you go by yourself. You've been through so much lately, I ain't leaving you alone. You been wrestling alligators, Louis."

They sat without talking, watching carhops delivering orders and taking away trays. The air was thick with the smell of fried food.

"Don't you want to talk about the storm, Louis?" Etta asked. "It might do you some good."

Louis shook his head. "Not right now. I'm just glad to be here with you, my beautiful girl, on this amazing day."

Etta slid from beneath the wheel to cozy up next to him. "Do you love your beautiful girl?" she teased.

"You know I do. Been thinking a lot about you lately. I've had some blessings in my life, Etta. I have to say you're one of the best gifts I've ever had. I feel like we belong together."

She looked up at his face. "We are together, baby."

"I want it to be forever."

"For real?"

"For real." He wrapped his arms around her and kissed her.

Etta pulled away, her eyebrows raised. "You gonna propose?"

"I thought I just did," Louis squinted. "I want you to be Mrs. Louis Fisher."

"Well, I ain't said yes, yet. Feels like some kind of hidden string . . . some big 'but' coming . . ."

"But," Louis said, grinning, "if we ever have a son, I wanna name him Jackson."

"Jackson . . . hmm," she said and rolled the name around on her tongue again, savoring the syllables. "Jackson . . . I don't know where you got it, but I love that name."

〜

In mid-April, Winston discovered an interesting article buried in the *Capital Democrat* about a group of private citizens who'd formed a coalition to watch over the governor and Cabinet's recently mandated water quality task force. A spokesman for the coalition—Citizens for Florida's Clean Water—said the group's concerns center around the *sincerity* of the government task force. They plan to keep a fire burning under the issue and insist that action be taken to clean up the current pollution, not just look at its effects on the future. The group is reaching out to private corporations, looking for creative ways to help. The spokesman indicated that the acclaimed Fellowship of National Underwater Archaeologists had expressed tentative interest in exploring the sinkholes and underwater caves, to shine a light on toxins that might be leaching into the waters from the dumping of chemicals, old appliances and even automobiles.

Winston folded the newspaper and stuck it deep inside his file drawer. He poked a toothpick between his teeth, reminding himself that ninety-nine percent of the things people worry about never come to pass.

Thank you so much for reading *Winston's Book of Souls*. If you've enjoyed the book, we would be grateful if you would post a review on the bookseller's website. Just a few words is all it takes!

Acknowledgements

When I started writing this story in December of 2018, I was amazed at the support and interest from others. You know you can count on your family to at least *act* interested (thank goodness), but whenever I talked to people outside my family circle, even complete strangers, I never felt anything but enthusiasm. I think the old saying, "it takes a village," applies to novel writing as well.

I could never have completed the book without my husband, Ben Haskew. Besides reading the manuscript twice and giving me advice on my 1950s/1960s car choices, he listened to so many of my ramblings about what I was writing that he surely could have written the book himself. He lived it and breathed it with me. And sometimes he had to send me to my writing room when I got too sidetracked. I'm eternally grateful for him, and not just because of the writing support. He's been my everything for more than forty years.

My kids were instrumental in several ways. They've always been fans of my writing, but this time they participated. My daughter, Michelle Daws Mecca, drawing from her highly successful sales background, advised me on sales work and sales competitions for my characters. My oldest son, Brian Haskew, who is an avid outdoorsman, helped me with passages on fishing in the Gulf of Mexico, including tides and bait. My youngest, Jason Haskew, knows *everything* about boats and gladly shared. He's also a strong writer and helped me refine some of my earlier pages. Alicia Haskew helped set up new social media accounts and the beginnings of a website. Claire Haskew, sympathetic to my lack of social media knowledge, has always been willing to talk me through that maze. My children and theirs (Tyler, Dylan, Emma, Charlotte, and Angelo, our bonus boy!) are my greatest accomplishments and greatest joy.

I'm thankful for other family members who shared critical knowledge—my brother, Wayne Cooper, advised on guns, ammo and all things hunting, and was an enthusiastic first reader. He, too, has been a lifetime supporter of my writing daydreams and in 1983 presented me with a brand-new *Writer's Market,* before I even knew what that book was for! My uncle, Jim Cooper, shared memories of his early insurance sales experience, giving me a good feel for debit routes and premium payments from back in the '60s. A special thanks to my aunt, Patricia Brown, for sending me vintage Gulf Life Insurance Company thimbles and sewing needle packets—holding them in my hand helped me cross the bridge back in time. Mark Haskew, a trucking industry expert, checked off on my writing of an important trucking "incident." Besides her manuscript reading, I so appreciate Kim Haskew's recounting of an unheralded Gulf Coast storm. By changing the actual year and circumstances, I was able to create a critical and believable ramp up to the book's climax.

A number of my friends were instrumental in the making of this manuscript. I am blessed by them all. Thanks to my teacher and great friend, Arthur McMaster; Dr. James Raff and Dr. Michael Crowley, for examining my story patients for injuries I might have missed; Ginna and Mark Vedder for the gift of a real buckeye, which is Winston's talisman; and Lee and Jeri Blair for reading and celebratory wines. I appreciate the gift of time and truth from other first readers: Tammi Hart, Sharon Ferruccio, and Sue McMaster.

My South Carolina Writers Association, Chapin/Irmo Chapter, made me believe I could go the distance. Thanks to all these passionate writers who twice a month read every word, sharing time and experience to help this novel stand strong: Jay, Arlene, Carolyn, Scotty, Charlotte, Vonnie, Sue, Don, Debbie, Cathy, Laura L., and Laura V.

Many thanks to Guy "Harley" Means, P.G., a respected Florida geologist and authority on sinkholes, caves, springs and natural bridges (called karst features), who patiently helped me understand the landscape where my childhood is rooted, which in turn legitimized my fictional "Blue Sink." I am indebted to Shelly Busky, sister of my dear friend Tammy Houtz, who offered expert input on dead bodies and criminal investigations.

My protagonist, Winston Taylor, drew his first breath in the short story, "The Book of Souls," published in the Winter 2012-2013 issue of *The Main Street Rag*. I am forever grateful for MSR's support of my writing over many, many years.

Last but not least, I am thankful for the team at TouchPoint Press for believing in my words and helping make one of my biggest dreams come true.

Author's Note

I almost didn't write this book. Early in the process, I became afraid of creating characters different from myself. As a white woman, how could I effectively write in the voice of a grown white man? What did I personally know about the struggles and horrors Black people faced during the 1960s, the time period of my story? I was just a child back then. But my main Black character, Louis Fisher, refused to be anybody but himself. The more he grew, the more I loved him. And I decided that as long as I treated him as fairly as my flawed white protagonist, Winston Taylor, we would all be okay. Afterall, they are both just men, and this novel is a work of fiction.

This story does reflect power and balance during the early '60s. It was a horrible time for so many, but the tale is not *about* the civil rights movement. It is not *about* equal rights for women either. It is just realistic fiction filtered through the eyes of Winston and Louis and Ruthie and Etta, and the time of their story was very different than today. I do believe the story shows how far our country has come and how far we still have to go.

If you would like to comment on this Author's Note, please contact me through my website: terresacooperhaskew.com.